DEADLY. SET. VEGAS.

A VEGAS VICTORY FC NOVEL

VANESSA M. KNIGHT

Deadly. Set. Vegas.

Published by Inked Publishing

Cover Art © 2024 by Qamber Designs & Media

Edited by Nancy Canu

ISBN: 978-1-963575-99-6

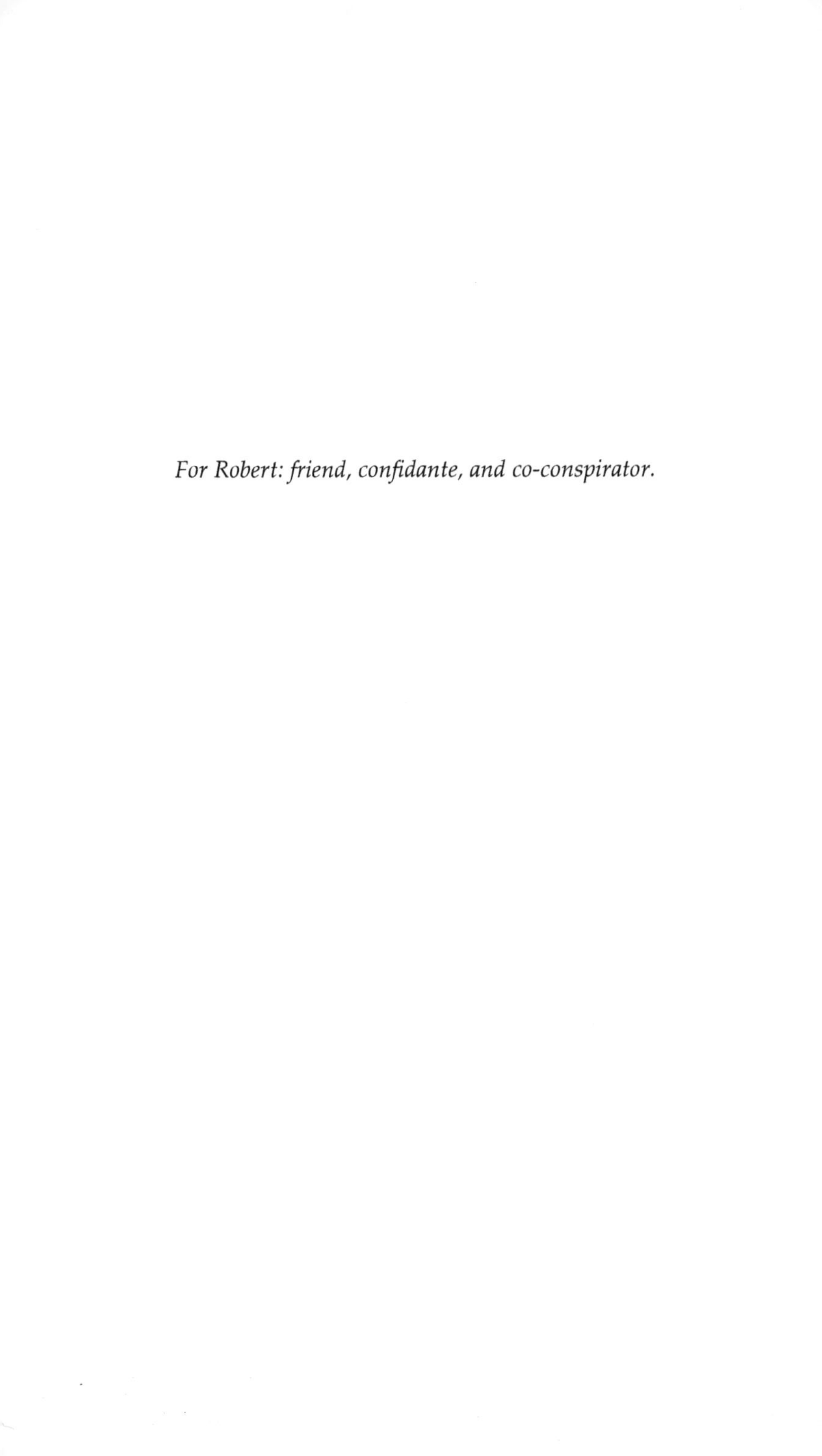

For Robert: friend, confidante, and co-conspirator.

CHAPTER 1

Silence buzzed as Kennedy Romero walked a long desolate hallway in the Vegas Victory soccer building. Normally the place would be filled with spectators and the scents of beer and popcorn. But today they were silent. Yeah, murder tended to silence a lot of things. Too bad it didn't silence the questions in her head.

Her dirty military boots scuffed along the concrete as she followed the security guard up the stairs to the owner's box. She'd always wanted to see how the other half lived, but not like this. The security guard opened the metal door to the box and cool air caressed her face before her boots hit the soft gold carpet.

A thirty-foot picture of Chuck and Craig Perrault, owners of the Vegas Victory Soccer Club, hung in the foyer. No matter his faults, Chuck was handsome. Had been handsome? Kennedy had no idea what to do with that. Salt and pepper hair, more salt than pepper these days, and bright blue eyes.

"I can't believe he's gone." Kennedy stared at the picture, her voice catching. "I watched him play in college, and then for the LA Galaxy. He was an incredible striker… unstoppable on the pitch."

"Pitch?" The security guard crossed his arms at the wrist and tapped his watch from his post in front of a hallway on the other side of the room. He seemed to be in a hurry. Kennedy was not.

As it was, the whole situation felt crazy. "Pitch is another word for field." Kennedy was explaining soccer to a security guard in a soccer venue while avoiding a crime scene. Not exactly how she pictured her day going. Had anyone told her when she'd gotten on the plane yesterday that she'd be checking on her friend after her best friend's husband was murdered, she would've told them they were crazy.

"Are you done, ma'am?"

She didn't know which to be offended by more—the tone or the ma'am. She turned her back on the giant picture and followed her impatient tour guide down a hall leading off the foyer. "He was an icon on the field." Even if nowhere else.

The guard took a deep breath. So he wasn't as unaffected as he pretended to be.

Chuck Perrault *was* an icon. Born and bred in the Vegas valley. The first guy handing out meals at the homeless shelter on Thanksgiving and driving truckloads of toys to the children's charities. Too bad his generosity didn't always stretch to his family, but then again, what happened behind closed doors didn't always match the public persona.

The murmur of police activity drifted to Kennedy's ears just before they reached the open doorway to the owner's box. Inside, dark blue paint contrasted with the white cabinetry lining the side wall. White furniture and mahogany tables faced a floor to ceiling window overlooking the field. It was all clean lines and opulence.

Or it would be if the room wasn't a crime scene.

Cops stood around the body. Red spatters stuck to the gold chandelier. A lake of blood curdled around Chuck's lifeless body. Chuck.

"Oh crap." Her stomach heaved and her heart cracked in her chest. No one deserved this.

"We need to move." Security guard stepped in to block Kennedy's view.

She blinked, and the scene burned behind her eyelids. She'd been to enough crime scenes to know this was personal. Multiple stab wounds. Too many to count.

Who could do this to Chuck? Or anyone?

Voices came from behind the wall of guard. "He was stabbed thirty-seven times in the back, Detective."

Apparently, they could count them.

"And that's just what we can see," someone who was probably the detective said. "We might find more once we turn the body."

"It takes stabbing someone in the back to new levels." The first officer's gruff chuckle faded and disappeared. Trauma affected people differently. Some threw up. Some cried. Some told horrible jokes.

"Who are you?" A man in plain clothes and a badge stood next to the bodyguard and growled at Kennedy. He actually growled like a surly bear. His six-foot frame was the only thing bearish about him. He had olive skin, and clean-cut dark brown hair. He'd be cute if he wasn't scowling.

The bodyguard flipped a thumb at Kennedy. "This is Darcy Perrault's friend."

"Bobby, who said you could bring a friend through here?" The detective's glare could melt steel. "This is a crime scene, not a show on the strip. We can't have civilians wandering around."

"She's not a civilian. She's a cop." Darcy must have told the security guard, AKA Bobby, Kennedy's profession.

The detective's eyes roamed up and down Kennedy's body. She'd think he was totally into her, but his body language said he wouldn't pee on her if she spontaneously burst into flames. "I've been with Metro for fifteen years. I've never seen you."

"You wouldn't have. I'm a cop in Chicago." A bit of an overstatement. She hadn't been on the streets in over ten months. Not since the *incident*.

"So, you're on vacation?" The detective's scowl morphed to a snarl. Misogynist or random anger issues… who knew?

"Yes." Not that she chose to take the time off, but he didn't need to know that.

He flapped his hand at her. "She's a civilian. Get her out of the building."

"Come on, ma'am." Bobby started toward the stairs they'd originally come up.

Kennedy didn't move.. "I'm going to see Darcy. Her husband was killed, and she asked me to come. Arrest me if you need to. I'm sure Darcy will be happy to post my bail."

The detective glared. Kennedy had stared down murderers and rapists. She could handle a jerk-face Metro Cop.

"Fine." Angry cop didn't look any happier now that he wasn't getting his way. It probably didn't help that Kennedy could feel the self-satisfied smile on her lips.

"This is going to be a shit-show when this gets out, so keep it quiet," the detective rumbled.

Kennedy pouted. "I was going to post this to my social media pages." She wasn't on social media, but he didn't know that.

"I can and will arrest you if you get in my way." He stormed across the room and stuck his big fat judgey finger in her face. It took everything in her to not bite it. She wasn't used to being on this side of the officer-ire. She wasn't usually the one being *ired* at.

Kennedy knew this would turn into a media circus, complete with soccer hooligans. The longer they put off the throngs, the better. And he was just trying to do his job, so she should let him off the hook. "It's the truth. I am here to see Darcy Perrault. I will not post, call, scream or send smoke signals regarding what I've seen here." She held up three fingers in the Girl Scout salute. Okay. So, maybe she wasn't exactly letting him off the hook. "Perhaps you want me to sign a nondisclosure agreement?"

The detective sighed and walked away. *Rude.* She couldn't really blame him. And bonus… she was getting to do what she wanted without his annoying scowl in her face.

"Let's go, ma'am." Bobby hit the elevator button once they were out in the hall and the door slowly opened. "She's in the office upstairs."

"How is she?" Death was never easy, but this, this was a whole other level.

"She found the body." Bobby followed Kennedy inside the elevator. "That's how she's doing." The door slid closed.

"So… bad."

"You could say that. She slipped on the blood and the cops won't let her take a shower until they're done talking to her."

"Slipped on the blood?" That sounded like a mess.

Bobby coughed. "Just try not to stare."

CHAPTER 2

ry not to stare.

Kennedy stared at her reflection as the elevator crawled up to wherever the office was. She hadn't had time to get herself together this morning. She was a hot mess— without the hot. Her dirty blond hair was pulled back in a ponytail. Had she thought about it, she might have brought something a little more appropriate for a trip to the glitz and glamor capital of the world instead of her usual blue jeans and T-shirt.

Better to get the staring out of her system now. Apparently, there might be a reason to stare when they got up to the office. Which really, they should have gotten to the office already. This was a brand-new building built for a brand-new team. One would think the elevator would move faster than a dumbwaiter with a pulley system. The car stopped with a jerk and the door slid open.

Try not to stare lingered in her thoughts as the room came into view.

The decor was professional-office chic. Black leather couches on one side. White desk with matching book-shelves on the other. Floor to ceiling windows overlooking the arena. But the hardwood floors and the blue and golden logo hanging behind the desk wasn't what caught her eye. It was the woman sitting on a dropcloth on the couch.

You gotta be kidding.

At least Kennedy thought it was a woman.

She looked like a victim from a slasher movie. A creamy white face topping a heavily used tampon, or maybe that was her body.

Kennedy looked over at the guard, but he was already back in the elevator and the door was closing. Wimp. She took a wild guess. "Darcy?"

The red covered swab moved and the pale face looked up. Her face was streamed with tears. Her hair was a balayage of crusted blond and red highlights.

Kennedy crossed the room and stopped short of wrapping her best friend in a hug. "Do you need an ambulance?" Or a shower?

"Oh, thank god, Kennedy." Darcy jumped up, a tear building in her eye. "I can't give you a hug."

"I'm sorry."

Darcy dropped to the couch. A red stained butt-print blemished the off-white cloth under her. "I need to take a shower, but we need to get this done first." She nodded to the cop walking toward her, a heavy-set woman wearing a collared shirt, dark pants, and sensible shoes. Her gold badge hung from a lanyard around her neck. Detective, not cop.

"I only have a few more questions and then you can take a shower." This detective had kind eyes, unlike the evil one downstairs. She slid her finger over her tablet. "You must be Kennedy Romero. I'm Detective Lester with Las Vegas Metro. Did you want to wait downstairs while we finish up?"

Downstairs with angry cop? If she had another run-in

with the man, there was a good chance she'd get thrown out of the building, or worse, thrown out of town.

Darcy saved Kennedy from being blacklisted in Vegas. "Can she stay?"

"Of course." Detective Lester was by far her favorite. So much kindness. "I know this is hard but, does anyone have a grudge against your husband?"

"Everyone loved my husband."

"No one was jealous or angry? No bitter ex-employees?" Detective sunshine appeared from behind Kennedy, adding his two cents. He was a black hole where kindness went to die.

"No. My husband has always been very giving to everyone." And from the fight Kennedy had witnessed last night, he'd been giving his seed to anyone that moved. Not that the cops needed to know that. Darcy wouldn't have killed her husband for that. He would've been dead a long time ago if that was the case.

"I find it hard to believe that a man with his stature didn't step on a few people along the way." The cranky detective was asking all the right questions, just maybe in the wrong way.

"What are you implying?" And Darcy was taking them in the wrong way.

"I'm implying nothing." The cranky detective moved closer.

"I'm sorry, Mrs. Perrault," Detective Lester said. "This is my partner, Detective Pagonis. He's just trying to figure out who might have had a problem with your husband." She was obviously choosing her words carefully. "The scene downstairs was very— gruesome. It implies a very personal attack. The person who did that would have been very angry."

"I just don't see how anyone could be that angry with Chuck." Darcy stood up and moved to the window overlooking the arena. Why they had an owner's box when they could watch everything from up here boggled the mind.

"Maybe they weren't that angry in your mind. But in theirs, he really hurt them."

Darcy sighed. "I don't know. The guy my husband outbid to buy the franchise might have been mad. The woman we outbid for the Rembrandt we bought was pretty steamed. I mean, none of that is reason to kill someone."

"I will need those names." Detective Lester wrote the names Darcy rattled off on a tablet with a Metro logo stuck to the back. In Chicago, they had to buy their own paper—there was no fancy electronic tablet. "What about players or fans?"

Kennedy hated to say she wasn't that up to date on the hot gossip about the Vegas Victory. If it wasn't a headline on Google, she probably didn't know about it.

"I don't think a player would do this. They're good men." Darcy wrapped her arms around herself and shivered. "We're in negotiations with Tad Markham. He keeps asking to leave, but we've built this team around him. I'm sure you've heard all the speculation on the news. We'd end up trading or letting go of most of the guys. A few of the fans aren't happy about all the talk."

If Tad was the one talking about leaving, that seemed like a reason to kill Tad. Just saying.

"What about friends or family?" Lester asked.

"No. His brother basically worshipped him. They fought, but who doesn't fight with their siblings. His parents are gone." Darcy turned her attention to the empty stadium. She pulled at a clump of hair and flinched—or maybe it was her mouth rejecting the Chuck being worshipped comment.

Detective Lester made another note. "What about—"'

"According to some witnesses," Pagonis said, interrupting her, "there was yelling coming from the office last night. They heard something about another woman."

"We were having a discussion. Kennedy was there."

Great, now angry cop's attention was on Kennedy. "So, you were the last people to see Chuck Perrault before he died?"

"Well, I left to feed the dogs," Darcy said.

Which was true, but it was more like Kennedy pulled Darcy off Chuck after he dropped the bombshell that he was in love with someone else.

Officer Smiley focused his attention on Kennedy. Great. "So, you were the last to see him alive?"

"I left a few minutes after Darcy. He was standing at the back windows—very much alive."

Pagonis scowled. "Can anyone corroborate your story?"

"She pulled into the driveway just as I parked in the garage." Darcy looked all happy with herself. Like her explanation took Kennedy's name off Detective Scowly Face's most-wanted list.

Shit, this looked bad. They were each other's alibi, and they both had a motive and means. They needed to regroup. Out of the corner of her eye, Kennedy saw Darcy squirm in her seat. The dried blood was a black stain on her skin.

"Can this wait?" Kennedy asked. The cops needed this information, but right now nothing was more important than Darcy getting out of her Carrie suit.

Pagonis sneered, which wasn't much better. "Since you're a police officer, you know how this works. The first forty-eight hours are critical to an investigation."

"I do, but since Darcy looks like an extra in a *Saw* movie, maybe you could investigate the names she's given you and let her take a minute to defunk. Maybe she'll even come up with other names if she's not peeling her hair off her skin."

"It's okay." Darcy attempted a smile. "I want to give them as much information as possible, so they can find who did this."

Detective Pagonis snarled again. Detective Lester smiled, the voice of reason. "I have all I need for now. We'll reach out if we have any other questions." She pulled a card from her pocket. "If there is anything you can remember, please call my cell."

Darcy took the card and tried to smile, but she was clearly heartbroken.

"I'm sure I don't have to say this. Don't leave town." Detective Sunshine walked to the elevator and hit the button, staring at Kennedy until he and his partner got inside, and the doors closed.

CHAPTER 3

Steam billowed from the bathroom down the hall. The crime scene people had sifted through the office, but hadn't found any evidence of a struggle. They cleared the room, which was good since Darcy either had to take a shower here or use the showers in the men's locker room. Darcy disappeared behind the bathroom door over twenty minutes ago, and the shower had been going ever since.

Not that Kennedy blamed her. If she was in there, she'd be looking at using all the soap and all the hot water—heck, maybe even some of the cold— to get the blood off.

Kennedy walked around the room, running a hand over the long white executive desk as she made her way to the floor to ceiling windows overlooking the field. The large skylight in the dome let in the setting sun, casting an orange glow over the synthetic grass. She couldn't get over the view. It was beautiful. A field of green surrounded by blue and gold seats. Chuck and Darcy had built something good here.

She moved back to the desk, running her hand along the

surface. Nine drawers with black knobs. The knobs were so smooth. She pulled one of the drawers open. Papers lined the top drawer. She should close it. She should go back to that window and watch the grass grow—although since it was synthetic that seemed like an awfully boring proposition. And since her best friend's husband was dead downstairs, she needed to do something to help. She needed to make sure this didn't blow back on Darcy.

The best way was to start looking at the facts—starting with this desk. She pulled out a stack of paperwork. On the top of the pile was a birthday card from Chuck's Aunt Judith. Next was an electric bill. A blank pad of paper.

"Find anything incriminating?"

Kennedy looked up at Darcy, who was standing in the bathroom doorway wearing a robe, a towel twisted into a turban on her head. All the gore was gone. Kennedy guiltily stuffed the paperwork back like a kid whose hand was caught in the owner's drawer. Well, it wasn't *like* that. It *was* that.

"Don't stop on my account." Darcy walked over to the desk and pulled out the papers. "I need to go through all this stuff."

"We don't have to do it now. Your boobs are about to fall out of that robe. Put on some clothes and we can come back tomorrow."

"Eh, who needs clothes." Darcy sat on the couch, her robe riding dangerously high.

Kennedy lifted her hand to block the impending beaver view. "I'm about to see something you haven't flashed me since college."

Darcy laughed as she tugged the robe closed over her naughty bits. Kennedy was almost afraid to look for fear of what might pop out and say hi.

Kennedy gathered another stack of papers. She sat at the

other end of the couch and flipped through her stack. A gas bill. A few memo pages with random lists. Post it notes with illegible scribbles. Another electric bill. Folded papers with notes. More lists and scribbles. A page from a coloring book with Dad scribbled at the top in bright pink. Fanny must have colored this when she was just a kid—at least fifteen years ago. She was going to be heartbroken. Not to mention their son, Charles.

"Have you told Fanny and Charles about their father?"

Darcy checked her cell phone. "I tried to call, but I can't get ahold of them." The disappointment on her face said there was no new message from her kids. "I texted them to come home ASAP, and I sent a car to their colleges to pick them up. It's probably best I tell them in person, anyway."

"Isn't Charles in Los Angeles?"

"He is. The plane is there to bring him home." Darcy said *the plane* like someone would say *the bus*—like everyone had a jet waiting on standby.

"Wouldn't they realize there's an issue and call since you sent a car out of the blue?"

"No, we've done this before. Usually when they forget some family obligation. One time we sent a car to their high school so we could go to Spain." Darcy leaned over and sifted through the Kennedy's stack of papers. "Those kids are going to be expecting something happy, and I'm going to destroy their world."

"Your world is pretty much destroyed, too." Kennedy moved back to the desk and opened another drawer. A box of granola bars. A few napkins. Nothing else.

"I know, but I'm just the mom. This is their father. Their whole world."

"Now you're their whole world." She closed the drawer and looked at Darcy.

"I guess." Darcy opened the card Kennedy had found earlier. "His aunt Judith always loved him. He was always her favorite. But then, Chuck was everyone's favorite. No matter what he did." She tossed the redundant paperwork toward the end table. "I need to get my mind off of the kids and what I have to do. What else is in the drawer over there?"

Kennedy opened the far drawer and laughed. "I found something." She pulled out a bottle of Jack Daniels. The good stuff, the Single Barrel Select.

"My man." Darcy stood up and took, clasping it to her chest. "This is why I loved him."

"Because he had whiskey in his desk?"

"Because he had the foresight to know I'd need this." Darcy picked up a glass from a side table. "Are you still on the wagon?"

Kennedy nodded. "Ten months." Ten months and twenty-four days, to be exact.

"I'm sorry." Darcy slid the glass through her fingers.

"Don't be." Kennedy was hoping to avoid this conversation for a while—or forever. She'd managed to dodge it yesterday while they got ready for the Glowing Hope gala. She'd managed to avoid it during the festivities at the gala. She'd even managed to avoid the conversation after the gala when Darcy was dealing with the heartbreak of fighting with her husband. Today, apparently, she wasn't that lucky. "We should be focusing on you."

"Please. I'm sick of focusing on me and my nightmare." Darcy sat on the desk next to Kennedy and crossed her legs, setting the bottle down behind her back. "What happened in Chicago?"

Kennedy shrugged. "With the Cubs? I'm a Chicagoan. We're used to them blowing their shot."

"Come on. You know what I mean. What happened with your job?"

That drink would be so welcome right about now, but a drink was what had led to the past nightmare of a year. "I was on a tough murder case… the victim was a child…" Darcy didn't need to hear the grisly details. Kennedy certainly didn't, not again. "It was bad. I couldn't go home. I couldn't be alone with my thoughts, so I went to a local bar just to be around people."

"Not the best idea. It must have been a rough scene." Darcy rested her hand on Kennedy's. She'd been there when Kennedy had gone through Alcoholics Anonymous back in college. The first time.

And she'd hoped it would have been the last time, but then that damn crime scene happened, and Kennedy fell off the wagon and shattered her life on the gravel. "It was a mistake. Not as bad as getting behind the wheel of my car. I don't even remember leaving the bar."

"Oh honey." Darcy leaned over and pulled her into a brief hug.

"I drove about a foot and hit the side of the building."

"What?" Darcy sat back, rearranging the robe.

"Yeah. Apparently, I put the car into drive instead of reverse."

Darcy leaned into Kennedy, frowning. "Were you hurt?"

"No. I was lucky. I'm fine. I didn't hurt anyone. Car was wrecked. Career is in shambles. I'm on desk duty at the station. Working the evidence locker. Can't screw that up."

"So you're still being punished?"

"Yeah, I have to go through twelve months of AA and counselling." And after today, she could definitely use a meeting.

"Twelve months?"

"The city of Chicago isn't fond of their police officers running into buildings while driving drunk."

"I can see that." Darcy leaned back and bumped the bottle on the desk. She reached behind her and stopped it from falling over. "What about Steve?"

The enabling ex-boyfriend. "He didn't quite make the cut."

"I'd say I'm sorry to hear that, but I didn't think he was right for you." Darcy never liked him.

Not that Kennedy could really disagree with that assessment at this point. He'd been easy to commiserate with about the job and even easier to drink with about the job. Unfortunately, beside the occasional romp in the hay, that was the extent of the relationship. "You and my therapist agree on that."

"I'll put this away." Darcy said, hefting the whiskey bottle.

Kennedy reached for a glass and handed it to Darcy. "Go ahead and have a drink. You've earned it."

"Are you sure?"

"Just keep it downwind. I'll be fine." Kennedy hoped, anyway.

Darcy got up and moved across the room before pouring three fingers into her glass, throwing it back before the liquid had stopped swishing. She poured another three fingers and then took a bottle of soda out of the refrigerator. She poured the soda into another glass and handed that to Kennedy. "Cream soda. Drink up, lady."

Kennedy sipped her sugary bubbles as Darcy took another gulp of amber liquid.

"What else is in there?" Darcy leaned against the desk. "If there's pot in there, I'm going to remarry that man." A high-pitched laugh laced with bitterness left her lips.

"Are you okay?"

"I miss him already. He had his faults, but he was my Chuck." Darcy drank again before shaking her head. "Not that I was his anything. We had history. We had two wonderful children."

"You did make some good kids."

"Yeah. That was the one thing we did right." Darcy

swirled the last of the JD in her glass. "What else is in there?"

Kennedy tilted her head to get another look into the giant drawer. No more booze, and definitely no Mary Jane. Which was probably good. Darcy was sucking down that whiskey like a teenager with a vat of Monster. Any more drugs or alcohol and she'd be in rehab before Chuck was in the ground.

"There's this." Kennedy pulled a dirty stuffed toy jalapeño from the bowels.

"Oh my goodness!" Darcy leaned over and ripped the pepper from her hand. "I can't believe he kept it."

"A filthy germ magnet?"

"No. I won this for him at the Sigma Chi mixer Sophomore year."

"Oh. My. Goodness! The wet T-shirt contest!" Kennedy remembered that mixer—barely. She'd gotten drunk and was tired waiting for the toilet, so she peed in the shower. The guys weren't too happy and banned her for a week—like the frat brothers never peed in the shower. That was the first time she was banned from a fraternity, but it wasn't the last.

Darcy stuck out her chest and shimmied. The jalapeño shook. "The girls won me more than a hot-ass husband."

"The girls are impressive."

Darcy's smile slowly deflated. Either the whiskey or the memories. Probably a mixture of both. Her eyes welled as she stared at the stuffed toy. It was a moment. A private moment.

And Kennedy didn't want to interrupt, so she shifted her attention back to the desk. A letter from the mayor, kissing Chuck's ass for being rich or a sports icon—or both. She pulled out a folded paper and opened it.

You need to get your head out of your ass. Are you sure you played football? You know nothing about the game and don't deserve the air you breathe.

"What's that?" Darcy asked.

"I'd say it's a hate letter. Somebody didn't like the way Chuck was managing the team."

"He would get some hateful shit from rabid fans." Darcy poured herself another three fingers of whiskey. Thankfully the bottle was empty, or Kennedy would have had to take the thing away.

Kennedy waved the letter at Darcy. "Shouldn't you have told the cops about this? This one is pretty bad."

"He's been getting them for years. You should have seen the one's he got as a player. You can't satisfy everyone." Darcy held out her hand. "Let me see it."

Kennedy kept it out of reach. There was no way Darcy needed to see that right now. "No. Let's see what else is in here." She opened another envelope. "Alex Volkov?" Did she say that out loud? The name sounded familiar.

"The winger?" Darcy walked around the desk. "What about him?"

"He wrote a letter to Chuck."

Darcy leaned over Kennedy's shoulder, blinking. "What does it say?"

Kennedy scanned the page. "He says he'll tell everyone Chuck's secret if he doesn't re-sign Tad Markham."

"His secret?"

"What secret? And why Tad?" Kennedy didn't think Chuck had any secrets. He was an open-book kind of guy. He did shitty things and wasn't shy about sharing them. It was one of the reasons Kennedy couldn't stand the man. She could never understand how he could cheat on Darcy, but to be fair, he never lied about doing it.

"I don't know the secret, but Tad Markham is our captain and our star player. We built the entire team around him. Alex is the team leader."

"Wouldn't Alex want him off the team, so he could move into the captain position?"

Darcy shook her head. "That's not how it works. Alex was brought in to support Tad. Without Tad, we don't need Alex."

That sounded like a motive. "What do you think the secret could be?"

"No clue." Darcy perked up. "We should ask him."

"Now?"

"Why not?"

"Maybe we should give this to the cops and let them ask."

"Why?" Darcy took the letter from Kennedy. "You're a cop. You know more than these people could ever know about interrogating the perp."

"Okay, *Law and Order*, you got the lingo down. But I wouldn't go that far." Kennedy's interrogating skills had disappeared while she was confined to the evidence locker.

Darcy rolled her eyes. "Okay fine. However, you do know Chuck and you know me. This will be personal for you."

"Which is why the experts should handle it."

"No, it's why you're perfect." Darcy bounced up and down. The twin reasons for the stuffed jalapeño prize bounced in Kennedy's face. "Come with me to talk to Alex. These cops will screw it up."

"They seemed fine." Well, Lester seemed fine. The other one was a narcissist with anger issues.

"Please help me." Darcy made prayer hands, doing alarming things to her chest. "For me."

Kennedy wanted to say no. She came here to get away from the shit-show that was her life. She'd gamble, see a soccer game or two, and eat her weight in buffet foods— mostly crab legs. She couldn't get a decent crab leg in Chicago to save her life. She also came to get away from cops and cop work. And she sure didn't want to fight with the narcissist about jurisdiction.

Darcy didn't pout, but it was so close. "You owe me."

And there it was. Darcy had never called in that chit before. This meant a lot to her.

"Okay, but you have to get dressed." Kennedy would do whatever it took to help Darcy. She owed Darcy her life.

CHAPTER 4

One hour, two lattes, and three cupcakes later, Kennedy followed a mostly sober and completely dressed Darcy down the hall, past the suite of offices and what appeared to be a medical center, to the locker room. "Why would Alex be here today?" Kennedy asked.

"They're training."

"The owner isn't going to get mad if they take a couple days off." Kennedy was pretty sure on that one.

"Chuck would want it this way."

"Really?" That sounded rather heartless, but maybe she didn't understand.

"He worked out a schedule to get them on track for the finals. He wouldn't want everyone slacking off. He loved this team."

Kennedy wasn't so sure about that, however Darcy knew him better than Kennedy ever could. "Don't they train at a training facility?"

"It's still being built in Henderson." Darcy pushed on a big metal door and walked through.

Kennedy followed her into a large room with a green

floor that resembled a field. White lines edged the outside and sliced down the center. A net was set on each side of the practice field.

"We ran into some zoning issues, so it's not going to be ready till next season. The guys practice over here, and they use the gym we have set up next to the locker room." She waved a hand at wall of floor to ceiling windows. On the other side of the glass, state-of-the-art treadmills and weightlifting benches were lined up, machine after machine.

"Mom, what are you doing in the bowels?" A young woman with red streaks in her blond hair approached Darcy.

Fanny? This couldn't be Darcy's daughter. Sometimes all Kennedy saw when she looked at Fanny was a tween with pigtails and braces, not this woman. "Fantasia!" Kennedy had called her Fantasia since she was born. The girl was magic from moment her lungs took in air.

"Aunt Kenn!"

"Oh my goodness, you are beautiful." Kennedy wrapped her best friend's daughter in a hug, and then pulled back. "How old are you now?"

"Nineteen." As old as Darcy was when she'd had her. It had been quite the drama back in the day. Darcy dropped out of school, and Chuck and Darcy had an actual shotgun wedding. Her father literally showed up to Chuck's fraternity house with a shotgun.

Despite all that, Chuck married her, and they had been happy until now. Happy adjacent, anyway.

"Sweetheart, you're back. Did you get my messages? Why didn't you come find me?" Darcy's eyebrows arched as she pulled her daughter into a hug. "I tried calling and texting," she said, her voice choked.

Fanny's tears slid down her face. "I was at soccer practice. Where's Dad?"

"Honey, there was an accident." Darcy swallowed. "Your father…"

"I know. Uncle Craig told me."

Darcy took a step back. "When did you talk to Uncle Craig? Where is he?"

Fanny shrugged. "He's upstairs hiding from the cops."

"What did he tell you?" Darcy asked, voice sharp.

"That Dad was murdered."

"How did he find out?"

Fanny frowned, looking confused. Kennedy was a little bit confused herself. Wasn't it a good thing that Craig told Fanny the hard news, so Darcy didn't have to? Kennedy had delivered this type of bad news multiple times. It sucked.

"Can I see Dad?"

"Oh honey." Darcy smoothed a piece of stray hair off Fanny's face. "I don't think that's a good idea."

"But Mom…"

"I don't think that's a good idea."

"Mom. I need to make sure it's him." Fanny's eyes watered, and she swiped at them.

"It is him, honey."

"Mom…"

Darcy stared at her daughter, looking like something was warring inside of her. Probably the urge to satisfy her daughter's curiosity versus the reality of how Chuck looked. "Follow me."

"Mom, they moved him."

"You were in the box?" Darcy asked. Kennedy completely understood her shocked tone. The box that looked like a horror movie set, soaked in blood spatter?

"I had to look, but they already took him away."

"Oh honey." The worry in Darcy's eyes was unmistakable.

"Yeah." Tears spilled down Fanny's face. "It was terrible."

"I know, sweetie." Darcy wrapped her in a hug. "That's why I don't want to take you to see Dad."

"I have to know."

"Know what?"

"If it's really him. It doesn't seem real."

Kennedy couldn't really blame Fanny for feeling that way. If it wasn't for her seeing Chuck with her own eyes, she wouldn't believe it was real either. Things like this happened on TV, or to other people. At least that was how it always felt… until now.

"Kennedy, can we start tomorrow?" Darcy said as she hugged her daughter, the words muffled by Fanny's hair.

"Tomorrow?" What were they starting? Oh. The letters. The threats.

"What's tomorrow?" Fanny pulled away from her mother.

Darcy looked directly at Kennedy. Over twenty-five years of friendship, and Kennedy understood Darcy was clearly asking her to shut the hell up. Which made sense. Some things your children didn't need to know. Darcy put on a half-smile. "We need to start talking to the staff and make sure everything is ready for the season."

"Of course." Kennedy smiled. Fanny didn't need to know that the talking had to do with her father. The murder was probably hard enough to deal with.

Darcy's phone dinged. "Charlie's flight just landed. I need to send a car…"

"Why don't I go get him?" Kennedy didn't want to sit around and infringe on the family moment.

"You don't mind?" Darcy felt at her jean pockets. "I don't have my keys."

Of course that wasn't surprising. She'd pulled on a spare pair of jeans and a team sweatshirt she kept in her own office for emergencies. "Do you have keys to any of the cars?"

"I have keys to the Range Rover." Fanny pulled out a fob and twirled it on her fingers.

"Can you give that to Kennedy so she can get your brother?"

"Sure." Fanny tossed the fob to Kennedy.

"Do you mind?" Darcy reached over and held Kennedy's hand. "I wouldn't ask if it wasn't important."

"Not at all." Kennedy had been in Vegas twenty-four hours, and she was already heading back to the airport. So far, this trip was anything but ordinary.

CHAPTER 5

Kennedy woke up to pitch black. She almost forgot where she was until she felt the softness of the sheets and the coziness of the pillows. Darcy's house.

The last time Kennedy had been here, they'd still been renovating. Now the bedrooms were gorgeous suites. Although she couldn't tell anything with all the dark surrounding her. It was obscenely dark. Darcy had mentioned something about this last night before bed. Something about auto-blinds and a remote. Kennedy flung her arm out, found the side table, and hit a random button. A television came on somewhere in the room, and the light from the screen showed her the lay of the land. Cream walls with burgundy bedding. Golden sconces on the walls, and a large white ceiling fan. She stared at the giant remote for a bleary second and clicked a button for the blinds before turning off the television.

The blinds slid to the side, and bright Vegas sunlight spilled into the room through extra-large glass doors. Kennedy tossed back the down comforter and the million-thread-count sheet, and then walked to the bathroom. From what Darcy said last night, every bedroom was a suite. Private bathroom. Private patio. Private view.

It was more opulent than a hotel. Even the bathroom had its own rain shower. Kennedy didn't even know such a thing existed until Darcy pointed it out. To be fair, she wasn't sure how she felt showering in the rain—even if it was Kohler-made rain.

After she did all the morning stuff in the bathroom, she took her minty-breathed self into the bedroom and looked out the largest sliding glass doors she'd ever seen. They had to be a good nine feet high. She pulled the latch, opened the door, and Vegas heat slapped at her cheeks. It felt nice after a night in the frozen air conditioning.

She crossed the patio and leaned against the stone railing. White stone steps led from Kennedy's room to a large crystal-blue pool with multiple small waterfalls along the far back wall. Palm trees lined the righthand side of the pool, and four wooden chaise lounges with tan cushions sat on the other side, on the deck.

A splash billowed in the pool, and Darcy's bottle-blond head popped out of the water. Her arms reached and pulled as her body sliced across the blue expanse, legs kicking.

Kennedy thought about going to see how Darcy was doing, but given the way she was pumping her arms, the woman needed this workout. And since Kennedy was currently wearing a tank top and underwear, she probably shouldn't be roaming the grounds.

An hour later, after a shower and wearing proper clothing, Kennedy left her room. The inside of the house was as beautiful as the outside. Wide hallways with extra tall ceilings. A majestic flight of stairs framed by etched glass led to the second floor. This house was amazing. The guest room was on the main floor, yet somehow it was quiet.

Until she reached another hallway.

Yelling. A lot of yelling. Kennedy followed the sound of Darcy's voice.

"Could you at least pretend to mourn? His body isn't even in the ground and you're planning your takeover." Kennedy hadn't heard her yell like that since she'd caught Chuck smoking three months after he'd said he quit. And then three years. Then twelve years after. He'd had a hard time quitting… over and over again.

A man's voice growled, "I'm trying to help you. You don't know. My father left us money before he was taken and now Chuck—"

"Craig, your father left you both the same amount of money. Chuck bought the club, and you bought hookers." Darcy sounded like this was an old argument.

Chuck had been very vocal about the problems his brother seemed to have with women and money and the law. Originally the two brothers bought the team, but Chuck ultimately bought out his brother when the rest of Craig's money ran dry.

At the moment, Craig seemed to have given up on words as he straight up growled in the kitchen, facing off with Darcy across a counter. Kennedy had met the man a few times, and each time he was usually drunk.

Darcy sneered. "I'm sorry the hooker industry didn't offer proper dividends."

"It has nothing to do with dividends." He grabbed at himself… well, the miniature himself. And from the pinch of his hands, it was very miniature. Which would explain why he was so cranky.

"Don't be vile," Darcy huffed.

Okay Kennedy was being a bit vile, but she had a feeling Darcy wasn't talking to her. Kennedy kept the vile inside her head where it belonged.

"You're the one talking about those ladies." He said

those ladies as if he was a prude whispering the town gossip. Like the words were bitter.

"At least I'm not keeping those ladies in stilettos and G-strings."

Craig jabbed a finger at her. "You're a racist. Those ladies are college students and parents."

"I think you need to try reading a book," Darcy said. "What I said wasn't racist. It was ignorant at worst, presumptuous at best."

"Chuck said you'd never understand," he whispered. "He knew they'd come, and you wouldn't get it."

"Who'd come?"

"He said you wouldn't understand." Craig shook his head, like his head was rejecting the things he was saying. "You're being a bit…."

"That's enough." Kennedy didn't mean to say that out loud, but she wasn't going to stand by and let him call Darcy a bitch the day after her husband was killed. You had to give a woman at least a month before you pulled that type of shit.

His growl was back. "Who are you?"

"Kennedy. Who the hell are you?" Yeah, she knew who he was, but he didn't know that.

"Kennedy from school?" He sounded surprised. Although, to be fair, her boobs had grown in since the last time she saw him.

"Yes."

The surprise turned to a scowl. "Well, I'm family."

Kennedy felt those words to her core. She wasn't family. Most people wouldn't have cared. Most people would have their own family.

"She's more family than you have ever been." Darcy's voice took on a tone that Kennedy had never heard, and her eye twitched—the sign that her fury was about to spill over.

"She was here when the kids were born. She was here when I was diagnosed with skin cancer."

"And I suppose it's a coincidence that she's here when my brother was taken." Craig looked up to the sky.

"Get out!" Darcy's mask of fury looked like a heart attack waiting to happen.

Kennedy wasn't sure if getting in the middle of family was a good idea. However, she had no desire to attend another funeral. It was too soon. "It's okay." Kennedy wasn't sure why, but this didn't feel right."

"No, it's not." Darcy was now glaring at her. Kennedy should have stuck with the first instinct to keep her mouth shut.

Craig sighed. "Maybe I should just leave."

"Maybe you should." Darcy walked around the island. The kitchen was a sea of white. White walls. White cabinets. White lights in the flower-shaped chandelier. The marbled brown counters offered the only color. And if Darcy got any closer to Craig, it would be covered in red.

No one wanted to clean that up.

Craig shook his head as he turned to leave.

"Stay away from my office." Darcy towered over Craig. "If Chuck wanted your help with the team, he would've asked."

"Well, I have to protect you and he's not here to ask." There it was again. Craig seemed hellbent on protecting Darcy.

"No. I'm here. And I am very capable of handling the team and everything else. I don't need your protection."

Craig huffed. He didn't appear too incredibly happy with her decision, but he looked like he was resigned enough to shut up for now. He left the kitchen, and a moment later Kennedy heard a door click closed.

"Are you alright?" Darcy said at the same time Kennedy asked, "Are you okay?"

Darcy's lips curled up, however there was no smile in her eyes. She looked tired. "Jinx. You owe me a Coke."

Kennedy grinned. "Why are you asking if I'm all right? You're the one who's dealing with the in-laws."

"Ah." Darcy waved it off. "I'm used to dealing with him and his brand of crazy."

"Is he gone?" Darcy's son Charlie walked in the door. Kennedy couldn't get over how much he'd grown. Last time she'd seen him he was a kid playing with toys. Now he was in his first year of college. She'd barely recognized him at the airport. He was six feet tall now. His dark brown hair reminded her of Darcy's hair, back before she could afford highlights.

"He's gone." Darcy walked over to the coffeemaker and poured herself a cup. "Anyone want?"

"Nah." Charlie walked to the fridge and leaned in. "Do we have anything to eat?"

"I don't know." Darcy poured a second cup and set it in front of Kennedy. "Grab your aunt some cream."

Charlie pulled out a bottle of cream, and Kennedy couldn't help her smile. Darcy remembered how she liked her coffee. She really was family.

"Can we order breakfast?" Charlie had given up on the fridge and was swiping at his phone.

Darcy took a sip of coffee. "I was going to run to the office."

"Mom, I think we should stay here." Charlie stopped running his finger along his phone.

"Kennedy and I have some work to do." Darcy looked at Kennedy like she held some secret. Although the fact that Alex Volkov held some magic information was probably a secret.

"I think Fanny needs us here." Charlie put down his phone.

Kennedy didn't think Darcy would go for it, but she had

to offer. "I can go talk to Alex." She didn't want to talk to him alone. She wasn't even sure what to say.

"Could you?"

She could. Did she want to? The voice in her head and the part that controlled motion appeared to be in disagreement. Kennedy nodded.

"That would be amazing."

And so Kennedy would go. She could handle one little interrogation. This seemed to make Charlie feel better. He picked up his phone and his face was bathed in the fake glow once again.

Fanny walked in the room. "What do you need to talk to Alex about?" Despite being upset, she seemed to have put herself together well.

"Nothing important." Darcy took a long drink from her coffee cup.

"Mom, I told you I want to be more involved at the club."

"And you will be once you're out of school, sweetheart." Darcy set her mug on the counter.

Fanny's eyes teared up. "Don't patronize me." She spun on her heels and ran back the way she'd come.

"I told you, Mom." Charlie didn't look up from his phone. "I'm ordering from Omelet House."

"I'll take a gyro omelet." Darcy shook her head. "I have to go deal with this," she told Kennedy. "Are you sure you can handle the meeting with Alex?"

No. "Are you sure you don't want to be there? We can talk to him tomorrow."

"I'd like to know what he meant today. Take the Jag. Go up to the main offices and ask for Belinda. She can help you get around." A door slammed in the house. "Shit. That's my cue."

"I got it." And Kennedy did.

Darcy grabbed her coffee mug and followed the path her daughter had just taken.

Part of Kennedy wanted to follow Darcy. The other part of her didn't want anything to do with the drama that was about to unfold. She grabbed Darcy's car keys from the hook in the kitchen and headed out the door, accompanied by screaming in the background.

Yeah. Leaving was the right decision, she had an interview to perform.

CHAPTER 6

Kennedy stood outside Darcy's office door talking to Bobby, the security guard. "Thank you so much."

"It's my job." Bobby smiled.

"Securing the building is your job. Helping lost women probably wasn't in the job description." Last time she'd gone past the owner's box, so she'd tried to follow the same path. But the owner's box was locked down. All the cops appeared to be gone, which meant police tape was currently holding out all the shenanigans.

Thankfully Bobby found her lurking around before she had to start wandering the halls and calling out for help. A *You Are Here* poster would have come in handy, but personalized delivery by security was nice.

He nodded. "I'm full service, ma'am."

"How long have you worked for the Vegas Victory?"

"Three months." He wasn't overly loquacious. Kennedy could appreciate that. It didn't mean she wasn't going to try to crack this nut.

"Do you like it?"

"It's a good job, ma'am." Nice guy. Good manners. It wasn't very often she was called ma'am in the big city.

Not that she liked being called ma'am. She was too young for that shit. "You don't have to call me ma'am. My name is Kennedy."

"Sorry, my momma wouldn't like that."

A momma's boy. Sweet. She was about to say that when someone asked, "Are you Kennedy?"

"I am." Kennedy straightened up when a woman sporting short black hair with pink tips ran into the foyer. Ran didn't do the movement justice. She was a like a tornado whooshing through the room. She was adorable, maybe late twenties, in a red ruffled shirt over a short bright pink skirt that accentuated muscular legs—to help with the whooshing.

"I'm Belinda." She dropped her purse on the desk in front of Darcy's door. "Darcy says you need to find Alex Volkov."

"Yes."

Belinda sat at her desk and booted up the computer. She opened drawers and grabbed things. She seemed to be in a hurry and incredibly focused on whatever she was doing. As the computer beeped and buzzed, Belinda clicked her nails on the keyboard.

She waited. Which meant she grabbed her water bottle from the bottom drawer. Then she poked at the keyboard again. She then got up and filled her bottle from the sink in the kitchenette to the right of her desk.

The woman was eerily efficient. And from the looks of it, incapable of sitting still.

Belinda came back to her desk and clicked and clacked her fingers on the keyboard with the efficiency of a maestro. She smiled. "Alex should be in the gym."

"Can we interrupt him?"

"Darcy is the boss. If she wants you to talk to him, he'll

talk." Belinda stood up and smiled. "Do you mind walking?"

"Of course not." Was there another way to get around the complex? She probably should have said yes, just to see what the other options might be.

Kennedy followed Belinda down the carpeted hall, past office after office. They came to a large metal door and walked through to concrete stairs.

They went down a flight... make that two... and Kennedy's thighs screamed as they kept going down, apparently to the bowels of hell. It was good they were going down the stairs. If they were going up, she might've told Belinda to leave her there and save herself.

Six flights later—six—Belinda stopped and opened another metal door. They walked past an elevator.

"There's an elevator?" Kennedy stared at the thing like it was her long-lost father. She could have taken an elevator. Her legs wobbled in disappointment.

"Yeah. I just like to get the blood pumping, don't you?"

"Umm..." Kennedy's blood liked to stay where it was, but now wasn't the time to talk about it. Since she'd been relegated to the evidence locker, her cardio had suffered. She needed to get back into the action before she forgot how to be a cop.

The hall was lined with nubby gold carpet, and two blue leather chairs sat around a brown side table. More chairs and tables could be seen up and down the long hallway. A coffee cup from a local shop sat on one table, and Belinda picked up the cup and dumped it in a golden garbage can.

Kennedy followed Belinda through the open door to the gym. The clanking of weight machines and male voices filled the air, as well as the stale smell of sweat. As they turned into the space they could see more of the machines and the men at them. Good grief, the gym was big. You could be working out at one end and not see anyone at the other end.

The machines banged and clanged as they walked toward an office area with two desks butted up against each other. A slim man with gray hair stood over one of the black metal desks. A nameplate on one desk read Coach Brighton. Not that Kennedy needed an introduction. She'd seen the man a time or two on television.

Belinda knocked on the door jamb before walking in. "Good morning, Coach. I want to introduce you to Darcy's friend Kennedy Romero. Kennedy, this is Coach Brighton. We're looking for Alex Volkov."

"Morning, sunshine." The coach's mustache curved as he smiled. "He's in the locker room. He just finished practice."

"Okay. We'll wait out here."

"They might take forever." Coach tossed a pad of paper onto his desk and waved at a side door. "Let's go." He pushed the door open and leaned his head in. "Volkov, out here."

Voices came from the locker room, but since Kennedy was standing back trying not to get a full-frontal view of changing athletes, she couldn't hear what they were saying.

"Seriously, you're not coming out?" The coach's voice turned menacing as he disappeared inside the room. A minute later he reappeared. "Ladies, come inside."

"Are you sure?" Kennedy didn't want to intrude on the guys as they got ready and left the stadium.

"They're used to the media being in here." Belinda followed the coach with no hesitation, so Kennedy did the same.

Men with lots of pecs and skin stood in front of cubbies. Belinda walked across the room to one of the men with a towel around his waist. His shoulder muscles were doing some serious bulging. But that wasn't what caught

Kennedy's eye. It was the scowl on his face. He was all sorts of angry.

"Alex Volkov." Belinda motioned to Kennedy. "This is Mrs. Perrault's friend, Kennedy. She has a few questions."

"Got warrant?" Alex seemed to be a jerky jock, but his accent was fun. The words sounded more like, "Gaut varrent?"

"No, but I'm sure you'd be happy to help since Chuck Perrault is dead." Kennedy hated to pull the whole death card so soon. Heck they hadn't even started the interrogation. This guy didn't seem to be agreeable at all, though. He needed a push or a slap.

"Why would I want help him? He did nothing for me."

Kennedy wasn't a prude or anything, but the towel needed to go. "Can you lose the towel and get dressed so we can talk?"

"Sure." Alex dropped the towel and stood there in nothing but his birthday suit. Stark. Naked. All his dangly bits dangling. The man was solid muscle. There wasn't much dangling. Except for…well.

That wasn't exactly what she meant by lose the towel. Kennedy didn't want to see all his body parts, she wanted to see less. However, she was a professional. She shouldn't be swayed by the dangly-bit lolling left then right. She tried to close her eyes. Her eyes wouldn't stop looking.

"See something you like?" Alex laughed as some guys laughed and some guys screamed at him to cover up.

"I'm not sure like is the word." Belinda made a scrunched face. "I get it's cold in here but cover it up. I'm starting to feel sorry for you."

The whole room erupted in laughter, and Kennedy held back a smile. She needed this guy, and laughing at the size of his, erm, member wasn't going to get him talking.

"Sorry enough to make it grow?" Alex smirked and let it dangle.

Belinda snorted. "Trying to get your stick stroked by pity?"

"I'll get stick stroked any way I can. As long as I don't have to rely on self-stimulation."

Everyone laughed, and even the coach had a bit of a smile on his face. "All right, guys. That's enough."

"Do you want to get dressed now, so we can talk?" Kennedy kept her lips from quirking up, but it was hard… since Alex was not. Even her subconscious was trying to get her to smile.

Alex sighed as he pulled on a pair of jeans and a T-shirt. "What do you want?"

"Did you want to go somewhere else and get some privacy?" Kennedy turned to see all the men staring at them. "No offense." The men turned back to their cubbies, pretending to ignore the drama.

"I'm good here. I don't hide things from teammates." Alex slid on a watch and fastened it.

"I read the letter you sent Chuck. Did you want to talk about that?" Kennedy kept it vague. She had a feeling he was hiding this from his teammates and the cops. No one wanted to be the guy who sent the threatening letter right before the recipient was killed.

Alex seemed to think about it for a moment, but must have realized the rest of the questions would not reflect well on him. "Fine." He shoved his cell phone and keys in his pockets before walking toward the door of the locker room.

Kennedy looked over at Belinda, who shrugged and followed him into the hall. This was going to be interesting.

CHAPTER 7

Belinda led them down the hall and back to the gym. The rest of the team must be in the locker room, because the room was as quiet as a coffin.

"I'm going to go back to my desk if you have everything you need," Belinda told Kennedy.

"Yes, thank you."

Belinda stopped. "Can you find your way out of the building?"

In theory. Maybe. "Sure." She'd follow the halls until she ended up on the outside. It couldn't be that hard. Right?

Belinda disappeared, and Kennedy was left alone with Alex Volkov. And he didn't look thrilled to be alone with her. Then again, he already knew the topic, so she wouldn't take his discomfort personally.

"Do you want to tell me about the letter?"

"You know so much. You tell me?" Alex was a real splash of sunshine… making Kennedy wish she had a splash of vodka. Why couldn't anything be easy?

"You mentioned a secret Chuck had been hiding." When

Alex didn't say anything, Kennedy continued. "What was the secret?"

"If I told you, it wouldn't be secret."

"Yes, but I'm sure he wouldn't mind you telling me." *Since he's dead and all.* She left that last part out because it sounded flippant.

"You don't know. He had reputation."

"Would his secret ruin his reputation?"

Alex cackled like an evil witch over a cauldron. "Oh yeah."

"Well, I'm a cop in Chicago." She didn't need to go into detail about what she did as said cop in Chicago. "And I need to ensure that the family won't be vulnerable to any threats if this secret comes out." That sounded so professional. Even she believed that was her only motivation, and not that her best friend thought her husband was a man-whore.

"Well, then ask his wife." Alex dropped onto one of the workout benches like a toddler told he had to go to church.

"She doesn't know."

He laughed. "So that's why you're asking question."

She didn't bother answering. They both knew that was why. And he wasn't giving her anything. She needed to get him talking about something else before she lost his attention completely. "What's your relationship with Tad Markham?"

"Relationship?" Alex almost seemed to be offended. "We work together."

She didn't think offending him was the key to his chatterbox. "I just meant that you two seem to be close."

Alex shrugged, his guard lowering. "Yes, he was my first friend when I moved to States from Russia."

"When did you move here?"

"High school."

"You're a good friend." Flattery should get her further.

In theory. "You threatened to tell Chuck's secret for him. That's a lot of loyalty for someone you just work with."

"What can I say, I want to win. He's good player." Alex pulled out his cellphone and began poking at the screen. His attention was heading in the same direction as her patience. Gone.

"Were they planning on trading Tad?"

"They must have been." Alex seemed enthralled with that darn screen. Maybe it was giving him instructions on how to annoy the hell out of her. "I read it on internet, so must be true." The phone was right. He was annoying the hell out of her.

She'd say this whole discussion was futile, but futility felt too optimistic. This was getting her nowhere. "So you don't know if he was going to be traded?"

"I know they talked about it."

See, nowhere. "Don't they talk about trading you guys regularly?" She'd accidentally sat through the sports report during the news her first night in town, and all they did was speculate on trades. Who'd make the cut? Who'd be traded before the trade deadline? They called it a transfer deadline, but it was the same concept. The scores were secondary to who was going to play where.

"Maybe the shitty players. I don't have to worry about that." His smirk was aimed at his hand.

She wanted to reach out and slap him with that cellphone. "Which was why you felt comfortable threatening one of the owners."

"I didn't threaten anyone."

"You threatened to tell his secret."

"I don't think you can arrest me for gossip." He sneered.

"I'm not trying to arrest you at all. I just want to know what he was hiding."

Alex sighed and looked up from the screen. "Not my story to tell."

"You said…"

"I lied. I wouldn't say anything." Alex slid his phone into his pocket. "What Chuck did on his own time was not my business."

"It was enough of your business to write a letter."

"If I could benefit from Chuck's bad choices, I would."

"Can you answer me this?" She paused because she really didn't want to know the answer—because she already knew. "Was he having an affair?"

Alex looked at his shoes, like they had some magic power to give him all the answers. So naturally, she stared at his shoes. Since this guy was answer-free, she might as well search anywhere that held promise.

"Look." Alex sighed as he stood up. "Everyone knew he was having affair. His secret had nothing to do with another woman. That wasn't secret."

"Another man?"

"No." Alex laughed. "Not that."

"Then what is it?"

"Ask his wife." Alex pulled his keys from his other pocket. "I have to go."

"She doesn't know."

"She knows more than she thinks." With those cryptic words, Alex walked out of the gym and out of earshot.

Kennedy needed more clues, and the one person who might have them was walking out the door. She dropped to the bench Alex just vacated and sighed. She needed help. Maybe some sort of annoying soccer player code book to put his cryptic-crack into English.

CHAPTER 8

"Bad day, huh?"

Kennedy jumped up from the bench and found the coach looking at her with a mixture of amusement and pity. Or that might have been her own interpretation. "Yeah." One could call it a bad day. Or one could call it a bad year. But this wasn't the time or place to get into all that.

"I've had one or two of those myself. Follow me." He walked through the gym, stopping outside his office. "Come on in and cop a squat." He was a good-looking man —short hair that was graying at the edges. Slim build, which probably helped him keep up with all the young soccer players. His skin was sun kissed, if not a little sun wrinkled. But it only made him more distinguished, in Kennedy's mind. He reminded her of her grandfather, or a trusted uncle.

"I don't want to impose."

"Not an imposition at all. I could use the company." He turned and walked into the small office. Aside from the two desks, there was a water cooler and a mini fridge. "Need a drink?"

"Water?"

Coach Brighton nodded and got her a cup of water from the cooler. "Do you mind if I drink something a little stronger?"

"Not at all." She hated to admit she'd like to drink something a little stronger, but talking to Alex and wondering what exactly Darcy was potentially hiding was weighing on her mind.

He poured amber liquid into his tumbler. "Best bourbon in Kentucky."

"We're not exactly near the Bluegrass State."

"You know the nickname."

"I might have taken a twirl on the bourbon trail a time or two. It's only a handful of hours east of Chicago." And each time she'd been hungover for only a handful of days. But the bourbon had been rather tasty.

"What's your favorite?"

"From the trail? Maker's. Yours?"

"This." The coach lifted the glass. "Pappy Van Winkle."

Kennedy tried not to inhale, but damn did that bourbon smell sweet. Honey and smoke. She wanted to take a drink more than her next breath, but that never ended well.

"It's my favorite." He sipped, then swirled the rest in the glass.

She couldn't seem to turn away. She was probably looking at him like she wanted to jump him—and to be fair, she did. She wanted to rip the glass from his hand and bathe in it.

Coach didn't seem to notice. "It would be even better with a cube of ice, but they won't give me a full fridge in here. Probably because I'd have to sit inside the damn thing for it to fit."

She laughed. And that broke the spell the bourbon had on her. She turned to the side and took a breath of clean air.

"So, what did Alex have to say?" Coach asked.

Kennedy wasn't sure how much she should share. No matter what, this was an ongoing murder investigation. But honestly, so far today was feeling like a bust. "Nothing. Somehow he managed to say a bunch of words and not say anything at all."

The coach laughed, a deep guttural guffaw. "That's Alex. I once asked him why he thought it was appropriate to stay out past curfew before a game and he went on a rant about stars aligning and the end of the crimson wave. I still have no idea what he was saying."

Kennedy raised her glass of water to her mouth. She didn't want him to know that she did indeed know what the crimson wave was, and basically Alex's excuse was that he needed to get some with his girlfriend since she'd been menstruating the week before. What a charmer.

"Did Alex have a problem with Chuck?" She needed to change the direction of the conversation before the coach asked about crimson waves.

"Alex has a problem with everyone. They didn't exactly agree on the team direction." The coach refilled his glass and sat back down behind his desk. "Alex has had trouble with nearly everyone on the team."

"He seems to like Tad Markham." She was assuming that, anyway. He was willing to go out on a limb to get him to stay.

"They went to high school together, so there's history. But honestly, they fight constantly. Tad gets all the attention that Alex feels should be his."

"Then why would Alex want Tad to stay on the team?"

"I think it's a family thing. They've been together so long, they don't know how to operate apart. It's like a bad marriage. Alex asked me to trade Tad at the beginning of the season, but they must have kissed and made up because he dropped it."

"Have you thought of trading Tad?"

"I didn't. If we traded Tad, most of the team would have to go." Coach took a sip. "We aren't ready to rebuild. We just put together this team."

"So maybe Alex figured that out and wanted to keep Tad on the roster so he wouldn't get traded."

"Alex probably wouldn't have been traded. No one wants to work with him anymore. He's nearing the end of his career and it's not because of his age. No one wants to deal with someone who has a bad attitude. His skills can't cover the checks his mouth tries to write."

"If Tad left," Kennedy asked, "would Alex stay on?"

"Not if I had anything to say about it." Brighton set his glass down.

"So keeping Tad means Alex could continue to play."

"I guess so." Brighton leaned back and motioned to the chair pushed against the other desk. "Have a seat."

"Do you miss Chuck?" Kennedy sat and took a drink of water. "I always wondered if he was a good boss." Since he was less than stellar in the husband department.

"He wasn't bad. He let me do my thing. Not all owners are smart enough to let the coaches do their job. Some stick their nose where it doesn't belong."

"Chuck didn't do that?"

"He had his opinions, but he'd let us do our job."

"Even with all the trade talk?"

Coach took a long pull on his drink. "I wasn't happy with the rebuild he was trying to push. But with the end of the transfer window approaching, I figured I'd just push it off till that passed and we'd be able to move forward. We aren't ready. And it's a waste of money. But he was hellbent on it."

"That must have been frustrating."

"Yeah. But I would've convinced him to hold off. We had a meeting scheduled next week."

"Did he have any enemies that you know of?"

"Not really. People seemed to like him, I guess. I had no issue. Then again, I wasn't his brother." He leaned forward in his chair and ran a finger along the edge of his glass. "I can't believe Chuck's gone." He finished the glass of bourbon and sat back. His face went from cloudy, to bright with a side of smile. "How long have you known Darcy and Chuck?"

"I was roommates with Darcy in college." Which felt like it was yesterday and not over ten years ago.

"So, you knew them when they met."

She did, so she nodded.

"I heard she was a bit wild back then."

"I don't know about wild." Although the time they tossed the bubble mix into Professor Wallace's front-yard fountain was wild. "She was young."

"As we all were." He laughed. "So many regrets, so little alcohol."

She couldn't stop her lips from quirking up. It sounded like something you'd find on a T-shirt.

"Is it true she trapped him into marriage?"

"Trapped?" Kennedy hadn't heard that in a while. It had been all over campus that Darcy had purposely gotten pregnant because she saw what a bright future Chuck had in soccer. No one saw the sacrifices she made so her parents wouldn't find out. Then the nights she'd spent crying once her parents did find out. No one saw the long nights, weeks or months she spent alone—the wife of a soccer star. "She didn't trap anyone. Chuck suited up and it must have broken. She was just as shocked as everyone else. And she had to give up her career to take care of the baby."

"Wasn't she in college?"

"She was, but she had an internship with an interior design firm. She couldn't take care of the baby and go to school and do the internship."

"Wouldn't her parents help?"

"No. They disowned her when she told them. Unwed, pregnant, and without a degree. She was an embarrassment to the suburban church set. She lost everything."

He nodded and there was a lot of knowledge in the look on his face. "We sacrifice a lot for our kids."

"She didn't regret it. Fanny is amazing."

He nodded again as he swirled the contents of his glass. "Do you have kids?"

"Not yet." It's something she'd like to do someday, but she'd always imagined she'd be further along in her career before she started a family.

"Her reputation seems to be worse than reality."

"Isn't it always." She emptied her cup, mind racing. Who was saying all of this? It would have to be someone who knew them back in the day. "I didn't know they'd hired anyone from the old days." Yes. She was fishing.

"The accountant. Miranda." He exhaled in a burst of air. "But given the fight she had with Chuck last week, I should've known better than to listen to her."

"A fight. About what?" And why was it that Detective Pagonis only talked about Kennedy's fight with Chuck? Apparently, he was fighting with everyone.

"I didn't hear. I just heard yelling, but by the time I got to his office, it had stopped." The coach finished his drink. "I should've known that she wasn't a reliable source."

Miranda and Chuck had fought. Interesting. Kennedy needed to talk to this Miranda person. The name didn't sound familiar, but their college had been huge. And she'd get to know her now. "You can't believe everything you hear."

"Very true." Now if she could get the cops to believe that.

CHAPTER 9

After a quick navigation lesson from the coach, Kennedy left for the upper offices—up where the building still smelled new and hadn't been permeated with sweat or beer.

The offices weren't empty, which was surprising since their boss died the day before. Apparently, soccer kept on. Chuck would actually like that. He was of the Michael Jordan train of thought—if you weren't wearing a toe-tag, you were well enough to get the job done.

Kennedy walked up to an office with a metal sign etched with Miranda Scott. No bells. No whistles. If Darcy and Chuck were going to hire someone from the college, she'd think it would've been one of their fraternity brothers or sorority sisters.

But Kennedy knew them all, and she couldn't remember a Miranda. And given the popularity of *Sex in the City* reruns in the quad, she would've remembered a Miranda.

The office was small but utilitarian. A set of windows lined the back wall, with a scenic view of the parking lot.

A woman sat at the desk inside the office—pale skin, red

hair pulled back into a bun, expensive silk suit. Her eyes bounced back and forth between paperwork in her hand and the screen of her computer. "Can I help you?" Apparently, her attention was also on the doorway.

"Are you Miranda Scott?"

"Yes." She looked up from the desk, setting her bright blue eyes on Kennedy. The woman was gorgeous.

"I'm Kennedy Romero, and I'm looking into the incident with Chuck."

"You mean his murder."

"Yes." Kennedy concentrated on her face so she didn't wince. She could handle the word murder, but the murder scene surged forefront in her mind. It was bright and horrible. And she didn't want to think about it. Not now or ever.

"Then you need to look into his wife." Miranda turned her attention back to the paperwork.

Dismissed. Too bad Kennedy wasn't so easily pushed aside. "Why?"

"Once a gold digger, always a gold digger." The contempt in Miranda's voice was unmistakable.

"I'm sorry, how do you know Chuck and Darcy?"

"I went to high school with him."

Kennedy didn't know much about Chuck when he was in high school. He didn't talk about his old friends that much. She met a couple of guys at the wedding, but they didn't really talk about high school. Well except for his serious girlfriend… "Mandy?"

"I did go by Mandy back in the day." She looked Kennedy up and down. "Do I know you?"

"No." But Kennedy had heard all about Mandy. If this was the right person... and it had to be. "You went to high school with Chuck? Did you date him?"

She laughed. "Yes. I was his first love."

Kennedy wanted to slap that laugh off of Mandy's face,

but the laugh was so hollow. She was obviously in pain. And Kennedy couldn't find it in her heart to kick the woman while she was down. "So, losing him must be hard."

"It's not easy. He's always been in my life." She stood from her desk. "Who are you?"

"I'm a family friend."

"Ah, right. Darcy's little minion." Miranda rolled her eyes. "The police officer. What can I help you with?"

Kennedy hadn't been called a minion before, but she was pretty sure it wasn't a compliment. "I wanted to talk about Chuck. Did anyone have an issue with him?"

"Of course you're trying to find someone else to put the blame on. Divert attention from the real murderer."

The woman was in pain. Keep remembering.

I am not a monster. I am not a monster. Kennedy would not kick Miranda while she was mourning. "And you think that's Darcy."

"Of course, it's her." Miranda's eyes rolled. Again.

Kennedy wasn't a monster but those rolling eyes were like a red cape waved in front of a bull. Any minute Kennedy's inner monster was going to lose its shit, and Miranda's eyes wouldn't be able to roll anymore due to all the inflammation. "How do you know Darcy killed Chuck?"

"I don't know for sure, but it's pretty obvious. He was miserable, and she was sleeping around. He was going to leave her, and she'd have nothing."

"If they got divorced, she'd just take half and move on."

"They had a prenup." Miranda smiled and crossed her arms. "That was my idea. When he was in college, he came to me and told me he'd made a mistake and slept with her. He begged me to forgive him. I told him he had to be with his kid. And I told him to make sure he had a pre-nup."

She stood up and walked to a window. "Part of me was proud of that, because she would have taken everything he had years ago. But another part wonders... would he be dead today if she had just disappeared from his life?"

This wasn't making sense. Darcy never mentioned that she was having extracurricular playdates, and that didn't align with what Alex had said. "If she was cheating on him, was he returning the favor? Was he seeing someone else on the side?"

"He wasn't like that."

"Are you sure?"

"He was loyal." If loyal had a new definition that included lying and cheating.

"Like he was loyal to you." Kennedy knew one thing to be true, a man didn't change his spots. Especially since he'd cheated on Darcy early on in their relationship. Heck, Kennedy wasn't sure he'd ever stopped. It wasn't in his nature to stop.

"We were young. He was naïve. And Darcy threw her boobs around, shimmied until he lost his mind."

"That must have pissed you off." Rightfully so, but she shouldn't waste her anger on Darcy. Miranda should be angry at Chuck.

"It did. I was heartbroken. She took everything from me." Of course Miranda was mad at Darcy.

Almost like a motive for murder, if Darcy had been the one to die. Thank goodness it hadn't been her.

"And before you get any ideas, I didn't hurt Chuck. I never had a reason to. If Darcy had ended up dead, I'd be the first to admit I would be at the top of the list. But Chuck was a victim. He deserved so much better."

"Someone like you?"

"No, that ship sailed long ago. We wanted different things." She stared out the window. "Well, we did want different things, but it was too late for us. Too much hurt.

You can't come back from that."

"Is that why you were fighting last week?"

"We had some differences on how capital was to be spent. I wanted him to invest in real estate in Henderson to take advantage of tax breaks and appreciation incentives. Which was why we bought the space in Henderson for the practice field in the first place, but I wanted to invest more heavily. Field. Sport store. Place for kids' teams to play. It would have been a whole experience. He wanted to waste money on another VIP area. Like the VIPs don't have enough space in this building."

"Ms. Romero." A voice that was way too recognizable and cocky and deep came from behind her. "Why are you harassing my witness?"

Detective Pagonis stood in the doorway. He looked good in his blue button-up shirt and black pants. His badge hung from his hip. If he wasn't glaring at Kennedy, he'd look downright edible. Instead he looked like an angry tax accountant.

She should have made sure she closed the door. That was an oversight on her part.

"I'm just asking questions." Kennedy batted her eyelashes at the detective. Well, she tried, but her game was way off.

The confused look he shot her said her game was further off than she thought. "Why are you asking questions at all?"

"I'm just assisting."

"Assisting whom?" It would be really sexy that he used proper grammar, if he wasn't such a dick.

And since she didn't think he'd appreciate who she was helping, she said, "You?" No, it wasn't him, but saying she was trying to help herself sounded so selfish.

"We have everything well in hand and don't need your interference." Jerk detective was still cranky. Maybe he needed to wake up on the other side of the bed. Or burn the damn thing and get a new bed.

"Ms. Scott, I have a few questions." He said that so pleasantly, and then turned to Kennedy and snarled, "Ms. Romero, you can go."

She almost asked if she could breathe or was she allowed to speak, but she had a feeling his answer would be no. He really didn't like her much. Which was weird because she was delightful. Just ask Darcy.

"Please, have a seat." Miranda motioned to the chair in front of her desk and smirked at Kennedy. She was a real cult of personality—if cult was spelled with an *n*.

Pagonis turned to Kennedy, ignoring the invitation to sit. It was nice to know he didn't just ignore Kennedy. "Wait outside." His tone said she wasn't allowed to ignore him.

She nodded, because any response she wanted to give would be sarcastic and jail-inducing.

"We need to talk," he said. The most dreaded words in the English language. But in this case, she wasn't going to get dumped. She was going to be interrogated and treated like a convict, because she didn't think he believed in innocent until proven guilty. He seemed to have already determined she was guilty.

She left the office and stood outside Miranda's closed door. Kennedy thought about pressing her ear to the wood, but that just felt pathetic. She closed her eyes. It sounded like the *Peanuts* teacher behind the door.

Waa. Wah-waa. Wah. Waa.

She wasn't learning anything standing here. Except that he still thought she was guilty. And he was probably going to yell. And she was standing outside Miranda's office. Waiting. To be yelled at by the Metro detective. To be fair, there was something about getting the interrogation over and just moving on—right on back to Chicago. But the alternative kept flashing through her mind. Jail. Being someone's bitch.

The whole loss of freedom thing and never having unfettered access to Haagen Dazs again, was enough to get her feet to stepping. She needed more time. She needed a meeting. She needed ice cream.

Which one, in which order, was the question.

CHAPTER 10

Kennedy sat on a folding chair in the basement of a local church. Scuffed flooring. The smell of stale coffee beans and sugar in the air. She'd thought about grabbing a donut, but made a deal with herself if she got through this hour, she'd get herself some of that ice cream she was craving.

She'd like to think that somehow Vegas meetings were more exotic, but really, it looked the same. Same smell. Same bad coffee. Same chairs arranged in a circle. Same types of people.

There looked to be an accountant, or some other desk jockey complete with suit and tie, sitting across the circle. His face was aglow from his cell phone. When his eyes weren't glued to the phone, they were staring at the clock on the wall.

A young woman sat a few chairs down, talking into her phone. Kennedy could only hear one side of the conversation, but so far there was a lot of *don't do that* and *put him on the phone.* The exasperated tone said there were multiple them on the other side and not one of them listened.

These were the days Kennedy thanked the heavens she

hadn't had kids. It almost made the gut-punching loneliness that hit her every now and again worth it.

A few chairs from Kennedy, a woman in lots of red spandex sat nibbling on a donut as she tapped the screen of her phone. She'd giggle, then type, then tear off another piece of sugared heaven.

A woman walked in the room carrying the *Big Book* and a folder. Her curly brown hair bounced as she glided to the head chair. Her chubby cheeks glowed when she smiled at the group. "Let's get started, everyone." Her voice was soothing. Her smile, kind. "My name is Betty, and I'll be facilitating today." She ran a hand through her curls as she read the Alcoholics Anonymous preamble, and then handed the *Big Book* to the mother who had hung up her phone.

The woman began reading out loud from the *Big Book*. It was the usual kickoff to a meeting. The words weren't always reassuring—half the time Kennedy didn't listen—but there was comfort in routine.

"Thank you, Joanna for the reading." Apparently, the mother was Joanna. "Any newcomers?"

Kennedy thought about raising her hand, but she had no intention of talking today. She wouldn't even know where to begin. No one else seemed to feel the need to raise their hands either—or maybe they were all old hats at this.

"We'll move on then." Betty opened her folder. "Today we're talking about step four. As we take an honest look at our good and bad traits, we need to take a moral inventory and shed all the preconceived ideas."

Moral inventory. Kennedy hated this step. She would shed her morals when she drank. She wouldn't question her decisions. Hell, sometimes she didn't even remember making the decision at all. It was like some deranged superpower. By day, a law-abiding coffee drinker making instant choices for the good of Chicago's citizens. By night, an alcohol-addled walking, talking dysfunction. It was why she stopped drinking—sober Kennedy and drunk Kennedy didn't exactly share the same values.

"Would anyone like to share?" Betty looked from one person to the next with a sweet, welcoming smile. Her attention moved to Kennedy.

Kennedy held her breath. She didn't move or smile. Nothing that would imply she wanted to share. She wasn't a sharer.

"I'll go first." Red spandex waved her powdered sugar-covered hand. "I'm Diandra and I'm an alcoholic." She licked her fingertips clean.

"Hi, Diandra," everyone said in unison.

"So, you all remember Zeke."

Kennedy could've sworn that Joanna groaned. But since AA held no judgement, she might have misheard it.

"So, Zeke told me he loved me again. And I don't know, maybe I should give him another chance. He's got a job over at Caesar's. He's not drinking no more." Diandra had a dreamy look in her eyes. "We used to drink all the time, but we can totally find other things to do."

Kennedy didn't know this woman or the whole situation, but two alcoholics who'd drank together, planning to not drink anymore? That was a recipe for disaster.

Kennedy had tried that. Kennedy had tried to keep her relationship with Steve alive after she'd hit rock bottom. Funny thing. When one person in a relationship hits rock bottom and the other does not, they can't move on together because they're in different places.

So now she was sober, and he was doing a five-month stint in county for multiple DUIs. It was one of the main reasons she was here, in this meeting—besides the whole court-ordered thing. She was only a couple DUIs from being in the cell next to his—well, in the women's facility. Cops didn't do well in jail.

"Zeke and I went to the gym together last night. It was so romantic."

"You know he's just going to suck you into his bullshit again." Joanna got it.

"Joanna!" Betty did not. Her smile had fallen from her face. "This is a safe space."

Joanna sighed. "It's a safe space, but someone has to speak up. We're enabling her to make poor choices. The last time she went out with Zeke they ended up passed-out, half-naked on a party bus."

Now that sounded like a story that would land a person in an AA meeting. Not that Kennedy was judging. She had a few of those in her back pocket. Maybe next time she'd pull a few out. But right now she was counting the minutes to ice cream.

CHAPTER 11

Kennedy couldn't find ice cream. Or maybe it was that she found frozen custard first. She pulled the Jaguar into Darcy's driveway and got out, flipping the plastic cover off her cup of pineapple cashew heaven before she hip-checked the car door closed.

She licked the side of the bowl to catch a drip, careful not to waste a bit. Only her terror of getting melted ice cream on the leather upholstery had kept her from eating while driving.

She walked through the grandiose outside entryway, flowers and palm trees lining the path to an oversized double front door. The unlocked front door. That was strange. Kennedy closed it behind her and listened. Silence. "Hello?"

Nothing. Eerily quiet. Which was weird since it was early evening. This was prime time in the Perrault household.

"Anyone home?" She shoved her spoon into the ice cream and scooped up a spoonful. Ate it. Still silent. Someone had to be home. The front door was practically hanging open, inviting thieves to steal stuff. Okay it wasn't hanging open, but it wasn't locked. And one would think they'd want to protect their stuff from walking out said front door.

She leaned up the stairs. "Hellooo." The sound bounced off the walls and vibrated back to her. "I'm king of the world…" *orld, orld, orld.*

"Excuse me." A woman with tied-back gray hair walked in the room, her feather duster held out like a weapon. Her jeans hugged ample curves and her T-shirt clung to more ample. She'd make a killing in a wet T-shirt competition.

Kennedy wasn't afraid of getting feather-dustered to death, but better safe than sorry. "I'm a friend of Darcy's."

"You're Kennedy?" The woman's face lit up as she barreled forward. She wrapped her arms around Kennedy and squeezed. "I'm Selma. I'm so glad to finally meet you. Miss Darcy told me all about you."

"Darcy talks about you as well." The words might have squeaked out of Kennedy's throat because Selma was currently trying to squeeze all the custard out of her. "I'm so happy to finally meet you."

"You too. You too." Selma pulled away, letting blood flow through Kennedy's body. From what Darcy had said, Selma was an amazing housekeeper and an amazing margarita maker. Oh, and she drank Darcy under the table a few times. "I really love her."

The smile on Kennedy's lips lit up her chest. "I love Darcy, too." How could she not? How could anyone not love her? She was a great person. "Where did everyone go?"

"They went to talk to the funeral home people."

Every time Kennedy felt normal, like eating frozen custard or meeting someone else in Darcy's life, Chuck's death smacked the normal right down. No matter what a crappy husband he was, he didn't deserve to be murdered. No one did.

"Why don't I make you something to eat?" Selma said.

"I have food." Kennedy held up her cup.

"You have junk food." Selma took the cup and spoon from Kennedy's hand. "Let me get you a sandwich. I have some honey turkey and ham."

A sandwich sounded pretty good about now. "That sounds delicious." Her stomach growled. Did she say both of those things out loud?

Selma laughed. "Follow me."

Kennedy followed Selma into the kitchen and sat on one of the stools at the counter while Selma gathered cold cuts, bread and a plate.

"So, do you miss having Chuck around here?" Kennedy tried to make small talk. Although bringing up Chuck wasn't exactly small.

"Not really."

"You didn't like him?" They should have started a club…

"Oh, I liked him fine. I just didn't like how he treated Miss Darcy."

Kennedy could relate. After Darcy found out she was pregnant, he would just disappear. He claimed it was to *clear his head*, but who actually left and went no-contact for a week at a time? "What did he do to her?"

"He had the redhead over way too much," Selma whispered, shaking her head. "He said they were working late, but it's impossible to work that late all the time." She wasn't the first one to mention he'd cheated.

"Did Darcy know?"

"Oh yes. Miss Darcy knows everything. But she was too busy with the bearded man." Selma layered meat on the bread.

"The bearded man?"

"Miss Darcy wouldn't tell me his name. Just said he was a friend." Selma rolled her eyes on the word "friend".

"If she said he was a friend, why don't you believe her?"

"Friends don't rub each other's back at the pool."

"Well to be fair, they do if they're putting sunscreen on each other." Kennedy had rubbed a few backs in her day. Hell, she'd rubbed Darcy's back many times.

"I saw her rubbing his front too. He was wearing pants over that part, so I'm thinking it didn't need sunscreen." Selma giggled. "When those kids weren't here, this place became a regular hotel."

"Was there anything else about the bearded man?" Since a name wasn't available, she'd settle for any distinct characteristic. "Hair color? Height? Anything that might stick out?"

Selma stopped, and Kennedy practically saw the wheels turning as she thought. "No hair on his head. But brown hair on his face."

"And Chuck was okay with this guy coming into his house."

"Eh, I don't think he noticed. They slept in separate bedrooms."

"And the kids didn't notice?"

"They only had sleepovers when the kids were at school." Selma took a knife out of a drawer.

"It must have been hard for them to share a bedroom all summer."

"Not really. Chuck spent more time at work and Darcy spent more time in the pool house."

"Why the pool house?" Please don't say she was doing the pool boy. That was so cliché. And so far this whole story was sounding more and more cliché.

Selma cut the sandwich in triangles, like Kennedy's grandma used to do, and then laughed. "Miss Darcy can get little loud when she's with her friend. If you get my drift."

Everyone got her drift. Darcy had always been a screamer. When there was a scrunchie on their college dorm room door, that meant she was entertaining a gentleman caller. And she'd be calling out his name for the dorm to hear. To be fair, though, it had usually been Chuck. Once she met him, the screaming was all for him.

"The pool house is sound-proofed." Selma pushed the plate with Kennedy's sandwich across the counter.

"Why?"

Selma shrugged. "Chuck tried his hand at rock and roll. He was taping in there for a while, but thankfully he realized he wasn't any good."

Kennedy had been privy to some of the music that had come out of those jam sessions. To call it music was insulting to music. Again, not a reason to be killed.

The problem was that Darcy wasn't looking good, and if the cops started looking at her, they'd find a whole forest of red flags. Which added another layer to why Kennedy needed to solve this. She didn't want to end up in jail with Darcy. She enjoyed rooming with her in college but had a feeling sharing a room in jail wouldn't nearly be as much fun.

Kennedy picked up half the sandwich. "How long were they unhappy together?"

"Who said they were unhappy? They loved each other but got to spend time with their little playthings. It was their way." Selma picked up a towel. "I have to get back to work."

"Can you tell me if you hear from Darcy?"

Selma nodded, and left Kennedy to eat her sandwich and wrap her mind around Darcy and Chuck's open relationship. Like it was normal. And according to Selma it was normal for them. But could it have caused Darcy to kill?

CHAPTER 12

Kennedy sat in the backyard, eating the best damn sandwich she'd ever had. Maybe it was the fact that someone else made it, or maybe it was the rhythmic splash of the tiny waterfalls carved into the far end of the swimming pool.

Either way, she was enjoying the heck out of the sandwich as she reclined in the lounge chair and soaked up the sun. Chicago in October was a crapshoot. One day it was warm enough to wear board shorts. The next day it was as dark as a Batman movie and you could feel the cold to your bones. There were very few days where the sun made an appearance, and even fewer days set to eighty degrees.

She dropped her head back and let the rays warm her skin. Soaking in the whole ambience of it all. Chlorine with a hint of eucalyptus tickled her sinuses. It was calming and pleasant. She couldn't help the smile that flitted at the edges of her lips.

"Miss Kennedy, the police are here." Selma's voice cut through the calm. And Kennedy's eyes flew open to find Detective Lester and her evil sidekick standing in the open doorway.

"Thank you, Ms. Schmidt." Detective Pagonis might be nice to Selma, but he had a smirk on his face for Kennedy—living up to the evil part of his name.

"Do you need anything before I go back to work?" Selma asked.

"No, thank you." Again, with the pleasantries. Who knew he even knew how to use the words *thank you*.

Selma nodded and walked back into the house, closing the sliding glass door and leaving Kennedy alone with Las Vegas's finest.

"Ms. Romero, do you have time for some questions?" Detective Lester actually seemed to care if Kennedy had time.

"You seem to be settling in." Pagonis, not so much.

Like a person wasn't allowed to eat. She stuffed the last bite of sandwich into her mouth. She'd get what little joy she could before Pagonis screwed it all up.

"Why did you come to Las Vegas?" Apparently, Pagonis was playing a game of ask the same questions over and over again to see if he could trip her up. He wasn't going to win.

"Vacation. Darcy was getting an award for philanthropy."

"That's it?"

"Well, she's also part owner of a soccer team. I wanted to see a game and do the whole MVP thing. Maybe gamble a little. Hit a buffet." What Kennedy wouldn't give for some Caesar's crab legs right about now. It was the one thing on her list. She needed to get her ass to the strip.

"When was the last time you saw Chuck?"

"The night before he passed." Yeah, she was well aware how guilty that made her look, but if she hadn't killed Chuck when he made a pass at her sophomore year of college— while his pregnant girlfriend was home sick with *after-dinner-morning-sickness*— she wasn't going to do it now.

That was one of the reasons she'd never jumped on the Chuck bandwagon. She didn't hate him, just thought he made really dumb choices when he drank. And back then he was drinking a lot. Not that she could really throw stones. Her decisions when she drank put her in a rather unstable glass house.

"So, you were the last one to see him alive?"

Kennedy did not roll her eyes, as much as she was tempted to. "No. I'm sure the person who killed him saw him after I did."

"Where did you see him?" Pagonis growled, face tense.

"At his office." Kennedy squinted as the sun pierced her eyelids. She'd ask them to move so she wasn't blinded, but she recognized their fun little interrogation tactic. They wanted to keep their victims off-kilter.

"What happened?"

So not working. She wasn't going to fall victim to their kiltering. "We talked, and I came back to the house."

"What did you talk about?"

"Normal stuff." How Chuck couldn't be bothered to show up for his wife's award ceremony because he was banging the help. Normal, right?

"So you raise your voice during normal conversations?"

"That's just how we talked." Kennedy and Chuck were like sharks and blood. Put them together and the water became choppy. Not that she'd say that out loud. "It was endearing."

"Some might say it was motive."

"Miss Kennedy." Selma opened the sliding glass door and stood in the opening. "You wanted me to let you know if Miss Darcy called. She's at the funeral home, and it's taking longer than expected."

"Thank you."

"How long have you been on the Perrault's staff?" Detective Pagonis moved his laser focus to Selma. Kennedy hated to admit it, but the breath hiding in her lungs evacuated in a large huff.

Selma shifted from one foot to the other. "Seven years."

"So you get to see the inner workings of the Perrault household regularly."

"I guess." Selma's fingers twirled around themselves. She kept averting her gaze, like she was getting ready to run.

I feel you. Kennedy was used to the police department's direct interrogation methods, yet this man discombobulated the hell out of her.

"Did they fight?"

"Everyone fights."

"From what I've heard, they fought every day." Detective Delightful was fishing. He was bobbing in the wrong lake.

"Well, I don't know about that. They didn't fight like that here." From what Selma said earlier it was because they lived completely separate lives at home. "They loved each other."

"Is that why she's running the team and not his brother?" The detective might be an ass, but that was a good question. Kennedy had wondered about as well.

"I don't know. You'd have to ask her."

That was a really good idea. She just had to ditch the five-oh. "Are we done here?"

Constable Crabby didn't seem to like that Kennedy asked that question. Or maybe it was that she asked any questions that chapped his ass. "We're done when we say we're done."

Kennedy stared at him and waited. What she was waiting for, she wasn't sure. Maybe she was waiting for the next question. Or maybe she was waiting for him to say they were done. She could honestly say she was hoping for the latter. This interrogation was exhausting and useless.

She didn't kill Chuck. Neither did Darcy.

"When did you say Darcy Perrault would be back?" Pagonis asked Selma.

"She didn't say, but apparently, they're having trouble with some paperwork at the funeral home." Selma gulped. "She said to eat dinner without her, so I'm thinking it will be a while."

"We'll come back tomorrow," Detective Lester said. Her scowling companion didn't seem to agree, but he followed her to the sliding glass door.

Pagonis stopped at the open door and turned to Kennedy. Something was hanging on his lips. Could it be another threat about not leaving town? Maybe pointing two fingers at his eyes then at her— *I'm watching you.* Fortunately, he did neither. He turned around and slid the door closed before disappearing.

Selma grabbed at her heart before leaning toward Kennedy and whispering. "Oh, thank God they left."

Kennedy agreed. "He's a bit much."

"No. I mean yes, but it's not that. Darcy will be here any moment."

"Nice work." Lying to the cops. "Great poker face."

"I don't play poker."

"You should. Where is Darcy?"

"She called to say she was bringing home pizza." Selma's face dropped. "What if they bump into each other?" She threw open the sliding glass door and went into the house. Kennedy followed.

"Are they gone?" Kennedy asked, as Selma checked the front windows.

"They're gone." Selma's face lit up in a smile. "She's bringing deep dish. I'll get the plates and sodas."

Kennedy couldn't help but smile back. Selma's excitement was contagious. Kennedy doubted Las Vegas pizza was going to compete with Chicago deep dish. But the pizza didn't matter. She wanted to talk to Darcy, because she needed answers.

CHAPTER 13

Kennedy sat on the couch rubbing her food baby. Surprisingly the Las Vegas version of Chicago-style deep dish tasted like home. And after the amount she ate, she might not need to eat until she got home.

The house was quiet again. Selma had headed out. Fanny and Charlie had left to be with friends. The best part of the night was the cops hadn't come back.

Darcy appeared through the kitchen door holding a bottle of wine in one hand and a bottle of cream soda in the other. "This is the best I can do right now."

Kennedy took the bottle of cream soda and poured some into the glass in front of her.

"Didn't you have cola in that glass?" Darcy's lips curled into a snarl.

"It did. I finished it."

"Gross."

"You didn't bring another glass."

"Where we're going, we don't need glasses." She lifted the bottle and took a gulp. "What did I miss while at the crypt keepers?"

"The cops were here."

"I'm sorry I missed that." Darcy dropped next to Kennedy, leaning against the arm of the couch and lifting her legs onto Kennedy's lap. "I don't know what's worse— burying your husband or dealing with the cops that want to talk about your husband nonstop."

"Either one sucks."

Darcy dropped her head to the side and breathed deep. "Amen." The bottle in her hand sloshed but didn't spill. "Did they leave when they realized I wasn't here?"

"Yes and no. I think they were tired of talking to me."

"I'm so sorry. Did they ask you more questions?" Darcy didn't wait for an answer, or maybe the look on Kennedy's face said it all. "They'll stop looking into you. They have to know that you couldn't do this."

"Darce, I was the last one to see him. We fought. There's a reason I'm at the top of the list."

"They'll move on when they realize you couldn't have done this. You pulled in right behind me."

"Yeah." Kennedy was glad Darcy was so sure. Because Kennedy didn't believe that at all. All the evidence pointed to her. Even if it didn't, she was high on the list of people who wouldn't cry if Chuck was dead. Thankfully there were a few others on this list. Like his brother.

Kennedy sat up. "They did have an interesting question. Why are you running the soccer club and not Craig? Isn't he part owner?"

"Chuck bought him out about a year ago."

"But the team just started."

"They've been working on getting a team for years. It was a long process." Darcy set the bottle in her lap and picked at the wine label.

"Why did Chuck buy him out?" Kennedy asked, thinking about the fight between Darcy and Craig. "He wasn't smart with his money?"

"Understatement. He was too busy spending all his money keeping the local drug dealers in iPhones. He wanted Chuck to bail him out. Free and clear. But Chuck wouldn't do it. Not again. Chuck was so sick of his bullshit. He complained all the time. So, he told Craig he'd buy a majority of his shares." Darcy took a pull from the bottle. "Paid him twice what it was worth, not that Craig appreciated that."

"That must have pissed off Craig to be pushed out. Maybe he wanted to soften the blow."

"Maybe, but it didn't work. He threatened to take the team by any means necessary."

"What does 'any means necessary' actually mean?"

"He tried to convince the board that Chuck was incompetent. Not that it mattered. Craig was no longer a full owner, so there was no way Chuck would ever let Craig get his hands on the team. He loved his brother, but this was too important to him."

"Would Craig kill his brother?"

Tears pooled in Darcy's eyes. "I'd hope not, but I don't know. I didn't think Craig would try to get the board to deem Chuck incompetent."

"It didn't work, right? So that's good."

"Yeah, but what kind of family does that? Craig is such a disappointment. But he's been that way Chuck's whole life." Darcy sighed. "Remember our wedding? He couldn't even bother to show up sober."

Kennedy remembered. She'd been securely on the wagon at that point, or as secure as one could be on that particular wagon. Which made it possible to remember Craig and the sober-free thing.

He made a pass at Darcy's cousin on the dance floor, in front of her husband. He then fought with Chuck's boss at the time and felt up Kennedy—until Kennedy throat-punched him. After that, Craig was nowhere to be found.

Later they found out he'd been crying to one of the wedding coordinators about how he'd been wronged. His usual narcissistic behavior. Kind of like dealing with Alex today. Speaking of which. "I forgot, I talked to Alex."

Darcy saluted her with the bottle. "Buried the lede. What did he say?"

How to broach this subject… "He said that he might know things, but he's not hiding anything."

"What the hell does that mean?"

"He said that you're hiding something and I should ask you about it."

"I don't know what he's talking about." Something in Darcy's tone said she knew—or at the very least she was sifting through the list of things that it could be.

"He said you would know. Think. Was there anything that Alex could hold over Chuck's head?"

"Oh." Darcy picked at the label. Little pieces of paper balled and dropped to her lap, the only sound the scrape of her nails. No excuse. Nothing. Alex's words hung in the air. The promise of an explanation dwindled with every passing second. Darcy hung her head and Kennedy could practically hear the gears turning. Probably because there were still no words coming out the woman's mouth.

Kennedy sighed. "Are you going to tell me or just leave me hanging here?"

"Charles has been having trouble at school, but I don't know what that would have to do with Chuck."

"He said you know more than you think."

"I don't know." Darcy shook her head as tears lined her eyes. Something was off. Darcy wasn't telling the entire truth. "I wish Chuck was here. I need him here to tell me what to do. He'd know how to handle all of this."

And there it was—the widow card. She needed space. There was no way Kennedy was pushing her now on any topic. Kennedy would give it to her. Today, at least. They needed answers, and Darcy couldn't hide behind her loss forever—especially since the cops could take away so much more from both of them.

But for today, there was one more question. "Did you and Chuck have a prenup?"

Darcy nodded. "Yeah, his parents made us sign one when we got married."

His parents… or his ex-girlfriend, Miranda? Who knew.

"Once the police find out, that will put you at the top of the list." And rightfully so. The-spouse-did-it was a tale as old as time.

Darcy shrugged. "Eh, they can try. I'll even hand over a copy. The prenup covered the money we brought into the marriage, not the money made or inherited during the marriage."

"Really?" That actually sounded like a large loophole.

"My lawyer was pretty good back then. We never thought Chuck would sign it, but we figured it was worth a try." Darcy shook her head. "It worked."

"Didn't his lawyer say anything?"

"I have no idea. Maybe the lawyer was on coke or something. Or maybe he hated Chuck. Either way, I benefited."

And if it was true, that would eliminate the larger motive. "So what do we do about Craig?"

"We need to see him." Darcy wiped at her tears, practically knocking herself out with the bottle in her hand.

"Let's go tomorrow." Given the outburst during a sober interaction, Kennedy didn't want to get the two together when Darcy was like this. No good could come from that.

Darcy's shoulders sagged. "I have a meeting with the finance team."

"I can go talk to him."

"You should wait for me. The neighborhood is rough."

"I can handle rough."

"It's not just the neighborhood, it's Craig." Darcy leaned

in and whispered. "You can try and get him to talk, but he's kind of an asshole."

Kennedy hated to say it again, but she was a cop in Chicago. Dealing with assholes was in the job title. She could handle it.

CHAPTER 14

The next morning Kennedy used her cellphone map app and drove the Jaguar to Craig's address in East Las Vegas. She pulled into a spot along the street and thought about turning around.

The sun was barely peeking over the trees, painting the neighborhood with splotches of light and dark patches. There were rundown houses with a few upkept yards thrown in. No driveways. It looked like the garages were in back behind the buildings. A staple in Chicago, but not something normally found in Vegas. She parked the car and looked around.

She was being watched. She could feel it. Not that she wasn't used to it. When she'd been on the beat, she'd gone into her share of questionable neighborhoods—being watched was a casualty of the uniform. However, she was normally driving a cop car, not a Jag.

When she'd said she could handle this environment, she'd meant it. But the Jaguar was an innocent. Kennedy angled out of the car and turned. She found the eyes watching her.

An older woman sat behind a window across the street.

She looked harmless enough. But the two teens standing at the corner in baggy pants looked shady as shit. One leaned inside a car, resting his hand on the windowsill. Kennedy could spot a drug deal from a hundred yards out. As the car drove on, he nodded and pulled away, slipping something in his pocket. And that was definitely the delivery of something illegal.

The kid licked his lips as he ran a hand through scraggly blond hair. The appreciation in his eyes was creepy—and hopefully for the Jag and not Kennedy's body.

She could handle herself. She couldn't handle Darcy's car wandering off.

Kennedy clicked the security alarm and kept her eyes on the kids on the corner. If they knew she'd seen them, there was a better chance the car would still be there when she was done. At least that was her story.

Craig's place was a rundown townhouse. Two stories of reddish-brown siding, with a cracked window on each level. She walked up the split sidewalk, past the silt lawn and knocked on the graying white door. Nothing. Maybe Craig wasn't home.

She knocked again.

"Hold up," a graveled voice called through the door. A lock tumbled with a scrape and the door flew open. "What?"

Craig stood in the doorway wearing a faded Van Halen T-shirt and sweatpants with air-conditioning holes at the knees and hip. Eyes half-closed. Scruff lining his face. If she didn't know better, she'd swear he was homeless. He took one look at Kennedy and the door flew toward her.

Kennedy's arm blocked it from hitting her in the face. "Can we talk?"

"Why?"

"Your brother was murdered."

Craig's normally stoic face morphed into sadness. This was a man in mourning. "Can I come in?"

He looked behind him and shook his head. "I don't think that's a good idea."

"Why? I just have a few questions." When he didn't budge, she kept going. "I want to find out who did this. Don't you want that?"

He squinted at her. "Of course, I do. He was my only family."

"You have Darcy and the kids."

"They don't like me very much."

"Maybe they just don't know you. If you want me to tell them the truth, I'll listen." And she would. She needed to get to the truth by any means necessary. Even listening to a jilted brother.

Craig opened the door a smidge, barely letting Kennedy in. She turned her body to squeak by. Inside, plastic covered every inch of, well, everything. Tinfoil lined the windows. This was not the residence of a playboy with hooker tendencies.

Craig twisted the lock closed and open, closed and open, closed and open. Then he stopped on closed. He motioned to a pleather couch covered by a plastic sofa cover. "Have a seat."

The seat crinkled and popped when she sat on the shiny material.

"I didn't kill my brother."

"I didn't think you did." She couldn't say that with conviction. There was something not right here. But Craig seemed to buy it. He sat in a chair across the room and relaxed. Kennedy leaned forward. "If you didn't kill him, who did?"

"You won't believe me. No one does." He ran a hand through the scruff on his chin.

"Try me."

"The aliens have been watching me for years."

Ummm... Kennedy wasn't sure what she expected to happen. But she could honestly say aliens were not anywhere near the top of her list. "When did they start watching you?"

"It started when I went to that hospital. They put chemicals in my body to mind control me."

"Chemicals?" Kennedy was pretty sure they'd given him meds while he was in rehab a few years ago. And she was also pretty sure that was the hospital to which he was referring. But why wouldn't Chuck have mentioned this was going on with his brother? He was painted as a drug-loving womanizing man-whore, and that was not what Kennedy saw here.

"Little space pebbles." He shook his head, like he was trying to catch scattering thoughts. "They're tapping my phones."

"Who?"

"The aliens," he whispered, like he was sharing some big secret.

"Why are they tapping your phones?"

He glanced back and forth. "Because I know too much."

She wanted to hold his hand or help him. Something. She'd watched people come off drugs before and it wasn't pretty. "Are you using right now?"

"I don't do that anymore. That's how they control you." He stood up and began pacing.

"Do you live here alone?" She asked the question, but she already knew the answer. Piles of clothes filled the corners—given the stains, there was no way any of it had seen the inside of a washer in years. Stacks of newspapers sat on every surface. Empty coffee cups rested on the stacks and on the floor. She had a feeling if they tried to move any of the piles around, they'd find plenty of critters were squatting in this house.

Kennedy didn't do critters. "Has Darcy ever been here?"

"No, she doesn't come to this side of town. Chuck said she was afraid of the aliens." Craig blinked. "I don't blame her. I wouldn't want to be part of this either. We have to protect the women and the children." He really believed everything he was saying. And protecting Darcy seemed to be high on his list.

"Did you see Chuck a lot?"

"Every week. I told him not to come by here." he whispered and leaned in. "Darcy is right, the aliens were watching me."

"Why did the aliens kill Chuck?"

"Because he wouldn't join them. I saw him arguing with a man."

"A human man?" She hated asking. It felt like she was making fun of him—but given the direction this was taking, she had to ask.

"Yeah, he works for them."

"The man works for who?" Kennedy was having a hard time keeping up.

"For the aliens."

"Why were you mad at Darcy for running the team?"

"Because she doesn't know about the aliens. They'll trick her."

Kennedy really needed to talk to Darcy. There's no way that she could have known what was going on with Craig. If Darcy was correct, they'd been trying to build the team for years—so before the hospital. Something happened to Craig in that hospital.

He was obviously worried about Darcy. Okay, it was worry about an alien attack, but it was still worry, which meant he cared. "Maybe we should talk to her together."

Craig shook his head. "I'm not allowed to talk to her."

"You talked to her the other day."

"But Chuck will be really mad."

Kennedy didn't have the heart to correct "will be mad" to "would have been mad." Craig didn't need a tense lesson. He might get a bit tense.

"I guess he isn't around to yell at me." Oh look. He figured it out all on his own.

"So maybe I can bring Darcy here." Darcy needed to see this place. Listening to him in these surroundings seemed to change the meaning of all his words. He went from a chaser of women to a chaser of intergalactic beings.

"No. Darcy can't come here. Darcy needs to stay where she is. Her house protects her because of the metal Chuck put in the roof."

Kennedy blinked. What? "Chuck put metal in the roof?"

"Yep, like Binion's."

"Like Binion's, the casino? Okay." Kennedy held up one hand, palm out. She needed to go easy. "How about we sit and talk?"

He nodded and relaxed, and somehow produced two bottles of water from underneath one of the piles.

Kennedy texted Darcy.

meet me at craigs

now

911

Why was every interaction ending with a necessary talk with Darcy?

When she had a few minutes to spare, she'd have to sit down and think about that.

CHAPTER 15

Craig and Kennedy sat drinking from their respective water bottles.

Craig shook his head. "I didn't like the ending at all. Nope. Nope."

"Best ending for a comedy." They'd just spent over an hour talking about all nine seasons of *Seinfeld*, ending with a critique of the series finale.

Craig laughed. Talking like this, he actually seemed okay. He wasn't scared or going on about aliens. Maybe inviting Darcy here was a mistake. She should text her.

Someone knocked on the front door.

Too late.

"Who's that?" Craig jumped up and pulled the blinds open. "Why is she here?"

"She's worried about you." Kennedy lifted her hand to stop Craig from accosting his sister-in-law. "Give her a chance."

"How do we know it's the real her?"

"Who else would it be?"

"The aliens are shifty."

"But you knew it was the real me?" He hadn't asked her to prove who she was. Kennedy felt vaguely insulted.

"You're not important. The aliens wouldn't pretend to be you."

Ouch. "There has to be something only the real Darcy would know."

Craig nodded and opened the door.

Darcy started to come in and he blocked her way. "Not yet." He looked her up and down, which might come across as lascivious, but given what Kennedy knew, somehow it wasn't sexual at all. He was probably looking for alien tentacles or blue skin.

Darcy tried to look around him. "Kennedy, are you in there? Are you okay?"

Kennedy stood up and moved behind Craig. "I'm fine. Just give him a chance. He needs to make sure you're who you say you are."

"What does that mean?" Darcy's eyebrow twitched. "I left a board meeting because I thought you were in danger." She pulled out her phone. "I'm getting Bobby."

"No!" Craig and Kennedy said at the same time. Craig could barely accept Darcy was who she was, if they added Bobby, he'd never relax and tell Darcy what was going on.

"What am I missing?" Another eyebrow twitch. Darcy was going to lose it if they didn't show her what she needed to see and be done.

Craig held his head—a hand on each side—like he was literally holding it all together.

"Craig, you needed to ask her a question."

"Okay." Craig let go of his head. "Where did my mother hide the good vodka?"

Darcy gave a huge sigh. "Why are you asking me this?"

"Darcy, I promise this will all make sense, but I need you to answer his question." Kennedy pleaded with her eyes.

"Don't give her the answer." Craig glared at Kennedy.

Darcy rolled her eyes. "How the hell would I know the answer to that?"

Craig nodded and turned to Darcy, who continued. "She kept it all over the house. She had a bottle in the vegetable crisper. One in the vase in the living room. There was one in the tampon box in the bathroom."

Craig frowned. "I didn't know about the bathroom."

"I went to grab a tampon and found a bottle instead."

"You forgot the one in her nightstand." Craig narrowed his eyes.

"I was never in her bedroom."

Craig nodded and looked over at Kennedy. He was obviously looking for her input. And this was obviously Darcy. She nodded.

With that, Craig opened the door. After Darcy walked over the threshold, he slammed the door shut, locking and unlocking the door three times until he finally slid the lock into place. "Have a seat."

Darcy's eyes widened as she looked around. Her silk shirt didn't match the ambiance of Craig's place at all. In this neighborhood, she looked like a high-class…

Never mind.

Darcy sat on the couch, her thighs producing a crinkle of plastic. "What's going on?"

Kennedy sat next to her. "We were talking about how the last episode of *Seinfeld* was genius."

"No. It was lazy writing." Craig tried to laugh, but he was too busy watching Darcy and Kennedy. She might have answered the question correctly, but he didn't seem to trust her yet.

Darcy was doing pretty much the same thing, looking totally confused. Between the stacks and piles on the floor, she had to notice something was off. "You brought me here to talk about *Seinfeld*?"

"No. I wanted you to see Craig's house."

That's when Darcy seemed to fully take in the room. Maybe she hadn't noticed before, but the way her eyes landed on the newspapers and the piles of clothes, she was seeing it now. When she got to the tinfoil on the windows, she visibly gulped. "You live here?"

Craig stared her up and down. "How do I know it's you?"

"What?"

"Craig, it's Darcy. She knew the answer," Kennedy whispered, because somehow whispering it would make him believe it. Or maybe she just didn't want to look insane in front of Darcy. "You have to tell her the truth." Kennedy nodded to Darcy. "She won't know what to watch out for if you don't tell her. Tell her about the man who yelled at Chuck."

Craig stared into Darcy's eyes for what felt like an eternity. He must have seen something that told him she was indeed his sister-in-law because he leaned in and whispered, "It's the aliens. The man works for the aliens. All the men do. You have to watch out for them."

"Which men?" Darcy looked over to Kennedy, and so many things were in that widened stare. So many questions.

Craig seemed annoyed she wasn't keeping up. "The angry man, he wanted to control the team."

Kennedy was confused. "I thought you said he wanted Chuck to join the aliens?" Controlling and joining were two totally different things, with different motivations.

"Well, yeah." Craig jumped to his feet and began pacing. Back and forth. He'd stop, tap his foot three times and pace again. "That's why the man killed Chuck."

"What man is that?" Darcy asked, voice rising.

Kennedy knew this line of questioning wasn't going to

get them very far, especially if they both got all worked up. "How should it have ended?"

"What?" Both Darcy and Craig said at the same time.

"You didn't like the *Seinfeld* ending. What would have made it better?"

The worry and agitation cleared from Craig's face like a lifting fog. "Well, they should have gone off together and lived happily ever after."

"Maybe they did."

"No, they were in jail. That's not happy."

Kennedy could honestly say that she'd never been in jail, but she had a feeling that jail was not happy. "True."

"Why are we talking about *Seinfeld*?" Darcy's eyes widened, and she turned to Kennedy and jerked her head. Kennedy looked as a something scampered across the floor. Smaller than a breadbox. Bigger than a hoagie roll.

"Do you have a cat?" Kennedy asked, throat dry.

"No."

"Dog?"

"I don't believe in animals."

Did animals require a belief? Kennedy didn't think so. But she did believe that whatever scampered across the floor meant diseases and who knew what else.

The look on Darcy's face would be comical if Kennedy wasn't sure her face mirrored the same terror. "Why don't you come stay at the house for few days?" Darcy asked.

"No!" He pushed his chair back and shook his head back and forth. "I can't. I just can't."

"Why?"

"The aliens are following him." Kennedy stood up and headed for a glint of blue sticking from a pile next to the chair.

It was a blue medication bottle with no logos or words. The sticker had been peeled off. The only indication that it might have held meds was the pill sitting on the side of the pile. At least she hoped it was a pill. She was pretty sure rats didn't poop out round yellow scat.

She looked at the top of the tablet. No medication name. Just some code. A08.

Kennedy wanted to take a picture of the pill. She wanted to Google it right here, but she was afraid of Craig's reaction. People who believed in aliens had some pretty intense phobias. Was he afraid of technology? Were cellphones okay? She didn't want to push it, so she'd look it up when they left.

"I hate leaving you here alone. How will you get food?" Darcy asked.

"I'm used to it." Craig stood and picked up a metal hard hat covered in aluminum foil. "Anyway, Chuck brought me this for when I go outside. I'll be okay."

Darcy was still trying. "Then why don't you come with—"

"Do you have a hat?" Craig shook his head, his tone mocking like Darcy hadn't thought this whole thing through. And maybe she hadn't. Alien-proofing herself would probably take a lot of energy that she didn't really have right now. "I can protect myself. I can't protect you and the kids."

"Are these yours?" Kennedy shook the empty bottle. If he was supposed to take these, he seemed to have run out.

"Yeah, Chuck brought them to me."

"Should I go get you some more?"

Craig shook his head. "Chuck was getting them from somewhere special."

"Your doctor?"

"That quack. No. I'll talk to that guy, but I don't trust him. He's working for them, too."

If he thought the doctor was working for the aliens, that was a problem. "What's the doctor's name?"

"Doctor Martin."

They needed a way to get him his meds that didn't include Doctor Martin.

Darcy's eyes lit up as the unfolding situation must have registered. "Did Chuck go through Louis?"

"Louis?" Craig made a thoughtful face.

"The team doctor." Darcy nodded. Ah, maybe that was how he got the meds. If the team doctor was prescribing them, then Chuck would be the one to bring them over.

Craig apparently agreed with that because he nodded. "I think so."

"I could talk to him and bring over the same type of medication"

"That would be fine. But only from him. I don't trust the other doctors."

"I don't blame you." Darcy nodded again, not one ounce of judgement in her tone. In fact, she sounded downright agreeable. "All those damn doctors care about is getting their next new motorboat on Lake Las Vegas."

"Right." Craig smiled. "I knew you'd understand."

Darcy stood up. "Let me see what I can do."

"Okay." Craig followed as they all walked to the front door. Kennedy stared at the ground like it might jump up and bite her. But to be fair, she wasn't worried about the floor biting her—it was whatever creatures lived along the floor that terrified the hell out of her.

CHAPTER 16

Kennedy and Darcy stood on the dirt-patch of a lawn at Craig's house. Surprisingly, both of Darcy's cars were parked where they'd left them.

Darcy looked back and forth, probably taking in the entrepreneurial teens on the corner and the woman sharpening her knives across the street. Literally sharpening knives. When Kennedy first drove up, the old woman looked so harmless.

"He can't stay here." Darcy's terrified stare earned her a mostly toothless smile from the old woman. Darcy spun to Kennedy. "He really can't stay here."

"He won't leave."

"We'll get him on his meds. Then he'll be okay."

Kennedy nodded. The nod wasn't a lie. She wanted to believe that was true. She just wasn't sure. "He mentioned that Chuck talked to a crazy man that was trying to control the team. Any idea who it could be?"

"If I would have heard that from anyone else, I would think it was Craig." Darcy shook her head. "I don't even know if the man exists."

"We should probably figure that out."

"I want him to have some magic answer. To find the person who did this and finish this, but..." Darcy couldn't even finish the sentence. "We need to find his doctor."

"I can Google it. We know it's a psychiatrist, and a man." Kennedy pulled out her phone and started searching for Doctor Martin. "There's probably a shitload with that name."

"Maybe you could cross-reference with alien sympathizers."

"If I can find him today, do you want to drop off your car and we'll head out?"

"I would love to, but I had to reschedule that meeting, so now I have a board meeting in an hour."

"Sounds like fun."

"No. I get to sit through at least an hour of everyone telling me to put someone else in charge because my ovaries make it impossible for me to make any decisions about a soccer club." Darcy pulled her keys from her pocket.

"Exactly, at least once a month we might lose our shit and start trading players."

Darcy laughed. "Trading? More like running them down with our cars."

"Isn't that a little stereotypical?"

"Well, stereotypes are a thing for a reason." Darcy shook her head. "We can sit here and joke about it, but it doesn't stop the fact that these assholes aren't joking."

"Don't let them get to you. Just prove them wrong."

"Why should I have to? Did Chuck have to prove them wrong?"

"No, you shouldn't have to, but that's the world we live in. And anyway, Chuck was a soccer legend." Kennedy wanted to believe that was the only reason they took his word as gospel and not Darcy's. But even she couldn't believe that.

"I just don't want to have another fight. I'm so tired. I need a break. I still have to clean out Chuck's office… ooh, come with and start helping me with that. I need to go through all the paperwork and try to get up to speed on everything."

"You're smart. You'll get it."

"I will if you come help me…" Darcy wrapped her arms around Kennedy and puckered her lips. The kissing sound was slobbery and snappy. "Please. Please. You can call Doctor Martin's offices while you sort."

Kennedy tilted her head back.

"Pleeeease…"

"Only if you keep your slimy kisses to yourself." Kennedy pulled back even further.

Darcy let her go with a laugh. "There was a time you loved my slimy kisses."

"They weren't as wet back then." Kennedy wiped at her face with the back of her hand.

"I'll meet you at the arena." Darcy's smile drooped. "I just need to get through this meeting, and then we'll clean while you try to find the psychiatrist."

Kennedy hated to see Darcy so broken-hearted. She bumped her shoulder "And then we'll find the alien."

Darcy's lips attempted a smile. It was half-hearted at best. "Don't remind me."

CHAPTER 17

Three hours later, Kennedy had a list of Doctor Martin candidates and she'd left a message with them all. She'd heard back from one. He wasn't the guy. So she focused on the office while she waited for her phone to ring.

She was currently cleaning out a cabinet. Another cabinet. She'd already been through five of them. Five cabinets sorted into three stacks. Three years. One stack for each year. Funny enough, it felt like she'd been working on this for three years.

She sifted through another pile of paperwork. Considering the soccer club started this year, why did they have paperwork spanning the past three years? It looked like they were paying and documenting things the whole time they were setting up the club.

Speaking of club… a sandwich would be good about now. Unfortunately, she'd have to leave the arena to get anything to eat. And as it was nearly three, she was too hungry to make the trek out into the world.

That might be a bit dramatic, but she'd really hoped

Darcy would be done with her meeting by now so they could go grab lunch together.

The door to the office flew open. "What a nightmare." Darcy stomped in, slamming the door shut behind her.

"Didn't go well?"

"If by well, you mean the board members are a bunch of jerkwads, then yes. It went swimmingly."

"Why are they jerkwads?"

"Poor upbringing. Their mothers didn't breastfeed them long enough. Their fathers didn't play stickball with them." Darcy dropped onto the couch. "I have no idea."

"Not how did they become jerkwads. What did they do?"

"Oh, that." Darcy leaned her head back and closed her eyes.

Ummm… Kennedy stood up. "Are you dead or just asleep?"

"Neither, but I'm up for the former. You own a gun, right?"

"I do, but it's back in Chicago."

"Dammit."

"Do you really need a gun?"

"No."

"Do you want to talk about it?"

"No." Darcy didn't way a word, but Kennedy could see thoughts spinning in her head, trying to break free.

"I have a degree." And here we go. "I get that I didn't get it till after my kids were born, but it's still a degree. It proves I'm not a complete idiot." Darcy opened her eyes and pointed at Kennedy. "Do not say a word."

Kennedy laughed. She almost commented on that a degree didn't necessarily mean the lack of idiocy, but Darcy looked like she wouldn't hesitate to kick Kennedy's ass right now. And Kennedy couldn't really fight back since Darcy'd had a shitty couple of days.

"They treat me like I don't know what a soccer ball is used for."

"It's used to sock her, right?"

Darcy's eyes actually rolled to the back of her head. "If I'd said that joke back there, they would have believed I thought soccer was some sort of domestic abuse."

"So, misogyny, huh?"

"Misogyny, with a little assholism." Darcy leaned her head back before it popped up again. "And don't forget the cattiness thrown in for good measure."

"Cattiness?"

"Yeah, Deborah is a raging bitch. You'd think girl power —let's stick together—but nope. She hates all women, or maybe just me." Darcy sat up and opened the top drawer of the side table. She pulled out a small plastic bottle and shook it. No telltale sound of tablets rattling. "Shit. It's empty." Darcy lobbed the bottle at the garbage and dropped her head onto the arm of the couch. "Why won't this headache go away?"

"Am I interrupting?" A Latin god stood in the doorway. Dark hair with gray at the temples and smoldering brown eyes. Yes—they smoldered. He had adorable dimples and wore a collared shirt that clung to his body like a second skin. He must love all things laundry, because his shirt was an ode to washboards. His arm muscles bunched as he fidgeted with a manila folder in his hands.

Don't even get her started on the hands.

Darcy sat up and smiled. The woman asking for a gun ten minutes ago was now all smiles. "You're not interrupting anything but my breakdown." She leaned back. "Do you have anything for that? Maybe some Paxil, or some cannabis?"

"Those are two very different things."

Darcy's smile was all for the Latin god. "I wasn't going to take them together."

His dimples danced as he smiled. At Darcy. Kennedy might as well not have existed.

Darcy smiled some more. "What can I do for you?"

"I have the test results for Tad Markham."

"The look on your face isn't promising."

He sighed and handed over the folder. "Torn meniscus."

Her sigh was much louder than his. "Shit." She glanced through the pages. "Surgery."

"Yes, that would be the best course of action. He'll be out for at least six weeks, barring any complications."

"And if there are complications?"

"It could be longer." Latin god shrugged.

Darcy tapped the folder. "Are there options?"

"We could focus on physical therapy but there's no guarantee, and then we'll just find ourselves back here in three months. It's not the best scenario for Tad. He deserves to have this treated properly so he can have a long career."

"What did Tad say?"

"I haven't told him yet." Latin god went into the adjoining bathroom. After a clink and some rustling, he came back out.

"I can't have him out for most of the season." Darcy shook her head. "They already think I'm in over my head. If he's out, we'll never win a game."

"Here." Hot doctor guy—Kennedy assumed he was the doctor, given the conversation—held out his hand.

"You are a god." Darcy took whatever he offered, popped it in her mouth and swallowed. That sounded much dirtier in Kennedy's head. How anyone could swallow pills without liquid eluded Kennedy.

"Thank you so much." Darcy's stare lingered a bit too long on hot doctor dude, and blood pooled in her cheeks. She sighed. "I'll have to talk to Coach Brighton."

"He won't be happy."

"No one will." Darcy poked at her cell phone and the

ring-back tone dinged through the speaker. After a few tones, the phone clicked. "Belinda, where are you?"

"Down on the field," Belinda replied.

"Are you near Coach Brighton?"

"Yes, he's meeting with the other coaches."

"Can you call me when he's available for quick talk?"

"Sure."

Darcy leaned back on the couch and closed her eyes. "Well, that's as done as I can make it for now."

"I'll stop by later to check on you." Doctor Hottie turned to leave, but his eyes caught on Kennedy. "I'm sorry. I didn't see you there."

Obviously. He was too busy oogly-eyeing Darcy. "I'm Kennedy."

"Ah, so you're the famous Kennedy. I'm Louis Guzman, the team doctor. I've heard all about you and your shenanigans in college."

She wished she could say the same, but Darcy seemed to have forgotten to tell Kennedy about Louis the Hot Doc.

"Nice to meet you, Doctor Guzman."

"Please, call me Louis." He focused his brown eyes on Darcy. "Don't do too much today." He ran a hand down the side of her cheek before heading out the door.

Speaking of doing… "How long you been doing the doctor?"

Darcy's face dropped. "Wait. How did you know?"

"Really?" Kennedy could feel her eyes pop out of her head. They didn't believe the words coming out of Darcy's mouth either. "I almost had an orgasm just watching you two."

"It's not that bad."

"Bad? No. Sizzling? I have scorch marks." Kennedy rubbed at the fictitious marks on her arms.

"He is nice to look at."

"Understatement. How long have you two been dating?"

"A few months, but no one knows… well, Selma knows, but she put two and two together."

"You mean she saw your hands roaming all over his body and figured out you were playing doctor?"

"You're judging me." Darcy's eyes filled with tears. She was about to cry, and given that her late husband wasn't exactly a saint, she didn't deserve this.

"No judgement. But Selma said the guy was bald."

Darcy shook her head. "That was someone else."

"Who?"

"It was a fling. Some guy from the country club. But he moved back in with his wife, and I don't mess with married men." Definition of irony right there—seeing she was a married woman. "You're judging again."

"Why would you say that?"

"It's in the eyes." Darcy held up two fingers and pointed them at Kennedy's face.

"I'm not judging at all. If you're going to play doctor with someone, he's a great choice." Kennedy hated to see Darcy cry again, but… "How did you and Chuck get here?"

"Get to a place where we were both getting some on the side?"

"Yeah."

"I don't know. It started as, you know, he cheated and I forgave him. When it happened again, the kids were in junior high. I didn't want to let him get away with it, but I also didn't want the kids shuffled between houses and everybody fighting over holidays. I couldn't put them through that. So I had to make a choice. Either I let him do whatever he wanted, or I left. Then I figured there was a third choice. What's good for the goose was good for the gander."

"Didn't it bother you, though?"

"Of course, but I couldn't do that to the kids."

"But what about you. What about your happiness?"

Darcy cocked her head to the side. "Eh. Happiness is overrated."

"What about Doctor Hottie? Does he make you happy?"

"Yeah." The smile on Darcy's face could power the scoreboard. "I'm in love with him, and I think he loves me."

"That was obvious. He didn't even know I was in the room."

"Right." Darcy giggled. An actual giggle, and it sounded so normal and good.

Someone tapped at the door to Darcy's office and her smile dropped. Detective Disagreeable stood in the doorway, and he looked about as welcoming as his name. His eyes were fixed on Darcy... probably on her megawatt smile.

Was it too soon for a grieving widow to smile without looking guilty? Given the look on his face, Kennedy thought that was a yes.

Shit.

CHAPTER 18

"Good afternoon. Am I interrupting?" Detective Pagonis asked, like he cared. His expression said he most certainly did not.

"No." Darcy blushed. Really? Was she supposed to be miserable forever? He'd probably say she should be miserable at least until the funeral. Which, okay, he might have a point there.

"What can I do for you, detective?" Darcy snapped her shoulders back, and her businesswoman mask was firmly in place.

"I've been speaking with some of your staff, and I wanted to talk about that fight you had with your husband on Saturday night."

"Didn't we talk about that?" Did Kennedy say that? Out loud?

"Yes, but we were cut short and I'd like to revisit it." His almost-sneer disappeared when he turned to Darcy. "You looked much better after your shower."

"Thank you so much for letting me clean up the other day. That was a nightmare." Darcy coiled her blondish hair between her fingers and laid it over her shoulder. "Red was never my color." She attempted a laugh, but anybody with half a heart could tell it was way too soon.

Beneath the detective's hard exterior, a glimmer of sympathy showed through. Maybe the man was actually human. Kennedy never would have guessed.

"The other night." Darcy sighed. "Chuck and I had our problems with cheating over the years."

"Is that why you were fighting?"

Darcy shook her head. "Not really. Well—sort of." She wrapped her arms around herself. The office wasn't cold, but Darcy chafed at her silk shirt like she was out in a snowstorm in Chicago. "A few years ago, we decided to have an open relationship. He couldn't seem to keep his, um, member to himself, and I couldn't break up our home."

"It's a nice home." His tone wasn't really judgmental, but Kennedy caught a whiff of…something. Like he was thinking about real estate values. And Nevada being a community property state.

Darcy didn't seem to pick up on it. She attempted another smile. "My kids mean everything to me. I couldn't do that to them. But Chuck? He changed."

"How so?"

"He met someone."

"So it got heated and you killed him." Pagonis might be fishing, but there was pity in the squint of his eyes.

Darcy just shrugged. "No, I met someone else, too."

"Then why the argument?"

A spark ignited in Darcy's eyes. "Have you ever won anything, Detective?"

He blinked. "Um, I won first place in diving."

"I've never won anything. Ever."

Apparently the wet T-shirt contests in college didn't count. Not that Kennedy blamed her. No one ever wanted to admit that their only claim to fame was that they had great tits.

Darcy took a deep breath. "Saturday night was my night. I had worked for months with Glowing Hope to feed and house the people in the tunnels. It was long nights and hot days, but I met so many wonderful men and women. We helped so many people. It felt so good."

Darcy's eyes lined with tears. "The Las Vegas Philanthropic Excellence award is given to one person a year, and they chose me. I just wanted my husband to be proud. Do you know how many awards my husband has?"

Pagonis glanced at the wall of gold and silver, everything from MVP to Good Citizen awards. All in Chuck's name.

Darcy stared at the shrine. "This is just a drop in the bucket. We have boxes of this stuff back at the house. And every award he won, I stood on the side— the proud wife clapping for his achievements. This award was my one chance. Someone finally noticed me for being more than Chuck Perrault's wife. And he couldn't be bothered to show up. Do you know how that made me feel?"

Pagonis didn't say anything. Didn't move, just watched Darcy.

"Do you?" She wasn't going to let this go. Darcy didn't lose her shit very often—and definitely not in front of strangers.

Pagonis shook his head. Given his widened eyes and tucked chin, he looked overall terrorized. He didn't seem to like dealing with a woman on the verge of a breakdown. It almost made it bearable to watch her best friend crumble... until a tear slid down Darcy's cheek.

No. If Kennedy could shield her from all of this bullshit, she would. Kennedy wrapped her arm around Darcy's shoulder, and Darcy snuggled into her.

Darcy swiped at her eyes. "It was supposed to be my night. All he had to do was show up. He couldn't even do that." Darcy leaned into Kennedy. "Kennedy flew thousands of miles to be here."

Seventeen hundred, to be exact. Not that Kennedy was about to correct Darcy when she was having a moment.

"Chuck couldn't pull his dick out of his girlfriend for one hour to celebrate what I'd done. I got angry and yelled. Who wouldn't? Then he got an attitude and said he had bigger problems, and that the world didn't revolve around me."

Kennedy latched onto the one word. "What kind of problems?"

"He never said. I don't know if it was club business or his girlfriend. All I know is that I wasn't important enough for him to take time away from whatever was going on."

"What's his girlfriend's name?"

Darcy pulled away from Kennedy. "I didn't want to know. It's one thing to know your husband is screwing someone else, it's a whole other thing to have to look at her. But I think it's his old high school girlfriend, Miranda Scott."

"The accountant?" Pagonis asked, which was the same question Kennedy had. Except Kennedy's version would have included a few swear words. "Why do you think it's Miranda?"

"She always glares at me like we're in middle school."

Kennedy said, "When I talked to her, I got the impression she wasn't with him." What had Miranda said? *Too much hurt.* The look in Miranda's eyes said she'd been telling the truth.

"Why?" Darcy glared at Kennedy—middle school drama, anyone?

Kennedy shrugged. "Miranda said she wasn't with him."

"She's a liar," Darcy spat.

"Maybe, but I don't think she's with him." Kennedy

tried on a tiny smirk. "But I can vouch for her being a bitch."

Darcy's annoyance faded as she attempted a smile.

Pagonis cleared his throat. "One more thing." He produced a plastic bag holding a piece of fabric from his pocket. "Does this look familiar? We found this at the crime scene."

The bag crinkled as Darcy took it and turned it over. "It doesn't look like anything special, but it's hard to see the color with all the..." She gestured at the bag, and Kennedy mentally finished *blood*.

Bobby appeared in the doorway, and knocked. "Mrs. Perrault." His eyes saucered at the bag in Darcy's hands.

"Bobby, is everything okay?" Darcy asked.

"Yes, ma'am." He gulped, turning an interesting shade of pale. Kennedy could understand. Blood wasn't her favorite thing either. It needed to stay in the body where it belonged. "You wanted Belinda to call you when Coach Brighton was available. Belinda is dealing with a food vendor issue, so she told me to tell you Coach is ready to see you."

Darcy glanced at Pagonis, who said, "I think I have everything I need. Please keep me posted if you find out the name of the girlfriend." He took back the evidence bag, turned, and Bobby stepped to the side to let him through.

Once he was gone, Darcy said, "Can you tell Coach I'll be down in ten minutes?"

"Yes, ma'am." Bobby disappeared, leaving Kennedy and Darcy alone.

"Shit." Darcy flopped back on the couch. "I don't want to have this conversation. It's not going to go over well."

"Do you need help?" Well, not help. "Support?"

"Thank you, but I need to handle my team." Darcy stood up and tucked in her shirt, tugged her pencil skirt back into place. She took a deep breath. "I should at least look my best when I tell the coach that the only reason we were winning is going to be out for the rest of the season."

"This is your first season," Kenney pointed out. "I'm sure they know there will be growing pains."

Darcy laughed without humor. "In theory, yes. In their heads, the fans know we need time, but in their hearts they want a winning team. And this first season is when we attract those fans. They're going to chase me out of the building with torches and pitchforks."

"It's not your fault."

"No. But I'm the messenger." Darcy gathered the medical folder from her desk.

"You got this."

Darcy nodded as she strode out of her office. Hopefully, Kennedy wouldn't need to have the car ready for a quick getaway.

CHAPTER 19

Kennedy lay on the couch, one arm resting on her forehead. Darcy hadn't asked her to make a prison break. Yet. Which was good, because Kennedy was exhausted. Her hands hurt. Her paper cuts had paper cuts.

"Darcy?" a deep voice called from somewhere over Kennedy's head.

She rolled off the couch and stood in front of a sports legend. Dark brown hair streaked through with sandy blond. Deep brown eyes and light black skin. The man was gorgeous, and so recognizable. He was the Michael Jordan of the soccer world.

Kennedy would know him if she saw him anywhere. Tad Markham. She especially liked him in that cologne commercial where he ran through the rain without a t-shirt. Nummy.

"You're not Darcy." The deep voice was the cherry on top of an already perfect male.

"Sorry, Darcy isn't here right now." That might have been obvious, but Kennedy's tongue was tied. All the drool in her mouth made her stutter.

Tad smiled. Her cheeks warmed as his eyes stayed riveted to her face. He was obviously into her. Which didn't make sense. She was a normal person and he was a sports god from middle America. She ran a hand through her hair, her fingers sticking to something at her temple.

She pulled whatever it was through the tangles. Ugh. Her hair must be a disaster. Yep. She crumpled the Post-It that had been in her hair and tossed it over her shoulder.

"Do you know where she is?" Tad asked.

Kennedy ran both hands through her hair to see if she was storing anything else. Nothing. Thank goodness. "I'm not sure, but she has to come back eventually."

"Why?"

"I have her keys." Kennedy took the Jaguar key out of her pocket and shook it. "She won't get very far without me."

Tad sat on the couch, his forearms resting on his knees. "You must be the friend."

"I must." She wanted to jump on his lap and talk about the first thing that came up. Crass. Yes. But so very true.

"What was she like in college?" She? Oh yeah, Darcy.

"Fun." Kennedy sat on the desk. It was so much safer than his lap.

"Weren't we all."

Kennedy nodded. She had been a lot of fun back then, too. The life of the party, until the night she'd come home drunk and her parents kicked her out. The night she almost lost everything.

"College was one long party with way too many drunken mistakes." Tad smiled.

"Amen." Kennedy really liked this guy. Back then, Darcy had just found out she was pregnant, she'd moved in with Chuck and left college. Yet she'd let Kennedy move in so Kennedy could keep going to school. The scholarship had covered the classes but nothing else. If Darcy hadn't taken Kennedy in, Kennedy wouldn't have finished college. Heck, she would've been homeless.

Tad smiled. "What was Chuck like?"

"Same. Why do you ask?"

"Curious I guess." Tad shrugged, doing interesting things to his shoulders. "I can't picture him being a party animal."

"Were you close to him?"

"No," Tad said immediately. Oh, there was a story there.

"What did you think of Chuck?" This was the perfect time to get some info, since he just appeared at Darcy's door and was all chatty.

"I tried not to."

"You didn't like him?" Kennedy asked, her curiosity building.

"I heard a rumor you didn't like him either."

"From whom?" It wasn't a secret she didn't like Chuck, but how would strangers know that?

"This place is worse than a knitting club. There's so much gossip." He leaned forward. "Nothing is a secret around here. You can't hide hate for a man who ended up dead.

His story checked out. "From what I've heard, we should've started a club."

Tad laughed. "We would've had so many members, we could've charged dues and been able to retire to the hills."

Kennedy laughed because it was true. They would have had to beat off new members with a stick. "Why didn't you two get along?"

"We didn't agree on a few things." Which was a very diplomatic way of saying Chuck was full of shit.

Kennedy nodded. "Me too. He liked to tell me how wrong I was all the time."

"Well, if you didn't agree with him, you were wrong."

"True." Kennedy laughed. Tad was pretty smart. "What were you wrong about?"

"My treatment."

"Treatment?"

"I hurt my knee over a week ago." Tad tapped at his knee and winced. "I'm sick of taking pain meds. They mess with my stomach."

Kennedy had taken pain meds a few years ago and her stomach completely revolted. She understood the problem. "Well, you'll be able to get it taken care of soon."

"Right." Sarcasm didn't look good on him. Which was surprising, since everything else did. "The way Chuck jerked me along, now they'll get their way. I'll be on meds the rest of my life."

Kennedy was here when Doctor Gorgeous told Darcy about the test results a few hours ago. They had even mentioned that Tad hadn't been told the results yet. "Didn't you get the results today?"

"We've known for a week. It's why they're trying to screw me on my contract."

Wait, what? "Can they do that?"

Tad sat back on the couch. "Either take six weeks, get physical therapy, and keep my contract. Or have surgery and they'll cut me loose."

She wanted to say that there was no way that Chuck would have done something like that. But over the past few days, she'd learned that she didn't seem to know him at all. But Darcy... "Darcy wouldn't do that."

"That's why I'm here. I need to talk to her and see where she's at on this."

"Where I'm at on what?" Darcy breezed into the office, her face all business.

"My torn meniscus."

Darcy glared at Kennedy, like Kennedy was some sort of gossip girl.

Kennedy shrugged one shoulder. "Apparently, Chuck knew about the knee and was using it in contract negotiations."

Darcy dropped a file onto her desk, obviously thinking. Which way those thoughts were heading, Kennedy had no idea. "Kennedy, could you give us a minute?"

"Sure." Kennedy wanted to be a fly on the wall, but this wasn't her business. She'd read about in the sports pages like everyone else. Anyway, she had work to do. Tad knew about his meniscus a week ago—which meant others knew too. She had some questions for the love doctor—like why he lied to the woman he supposedly loved.

CHAPTER 20

ennedy headed down the stairs and followed the hallways to the doctor's office. They'd only passed it once, but she was pretty sure this was the way. A few minutes later, she arrived at a white door with a sign above it that said medical center.

She opened the door and was greeted by the smell of antiseptic and menthol—heavy on the menthol. Someone must have been bathing in that crap. Or they just used it to wipe down everything. A couch and side tables occupied one wall. There were three doors, but only the center one was closed. The two rooms beyond the open doors held examination tables.

The center door opened. "May I help you?" A woman in pink scrubs appeared in the doorway. A beautiful girl. Probably twenty-something, with dark skin that glistened as she smiled. Ombre twists hung down her back.

"I was looking for Doctor Guzman." Kennedy's nose twitched as a strong whiff of menthol hit her.

The woman laughed. "Sorry, about the smell. We just did a rubdown with a bit of Icy Hot."

A bit? That felt a bit like an understatement. Kennedy

tried to laugh, but the smell tickled her throat, making her want to cough. The minty smell grew stronger as broad shoulders came into the room. The broad shoulders were attached to so many muscles—and they were all on display. Did Alex wear clothes outside of the soccer field? Because all she ever saw him in was a towel. Or without. Not that she was complaining. It was nice view.

"Desty, my shoulder is still hurting. Can I get that needle thing?" he asked the nurse.

"Dry needling?"

"Yeah, that thing." Alex winced when he moved his shoulder. He either didn't see Kennedy or didn't care.

Desty—was that her name?—sighed. "The operative word is dry, Alex. I can't use the needles after menthol treatment."

"Can we do something?" Alex rolled his shoulder as another wince twisted his face. Deeper. The man was obviously in pain.

"Of course." The woman sighed again. "Go back in and I'll work on it a bit more."

Alex attempted a smile as he turned and skulked back through the center door. Unlike the other two, this one led down a hall.

"I'm sorry about that;" the woman said. "Athletes can be a handful."

"No problem. Are they always like that?"

"Whiny? The center of the universe? Yes." Desty laughed. Desty. Interesting name.

"Did he call you Desty?"

"Yeah." Her dark skin glowed as red crawled over her cheeks. "It's a nickname. My real name is Destiny."

"It's beautiful. Although so is Destiny."

"Thank you." Destiny nodded. "So you're looking for Doctor Guzman."

"I am."

"He's actually busy at the moment. Can I help?"

"I'm Kennedy Romero, and I have a few questions for the doctor."

"Kennedy, Darcy's friend?"

"Yes."

"I'm the nurse practitioner here." Destiny smiled. "It's so great to meet you. I've heard so much about you."

Kennedy wasn't exactly sure that was a good thing. After all, the cops considered her a suspect, and other people thought she was Darcy's minion. Not many others had met her.

"What questions did you have for the doctor?" Destiny asked.

"I was hoping to see the knee report for Tad Markham."

"I can't really share that information." Destiny shrugged. "You know, HIPAA."

"I can go get Darcy and have her show it to me." Kennedy was going to play her cards, even if it made her sound like a tween. "I am her best friend."

"The doctor said you went to college together." Destiny seemed to be digging, but that was okay, as long as things went in Kennedy's favor.

"We did. I lived with her when her children were born. I'm their godmother." How many more labels did Kennedy have to pull out?

"Darcy would probably just show you."

"She did send me down here to get the information." Mostly.

"Follow me." Destiny led Kennedy down the middle hall, past a set of offices. She turned into a room with a desk. And an entire wall of filing cabinets. Kennedy almost hyperventilated. So many cabinets. It would take days to clean these out.

"We just got Markham's report today." Destiny sifted through a pile of papers on the desk.

"Was it today? Tad said he was working with Chuck on his treatment plan."

Destiny didn't look up. She kept sifting through papers. She finally handed a sheet of paper to Kennedy. "I don't know about anything like that, but this is the report we got today."

Kennedy looked it over. She held it up to the light, but there was no Wite-Out or cross-outs anywhere on the page. The date was today's date. "Could there be another report?"

"If there was, I haven't seen it."

"Kennedy, is Darcy okay?" Louis Guzman stood in the doorway.

"Yeah, I left her talking to Tad Markham."

"Destiny, can you go work with Alex? He's whining that his shoulder is going to fall off if you don't come help him soon."

Destiny nodded to Kennedy. "It was nice to meet you."

"You, too." Kennedy walked over and handed the paper in her hand to Louis. "What is this?"

"The MRI report for Tad Markham."

"With today's date. I wanted to know if there was another test taken before this."

Louis glanced at the page. "This is the only test that was done. With the problems he was having, we figured the MRI was the best course of action. Why?"

"According to Tad, Chuck knew about the meniscus and was using it to renegotiate Tad's salary."

"I don't know how he would have known. My office gets the preliminary report, if there is one. This is the first report I've seen."

Unless he was a professional liar, something in his eyes said he wasn't lying. Somehow, Kennedy believed him. "Is it normal not to get a preliminary report?"

"No, but nothing about this was normal." Louis sat at

the desk, and moved files to the side. "Our usual lab is in the middle of a renovation, so we used a different one. They said they lost the paperwork. We usually know within twenty-four hours what's going on."

A very pregnant woman with blond hair waddled into the office carrying a stack of file folders. She rested the folders on her sizeable bump. "Doctor Guzman, I have to get to my other job." She seemed surprised to find them in the room—or maybe she was surprised at the mess. Her eyes widened, darting from one side of the desk to the other.

"Beth Haas, this is Kennedy." Louis was still sifting through files. "Before you leave, do you know where the Tad Markham file is?"

Beth set the folders she carried down on the corner of the desk, reached out, and pulled a single file from the clutter. Kennedy was impressed. They could have used her in the evidence locker.

"You are amazing, as always." Louis smiled. "I don't know what we're going to do without you when you're gone."

"Are you quitting?" Kennedy leaned against the chair in front of the desk.

"Maternity leave." Beth shook her head and started restacking the paperwork Louis had moved around. "I'm the office manager."

"Best office manager ever." Louis s stood up, still holding the file. "I'm really sorry. We seem to have made a mess."

"That's okay." Beth attempted a smile, but there was no way that the desk being a mess was okay. Given the jitter in her movements as she cleaned, it was the furthest thing from okay.

"It was nice meeting you." Kennedy followed Louis out the door.

"Beth likes things kept in order," Louis whispered as he crossed the hall to what appeared to be his office. A desk sat in the center of the room, and two framed diplomas hung on the wall behind it.

"I could tell," Kennedy said, squinting to read the diplomas. The University of Illinois at Chicago, and Columbia University

"I would complain, but she's the only reason we get any of our insurance claims done on time."

"You take insurance?"

"Not exactly. I'm the team doctor, and we handle physical therapy and basic care. Anything more than what we can handle, I write a referral and the player's private insurance takes over."

Interesting. Kennedy had no idea. "So when players need a test or an MRI…?"

"The doctor or facility performing the test would submit the claim."

"Can we find out when insurance got billed for Tad's test? Or at least the meds?"

"Meds?" Louis frowned as he sifted through the file. "I don't see that any medication was prescribed by an outside doctor, and I didn't prescribe any, either."

"Wouldn't pain meds be a part of the treatment plan for a torn meniscus? Initially, anyway."

"Unless a patient doesn't want any medication."

"Tad didn't mention not wanting medication. He just said he didn't want to be on the pain meds forever."

Beth cleared her throat from the doorway. "Doctor Guzman, you have a phone call."

"Okay." His brow was snarled in confusion as he read and turned a page. "Beth, do you know if Tad Markham was given any medication?"

"Um… if he was it would be listed in the file."

"I don't see anything here, but Tad is saying he was given pain meds."

"May I?" Beth took the file. "Maybe one of the nurses gave him some meds for pain. They sometimes forget to put it in the file. Do we know what was prescribed?"

"Did he mention the medication name?" Louis was looking at Kennedy—like she had an answer.

She most certainly did not. "No. But wouldn't you have to have something on file if a narcotic was prescribed?" That felt incredibly illegal.

"We don't keep narcotics on site." Louis shook his head. "The most we would have given him was a high dose of acetaminophen. I guess it could be an error, but I don't see anything." Louis shook his head before focusing on Beth. "I know you're on your way out, but can you call the lab tomorrow and see if they've submitted the insurance claims for Tad? And verify if there are any prescriptions?"

"Also, can we find out when the test results were originally provided?" Kennedy added. Might as well get in on the request.

Beth nodded as she took notes on the back page of the file. The pharmacist might not know what medication was prescribed, but they had to know something. This was not adding up. Someone had to be lying. But whom?

CHAPTER 21

Fifteen minutes later, Kennedy was taking the elevator up to Darcy's office. It had been a long day. She just wanted to go to bed.

Kennedy rested her hand on her grumbling stomach. Maybe she should eat before she headed to bed. She was pretty sure those grumbles translated into "I'll start eating useless organs if you don't feed me."

So, sleeping wasn't going to happen until she ate. Maybe she could talk Darcy into hitting a buffet. Kennedy walked through Darcy's open office door. "Feed me," she said, dropping onto the couch.

Darcy waved a hand. "I would love to feed you, but I have this pile of work."

"You have to eat dinner." Kennedy didn't whine. She didn't.

"I will, but it's going to be a while. I might just grab a granola bar from one of the machines."

Really? Darcy was in the middle of a city with some of the best chefs in the world and chose to eat stale granola. But sometimes you sacrificed for friendship. Kennedy prepared to crawl off the couch. "Okay, I'll grab us some snacks from the machine."

"They have a great burger place next door. You go."

"Do they have crab legs?"

"No." Darcy opened a drawer and took out her keys. "Take my car to Joe's, or Caesars has an amazing buffet. If you don't feel like driving, there's the tram."

Caesar's crab legs. She'd been dreaming of those things for a few days now.

Darcy tossed the keys, and Kennedy barely managed to catch them before her eyes were skewered. "Are you sure I can't help with whatever you're doing."

"No. You go." Darcy held up some papers. "These numbers are not adding up. Did you become a number guru?"

"I know all the numbers." Kennedy held up her fingers. "One. Two. Three... Does that help?"

"Not even a little. Go find yourself a nice set of legs."

"Are you sure? I really can help." She might not be able to help with numbers, but she could cheer Darcy on or something.

"Absolutely. I'll get more done if I don't have to worry about making sure you're having fun. It's about time you enjoy your vacation."

"I'm going to find dinner, then." Kennedy tossed the set of keys back to Darcy.

"Don't you want to take the car?"

"Nah, I'll take the tram."

"You can pick it up at the hotel next door. But take my jacket." Darcy dropped her keys into the open drawer and pointed toward her coat with her other hand. "It gets cold at night. Call me when you're done, and I'll take you back to the house."

"I will." Kennedy waved before taking Darcy's pink

jacket off the end of the couch and slipping it on as she headed out of Darcy's office and left the building.

The sun was setting, and cold air tickled her neck. Two blocks to the tram. She didn't care. Kennedy was going to find crab legs if it killed her.

She wrapped her arms around her waist and tried not to shiver. She was from Chicago, for heaven's sake. Sixty degrees was practically a heatwave. In her defense, people passed her on the sidewalk with winter coats and gloves. She was wearing a pink leather blazer.

Kennedy walked up a ramp to the hotel and opened one of the double doors. A wall of air conditioning met her, along with indistinct chatter plus machine squeaks and beeps.

The sweet smell of milk and sugar wafted from the ice cream shop next to the front door. Her growling stomach probably made a noise, but she couldn't hear a thing over the casino noises. Ice cream was almost healthy. It had milk. She hesitated, but visons of crab legs danced in front of her eyes, red claws snapping and clicking.

The buffet probably had ice cream.

A sign pointed the way to the tram, so she turned away from the sugar factory and followed the worn red and blue carpet, dinging machines on both sides. People sat on black swivel chairs in front of each one, pushing button after button. Some people frowned. Some jumped up when their machine lit up like a fireworks finale.

Kennedy stopped when the passageway split. No helpful sign or arrow anywhere. A woman sat at a Wild Cherry machine, a cigarette dangling from her lips. An oxygen tank sat to her left on a little wheeled cart-thingy, plastic tubing leading to the plastic nose piece. At least she was keeping the lit cigarette away from the flammable tank. Mostly.

The woman glared at Kennedy and stabbed at the

machine, her finger jabbing at the buttons. No lights. No beeps. The machine whirred and the woman glared. "You're standing too close," she rasped.

"I'm sorry?" Kennedy could have sworn the woman was talking to her.

"You should be." The woman's voice was all gravel as she poked a button and the machine whirred with no pomp or circumstance. "You're bad luck."

Kennedy almost said something rude, but honestly? Kennedy's bad luck aura seemed to be the least of the woman's problems, what with the fire near flammable gas and all.

The woman hocked up a lung as Kennedy stepped back and chose a direction at random. Anything to get clear of the blast zone. She found another sign, and sped up. She had a tram to catch and buffet to hoover.

A set of automatic doors let her out onto an enclosed path leading to an empty platform, with glass doors between her and the tracks. Back in Chicago, five PM was prime rush hour. Here, not so much. At least not today.

Five long, drawn-out minutes passed. She checked her phone for messages. Ten minutes passed. Well, maybe it was only seven minutes, but it felt like seventy, so there was that.

She tried to look down the tracks for an incoming train, but palm trees and the building next door blocked the view. Then she checked the website to see if the tram was running today. Nothing indicated it was down.

As if she willed them, the glass tram doors opened. Finally.

She took a step back, waiting for the tram to pull up to the platform. No tram. Maybe she was missing something. She leaned past the doors. Nothing. No tram was in sight.

A shove at her back and she fell forward—toward the

tracks. Her arms flailed. She was falling. And there was nothing she could do about it.

Not.

One.

Thing.

Her knee bent, banging into a metal rail. Her hands shot forward, her palms smacking into the other rail. Her forehead thumped against metal. Everything rocked with darkness.

Raw pain burned along her palms. Not to mention the throbbing in her knee. She swore she heard voices yelling behind her. Maybe the person who pushed her. Maybe she was hearing things. Her head was ringing. The whoosh in her ears was so loud, she might be mishearing the ringing in her ears as voices.

Maybe she finally lost her marbles and the marbles were actually talking. Who knew.

Her body vibrated. Two sets of hands wrapped around her upper arms. The tracks disappeared, replaced by a blur of palm trees and sky. She flopped like a rag doll as a silver wall flashed by. Two men stood over her. "Are you okay?"

She wanted to say yes—because she was pretty sure the men were talking to her—but her mouth wouldn't move. Her body was coming back online piece by piece and she couldn't seem to form words.

"Someone call an ambulance," one man called out.

"I got it," another man said.

"Did you see the guy push her?"

"We need help…"

Kennedy tuned out the words and concentrated on making her mouth work. "I'm okay." She heard the words come from her lips and she almost believed them. She tried to sit up, but the men held her down.

"Don't get up." The one on the right smiled. He had a

nice smile. White teeth. Tan face. "We're getting you some help."

"I'm okay," Kennedy insisted.

"You mentioned that," the guy on the left said. He was cute, too. Blond hair. Blue eyes. He looked like he belonged on a billboard—or maybe in an all-male review. "Just lay back until the paramedics get here."

Her head throbbed. Her back pulsed. That didn't exactly feel normal. She probably could use the paramedics. Kennedy laid back—not because he said so. Because of all those other things.

Blond Hair Cutie pushed hair from her forehead. She melted. Okay, it was partially because he said so. This was going to be one hell of a meet-cute to tell their grand-children.

"I told you coming to Vegas was a bad idea." Blond-haired cutie sighed and looked at Nice Smile.

"I thought you wanted to get married here." Nice Smile couldn't hide his disappointment if he tried. It was like he just found out there was no Santa Claus.

Kennedy probably had the same look. No meet-cute for her.

"I don't care where we get married." Blond-Cutie grabbed Nice-Smile's hand. "As long as you're there, the wedding will be perfect."

"Even if we have to nurse a lady back to health before the ceremony?"

The men's words were jumbled as they leaned over Kennedy and began kissing. Their shirts were pushed against her ear—she hoped it was their shirt.

"Where's the patient?" A voice broke through the adorable couple, and they parted. Blond-Cutie and Nice-Smile stood up and made room.

A paramedic kneeled down next to Kennedy. "What's your name?"

She was pretty sure she knew that answer. "Kennedy Romero."

The paramedic pushed Kennedy's hair aside and smiled. Everyone was so nice.

It was a bit weird though, that everyone had some kind of obsession with her hair. Kennedy closed her eyes as the woman looked her up and down. "Where does it hurt?"

"Everywhere" was the answer. But Kennedy had a feeling that she needed to give a more detailed answer. She was going to be here awhile.

CHAPTER 22

A half hour later, and she was a living, breathing spectacle sitting on a gurney at the tram stop. When she'd walked up, there was no one on the platform. Well, that had changed. It was now the hopping-ist place on the strip.

People stood around in a half circle watching the paramedics take her blood pressure. *Oooh.* And watching the paramedics part her hair so they could clean the gash over her eye. *Riveting.* At least one would think it was riveting the way everyone was watching and holding up their cell phone. Although it did explain everyone's obsession with her hair. At least her forehead didn't need stitches—so not spending hours in an ER was a win.

Nice-smile and his fiancé were standing around telling the story of the last hour. "We walked up to the casino doors and this woman was looking over the edge of the platform. The tram platform doors were open, but there was no tram. Some man ran up behind her and pushed her."

The fiancé interrupted. "Well, we're assuming it was a

man. They were wearing a hoody and running away from us."

"Of course it was a man, did you see his shoulders? Anyway, they ran off. We pulled her onto the platform just as the tram pulled up."

Kennedy had already heard the story a dozen times. They'd told the paramedics and the numerous cops that had come through. She hated thinking how close she'd come to being a tram hood ornament.

Even worse, she just knew she was going to be a meme on social media. *Chicago cop can't handle her Vegas, news at eleven.* Maybe if she kept her face down, no one would recognize her.

"Please keep your chin up." The paramedic waited for Kennedy to look up and then rubbed cream over her forehead. "Don't worry, no one will recognize you through the bruising and the gash here."

If that was supposed to make Kennedy feel better, it was a fail. She apparently looked like a cut-up punching bag. Not exactly how you wanted to be seen… ever.

"Why are all these people here?" That voice. It was like her own private nightmare that followed her everywhere. "Romero." Detective Cranky-pants was here. The last person she wanted to look like the loser of fight club in front of, so of course he was here.

Kennedy attempted a smile, but her face was too sore to really mean it. "Detective Pagonis. Isn't this a little below your paygrade?" Funny enough, her sarcasm was still working.

"I heard your name."

"So you missed me." She knew she was giving him a hard time. She got so little joy in her life, she needed this.

"Sure." Pagonis smirked. "I do like spending time with the main suspects in my murder cases."

"How can I still be the main suspect? I was pushed onto train tracks."

"Tram tracks."

"Is there really much of a difference?" Kennedy had got a close look at the tram. It looked rather train-like to her.

He didn't answer, just smirked his smirky face.

"Here are the notes for my report." An officer handed Pagonis a pad of paper. "If you can read my writing."

Pagonis was the quietest he'd ever been. He turned pages and nodded his head. "Someone pushed you onto the tracks." He looked up and stared at Kennedy, like he wanted her to answer.

"Yes." She'd already said that, but who was counting.

"Thank you for your notes." Pagonis handed the pad back to the officer. "Are you done?"

"I'll finish up and head out."

"Send me a copy of that after you submit it." Pagonis waved off the crowd. "Nothing left to see here."

The paramedic finished repacking the large bag at her left. "After you get something to eat, take a couple more aspirin. Just two."

Kennedy nodded. "Two. Got it."

Detective Pagonis turned to the paramedic. "Are you done with Ms. Romero?"

"She's good to go. Would you like some help down?" she asked Kennedy.

"No, I'm good." Kennedy slid down from the gurney.

The paramedic steadied her. "Are you sure you won't let us take you to the hospital?"

"No, thank you." Kennedy had already refused their invitation twice. She was a bit rocked from being tossed around, but she was okay.

The paramedic handed Kennedy Darcy's pink jacket, now with blood spattered all over it. A wardrobe disaster. DOA.

The paramedic folded up the gurney and left. People disbanded. Pagonis seemed to have a gift for scaring away spectators. Not that Kennedy was complaining. She didn't want to be the center of attention any more than she wanted to be poked and prodded.

"You're getting too close, Romero."

"What?"

"Someone wanted to stop you. Who did you talk to?" Pagonis stared at her like he could see into her soul. Since he was still looking at her like she needed to answer, he obviously couldn't actually see.

She'd talked to so many people. "Alex Volkov, Tad Markham, the medical staff…"

"Players? Did they have anything to say that would lead you to believe you were onto something?"

Her stomach gnawed on itself with a growl. Almost getting squished by a tram hadn't curbed her appetite.

"Are you hungry?"

"Yes." She was even too tired to say something snarky.

The detective rested his hand on her back and motioned toward the casino doors. "Yes?"

She might not have been exactly clear. "No to the players getting too close. Yes to hungry. I was heading to Caesars."

"Caesars?"

"Crab legs," Kennedy said.

Pagonis nodded. "Ah. Are you okay taking the tram?"

"Yeah. Why not?"

"Just making sure you're not traumatized."

"No." She stood a good ten feet from the glass doors. And there was no possibility she'd get closer—unless she saw open tram doors. And a tram.

So far, no open doors. When she was splayed out, everyone was there with camera phones. But now? Nothing. The platform was empty.

Eventually the tram pulled alongside the platform and stopped with a high-pitched screech. The glass doors opened at the same time the tram door opened. Pagonis held the door open as she made her way across the platform. He rested his hand on her back and guided her inside.

It was incredibly sweet, but she didn't need help. "You know I can get on the tram by myself."

He smiled as he followed her on board. "I'm not letting you hit the tracks on my watch."

"Then just don't push me." It wasn't like she couldn't get on train. She rode the El every day on the way to work.

The tram lurched forward, and Pagonis laughed as he grabbed a pole. Kennedy latched onto the pole like a scared cat, her arms wrapped around it like a vise. She leaned her bruised face on the cool metal.

"Are you okay, Romero?" The detective was so close, she could practically feel the tremor of laughter in his words. His arm was around her shoulders.

"I'm good." She got her balance and leaned back. She could do this. *Be cool, Romero.* She was so cool. She held the pole with one hand.

They stepped out onto the platform at the next stop, which turned out to be Bellagio. "This isn't Caesars." If Pagonis thought getting her lost in Sin City would deter her from getting her crab legs, he was mistaken. She was getting them if she had to pay a homeless man to steal them from the kitchen.

"This is the way." Pagonis smiled. "Trust me."

She had almost been assaulted by a wannabe Thomas the Tank Engine. Her trust was splattered on the tracks. But since Kennedy had no idea which way to go from here, she let Pagonis lead her to an elevator down to the main floor.

Kennedy hobbled past Chanel and Dior and all the other stores she couldn't afford on a cop's salary. Well, she couldn't afford it and pay her mortgage. Life was full of choices, and she liked having a roof over her head during Chicago winters.

They walked outside, over the Flamingo bridge, through the hotel hallways, and into the casino at Caesars. Her knee throbbed, out of sync with the bells and lights. They'd given her pain meds, but they hadn't quite kicked in. The pain had, though.

Her stomach growled. Food had to be close. She could smell fried chicken, or maybe just fried food. Her stomach gurgled again. Louder. More insistent. Thank goodness for slot machine noises.

She followed Pagonis to the entrance to the buffet, and reached for the credit card in her back pocket.

"I got this." The detective pulled out his own credit card.

"Are you sure?"

"You've had a rough night in Sin City. You deserve a free meal."

The smell of fried everything and steak and fish permeated the air. Kennedy's stomach did a jig as she inhaled a deep breath of heaven.

"This way," said the sweet old lady who'd run his card, and led them to a table at the far end of the buffet. There were no windows in the huge room. No clocks. The usual casino décor, so you'd lose track of time.

Once the woman left, Kennedy dropped Darcy's bloody coat on a chair next to hers. Her knee screamed. Her stomach screamed. Her stomach won. She hobble-ran to the buffet, and grabbed two plates—both for her. She was going to get the detective's money's worth.

CHAPTER 23

Kennedy had one plate in front of her piled with crab legs, and another filled with everything else. Pagonis only had one plate—which would be embarrassing if she cared. At the moment she was so hungry she could eat the food on her plates and his. That would be embarrassing, so her restraint was admirable.

That's what she was going with.

Pagonis sat back in his seat. "So you talked to Markham and Volkov. Do you think either one of them pushed you onto the track?"

"I don't think they pushed me." Kennedy wasn't completely sure, but she couldn't see them doing anything like that. It wasn't like she found out anything earth-shattering.

"Are you sure?"

"They didn't say anything that was incriminating. They didn't seem to be lying." She cracked the crab leg and picked out the meat. "They were pleasant and forthcoming." Well, Volkov was neither of those things, but being an asshole didn't mean the guy would shove a woman in front of a moving train.

"Didn't you mention a medical office?"

"I talked to the team physician." She dipped the crab into butter and smiled. Did she mention heaven? "Although it was strange."

"What was strange?"

"Tad Markham was told about his injury one week ago. But according to the team physician, they just got the results today."

"That is strange." The detective dug into his plate of steak and vegetables. "Someone must have gotten the results then."

"So far, no. According to Tad, he received the information from Chuck."

"So who gave Chuck the information?"

"That would be the question."

Kennedy broke open a crab leg and pulled out the meat. Dipped it into a bowl of butter. Moist, buttery crab coated her fingers. She slid the goodness into her awaiting mouth and licked the golden drops from her fingers. Her eyes closed as she chewed. "Hmm." It was so good. Her eyes popped open and met Pagonis' stare. "Sorry." Red clawed up her cheeks.

He cleared his throat. "Don't be. That was interesting to watch."

"Interesting?"

He smiled. "Enjoyable."

"I really like crab legs." Her lips curled up. She did not mind being thought of as enjoyable.

"I can see that." He smiled. Two smiles—did she miss something? "Speaking of things you like, and don't like. Why didn't you like Chuck?"

She knew they'd get to this. And there was no way she didn't come out looking like a suspect. But she refused to lie. "Chuck never liked me. To be fair, I was a bit wild back in the day."

"You, wild?"

She'd like to think the truth would set her free, but not her truth. Her truth landed her in rehab. "I have a drinking problem. It started in college. I was out of control back then. Chuck didn't like Darcy being around me. Rightfully so. Sophomore year of college I hitchhiked all the way home to my parent's house. I was so drunk I forgot which bedroom was mine. I shoved my sister out of her bed. Broke her arm. Mild concussion. My parents kicked me out."

"How old was your sister?"

"Four." Bile just about choked Kennedy. She cleared her throat. Again. And again. Her sister had been terrified. And her parents… they'd been fed up. "It was awful. After taking my sister to the hospital, the next morning they kicked me out."

"That was an extreme reaction." Pagonis sat back, actually looking pissed on her behalf.

"Yeah. I thought so. And after Darcy had Fanny, I don't think I could ever understand. Fanny wasn't my own my own daughter and I could never kick her out of my house. I would have gotten her help and fought for her. But I had never been worth the effort." That realization had hurt the most.. "I'd done a lot over the years. In high school I wrapped my dad's bike around a tree. I'd come home drunk and throw up in various places. We had this rattan basket in the living room where we kept blankets…"

"You didn't."

"I did. For a week, my mom couldn't figure out why the living room smelled like vomit." She couldn't help the laugh that bubbled out of her chest. "It's not funny at all, but she'd walked around the living room, her nose twitching. 'Doesn't anyone else smell that?' She was so mad when she went to grab a blanket and found what I left there."

The laughter dried up and a tear poked at the back of her eye. "I tried not to drink. I watched other girls around me go out and party without drinking or just go out and have fun. Somehow I just couldn't do it. I would feel so bored and boring. It was like I was walking around invisible. I'd talk myself into just one, and then it would snowball until I was bleary-eyed."

Pagonis reached across the table and laid a hand on hers. It was a simple act, but so sweet. "That had to be rough being left on your own like that in college."

"It wasn't easy. I was nineteen, with nowhere to go. They were my only family." She shrugged, not looking at him. Her eyes were focused on his hand on hers. It felt so warm and strong. She hated how good his hand felt on hers. She wasn't the type to get all mushy at the slightest bit of attention from a guy. "I don't blame them. I hated myself for hurting her. I was so lost, but it wasn't their fault."

"It might not have been their fault, but you were their child too." The anger in his eyes about tore her apart. No one else ever felt sympathy for the poor little rich girl who couldn't stop drinking. No one cared how her life was destroyed. She was the evil one and her parents were the saints who put up with their terrible teen. "You didn't deserve that."

No. She didn't. Kennedy pulled her hand away. She didn't want him to feel her hand shaking from anger or the desire for a drink or an overwhelming urge to slap her parents on her younger self's behalf.

"What did you do?"

"Darcy. She saved me. She took me in and helped me get sober. I lived with her in her dorm until she got a place with Chuck. Who was... a bit flighty in college." Flighty was an understatement. Throw a nineteen-year-old boy on a soccer field with adoring fans, and you ended up with a boy who thought he was God's gift to the world. "He was this hotshot soccer player, and he could sleep with anyone he wanted—and he did. After Darcy had the baby, she needed help. Chuck was away a lot, and Darcy was alone. We had a 'two women and a baby' thing going on while he was on the road. We stayed in school and raised Fanny."

"It sounds like you two are close." Pagonis dug back into his plate of food.

"I never would have graduated if not for her, let alone have become a cop. And I'd like to think she'd have had a hard time navigating the first year of motherhood without me." Kennedy cracked another crab leg and pulled out the meat. "We're both where we are today because of each other. Darcy never gave up on me. She's my family."

"That's how you became a Chicago cop?"

"Yes." Although she wasn't in the best place right now. She dipped more crab meat into the awaiting butter and brought it to her lips. She avoided making any noises that might lead to Pagonis staring.

"You mentioned you're riding the desk."

"You remembered that?" Kennedy almost stopped eating from the shock—but, food.

"Professional hazard. I listen and I remember."

It was the darkest point in Kennedy's life. "I had some personal problems and had trouble maneuvering… But, that's a story for a different time." Or never.

"So is it blind loyalty that makes you think Darcy is innocent, or do you have something to back that up?"

Kennedy would like to think she wasn't blindly doing anything, but this was Darcy. "I think she's innocent because she wouldn't hurt anyone. I've watched her throw Chuck's trophies—not at him, although he deserved it. I've watched her put up with all the shitty things he's done over the years, and she rolled with it."

"Like?"

Chuck was dead, so why not throw him under the bus? It was for a good cause. "He spent an entire month's pay on hookers and blow in Monte Carlo when he was in Europe for the Olympics."

"He played soccer in the Olympics?"

"He did. They came in last." Kennedy still couldn't believe it. Who had a total breakdown after losing one game? Chuck, that was who. "He wasn't used to losing, hence the hookers and blow. Darcy was beside herself. She almost flew there to kill him." Maybe not the best choice of words. "She didn't, though. She waited till he got home and threatened to leave him. She was mad enough to do it. But he talked her out of it, and they've been going strong ever since." Depending on your definition of strong. "Do you still think she's good for this?"

"It's always the spouse." He was so sure.

She was not. "Not this time."

"Why don't you think she did it? She was one of the last people to see him alive. He was stepping out on her."

"She was stepping out on him, too. Darcy and Chuck practically split the house down the middle, and they'd have their significant others stay over. According to Darcy, she's in love with the guy."

"Which guy?"

Kennedy didn't think this was privileged information. "The team physician, Louis Guzman." Pagonis would find out eventually, if he was any good at his job. And she had a feeling he was really good at his job.

"The doctor." He shook his head.

"You don't think I'm telling the truth?"

"No, I do. It's…I didn't think she was dating the doctor, but my partner did. She always has my back, but she's never going to let me live this down."

"Partners are good like that." She finished off the last crab leg. So sad. "You know I could have your back."

"Yeah." He laughed. A throaty, deep laugh that made

his face light up. Who knew he could be so cute? "You need to step back. You could get hurt."

"I can take care of myself."

"Clearly." He stared at her forehead— and presumably the bandage— as he ate a piece of bacon from the stack on the side of his plate.

Her face must have conveyed her annoyance, because he dropped the bacon and actually frowned before shaking his head.

She needed to change his mind. "I've been working this case and I've given you information. I'll follow the clues wherever they lead. We can learn more if we work together."

"Are you sure you can follow them even if they lead to Darcy?"

"Even if they lead to Darcy." She wasn't sure she could stand behind those words, but they must have sounded convincing because he nodded.

"This goes against every logical thought."

She tried not to smile. She didn't want scare him into reconsidering.

"If you get in my way, I will arrest you."

"I won't." She just had to pray that Darcy wasn't implicated in any way. Darcy swore she didn't kill Chuck. Darcy wouldn't lie.

At least Kennedy hoped not.

CHAPTER 24

nother plate of crab legs later, and Kennedy was pretty sure she'd need a forklift to get her back to Darcy's house. She'd eaten more crab legs tonight than she had in her entire thirty-eight years of life. More than she ever needed to eat again. But they were right here, and so good.

"Did you want some more?" Pagonis seemed to be gloating as he compared his one plate of food to her two-plus.

"No." Even the thought of more crab made her queasy.

"That's good. I think they ran out." He smiled, and then his phone buzzed. He looked down. "The video from the tram platform is here. Want to see?"

Kennedy pulled the chair to the other side of the table and inched her chair closer to his. "Absolutely."

On the grainy video, the glass doors opened and Kennedy peered around the corner. It was blurry enough for her own face to be barely recognizable. Unfortunately, she'd lived it, so she knew what came next.

A fuzzy man— or woman— came up behind her and shoved her. Their jacket was nondescript. A hoody, maybe black. Black jeans. Nondescript shoes. Nothing that really stood out.

Pagonis sighed as the video clip ended. "That isn't much help."

"Next time I get pushed in front of a train, I'll make sure to get their name and address first."

"That would help. But if you could avoid getting pushed in front of a train, that would be great." He smiled.

"Was that a joke, Detective?" She didn't know he knew how to joke. But so far tonight he'd been full of zingers.

"I have a hell of a sense of humor, Romero."

"You hide it well."

Pagonis laughed. "Well, it's hard to joke with the main suspect in a murder investigation."

"Well, then it's a good thing I'm not at the top of that list any longer."

"True." He nodded. "If you like my type of humor."

Truth was she did, but one things still bothered her. "But Darcy is on your list."

"Yes." He seemed to think about his next words. Some inner decision must have been reached, because he added, "But we have other leads."

"Like?"

"We have a lead on one of the super fans." He leaned sideways, and rested his arm along the back of the chair.

"Well, let's go talk to him." Kennedy thought about standing up and running for the door, but honestly, she was still waiting for that forklift.

Pagonis checked his watch. "It's eight o'clock at night. We'll go tomorrow."

Eight. Talk about losing track of time. They needed to get as much information tonight as possible. At least Kennedy did. Tonight the delightful detective was playing nice, and tomorrow he could be back to asshole. "You'll blow me off."

He held up one hand and gave her the Boy Scout three-finger salute. "I promise to pick you up by car, bus, train, or plane and not blow you off." If he wasn't such an ass, the whole Boy Scout thing might be cute.

"Are you okay? I got your text." Darcy whirled into the buffet dining room like a designer tornado. Her eyes first found Kennedy, but then laser-focused on Kennedy's chair next to the detective.

Kennedy felt that stare like a mama bird catching her chick stealing a worm. She wanted to jump up and move the chair. She wanted to swear she wasn't conspiring with the enemy. Kennedy didn't know what to say, so she went with, "I ruined your jacket."

"I don't care about the jacket. Look at you." Darcy lifted Kennedy's bangs and winced. Not a surprise. A face versus train tracks was never good. The train tracks always won. "Why didn't you come home?"

"I had to eat." Kennedy pointed to the crab leg carnage.

"I would have fed you." Darcy dragged a chair over and practically sat down on top of Kennedy. "You should be in a hospital."

"The paramedics looked me over. I'm fine."

Darcy seemed to be placated, at least until she re-noticed Kennedy's eating companion. Her worried face morphed to angry. "And why are you with him?"

"Good to see you too, Mrs. Perrault." Pagonis stood up and pulled out his wallet.

Kennedy really didn't want tonight to end. Not because she liked him or anything. It had to do more with getting information. "You don't have to go."

Pagonis took two bills out of his wallet and dropped them onto the table. "Yeah, I do."

"Thank you for dinner."

"Yep." He slid his wallet into the back pocket of his jeans.

"Tomorrow?"

He saluted her with three fingers and walked away.

"What's tomorrow?" Darcy picked at the fries on Kennedy's non-crab plate, popping one into her mouth.

"I'm going to tag along with him."

"Are you serious?" Darcy's eyes raged with fire as her teeth slowed their chewing. "There are millions of men in Las Vegas. Why are you trying to get with that one?"

"I'm not trying to get with anyone. I'm trying to make sure they follow through with the investigation and you don't get railroaded." Ooh. Too soon. Although maybe it was the pain shooting up her arm. Now that she wasn't famished, she felt the effects of her run-in with the tracks. It could also have to do with the fact that the meds were probably wearing off. And Darcy was being an ass. "Is that really what you think of me? That I'd be looking for a hookup while the cops are looking at you for murder?"

"Of course not." Darcy stood up. The words sounded right, but she didn't even look at Kennedy. "We need to get you home."

Part of Kennedy wanted to talk all this through with Darcy, but a bigger part of her was ridiculously tired. She wanted to go home and sleep. Or better yet, she wanted to go home and drink. But one drink always led to two, and two always led to nothing good. Sighing, she followed Darcy out of the restaurant.

Tonight had been rough—nearly getting run over and being called a ho by her best friend. She needed another meeting. Sooner rather than later. There was no way she was falling down that liquor hole again.

CHAPTER 25

The drive to Darcy's last night had been quiet. Kennedy was exhausted after the train incident and Darcy was lost in thought. If Kennedy didn't know her best friend better, she'd think the woman was hiding something. Although Darcy hadn't hid her annoyance at Kennedy having dinner with Pagonis. She'd made that pretty clear.

Kennedy tried to get up early enough to talk to Darcy. Who, apparently, had run out the door before the sun came up. So Kennedy sat here, at the kitchen counter, checking the phone in her hand for the millionth time. No calls. No texts. No smoke signals. Pagonis swore he'd come get her today. He Boy Scout saluted, for goodness' sake.

He knew Kennedy was staying here at the house, but he should have called. She'd think he was sick from all the crab legs, but he hadn't eaten any. It must have only been her. Now she was just angry.

Who was this guy to Boy Scout promise and then stand her up?

What kind of cop does that? What kind of man?

The doorbell rang, and she checked her phone. Would

he just show up at the door? As Kennedy stood up, she heard the front door open.

Selma's voice came from that direction. "Detective, we... we weren't expecting you. Miss Darcy isn't here, and I don't think anyone else is home." She sounded terrified. "Fanny is at a friend's house and Charles is with his uncle or something." The poor woman was rambling.

Kennedy hurried to the front door—just a little jog. "It's okay. He's here for me. Right?" She smiled at Selma, trying to calm her down. The woman was so high-strung.

It wasn't Selma's fault the detective's broad shoulders and tall frame took over the doorway. It didn't help that his collared dark shirt and equally dark pants made him look domineering. He commanded a room, which was a great quality for a cop. Selma just didn't seem to appreciate it.

"If you're ready?" He looked Kennedy up and down, but not in a hot and bothered kind of way. It was more of a clinical any-new-bruises kind of way. And from what Kennedy saw in the mirror this morning, there were no new bruises, but the old ones were still there.

The detective's eyes roamed downward. She mentally followed along. Jeans and a T-shirt. The go-to outfit of the vacationing crowd. And since she thought she was coming here on a quasi-vacation, totally appropriate. Maybe not the best for interrogations, but whatever.

"I'm ready." She stared directly into his eyes and willed him to argue with her. She'd been dealing with the stress of waiting for two hours. She could use an outlet for her frustration.

He didn't take the bait. "Let's go."

Darn it. "I'll see you later." Kennedy nodded to Selma as she followed Pagonis outside into what was left of the cloudy morning. The air held a chill without the sun poking out to flambeau the desert.

He opened the door on a black Ford Explorer and held it

while Kennedy slid inside. It was incredibly sweet, but it looked way too much like a date. And this was not a date. All she needed was Selma to be watching and it to get back to Darcy that Kennedy was dating the detective. She straight-armed the door to hold it open. "I got it."

He held his up, palms out, and walked to his side. Once he was situated and the car started, Kennedy asked, "Where are we headed?"

"Barrett Fisher Coleman." Pagonis drove toward the gate.

"Who is Barrett Fisher Coleman? Your investment banker?"

"Sounds like it, doesn't it?" The detective laughed as he stopped at the gate and opened his window. Leaning over, he pressed the button to open the gate. "He's our rabid fan."

Ah. She was glad Darcy was surrounded by walls, and guards surrounded her subdivision, no matter what the fan's name was. "That name doesn't exactly scream psycho fan."

"What does it scream?"

"That he ate paste in grade school." Okay, she was being an ass.

Pagonis laughed as he headed north, up through Summerlin. The houses were large. Palm trees lined the streets. They drove up to the Ridges, another gated community, and stopped behind a line of cars.

"Are we driving through here?" Although that seemed like fun, she didn't think the people in these fancy neighborhoods appreciated it much—given the stacked security guards vetting every car. The place was locked up like Fort Knox.

"No. Mr. Coleman lives here." Their car inched forward as the one in front of them was allowed into the inner sanctum.

Really? Creepy super fan lived in Extreme HOA Land? "Here?"

"State your business." A guard stood next to the car.

Pagonis flashed his badge. "Detective Pagonis to see Mr. Coleman."

"Address?" The guard tapped at his tablet.

"It's 105 Promon..." Pagonis kept speaking, the guard kept typing, and Kennedy couldn't believe it took this much information to get into the subdivision. The guard stepped back and talked into his phone. Kennedy couldn't really tell what he was saying, but it felt all kinds of judgey. She would have never gotten into this neighborhood alone. Having a cop guide was a necessity around here.

"Go ahead," the guard finally said as he motioned to a guy inside the guard station to open the gate. Darcy's community was fancy, but not like this.

Pagonis drove through and followed the curved road. Houses sitting high on hills lined both sides of the road. Every one of them huge and modern, with floor to ceiling windows and soft angles. He turned onto a side street that climbed further into the hills, past more sprawling homes.

Didn't Las Vegas have any normal-sized houses? So far, every house she'd seen was either tiny or a monstrosity. These were obscenely huge. Pagonis turned off the road onto a half-moon drive and parked near the front steps of a mega-mansion done in white, brown, and black stone.

Kennedy got out of the car and followed Pagonis up the large stone steps to the oversized carved wood front door. When the detective pressed the doorbell, what sounded like the song the Victory used when the team scored played inside the house. Although that could have been Kennedy's imagination.

A short, balding man with large headphones hanging around his neck opened the door. He looked Pagonis up and down and then Kennedy. He must have decided she didn't matter, because he turned his attention back to Pagonis. "My guards tell me you're with the local constabulary. To what do I owe the pleasure?"

"I was hoping to ask a few questions."

"Come on in, mate." Mr. Coleman was either from Australia, or he was really good at faking an accent. He motioned them through the door. Inside was as spectacular as the neighborhood would suggest. A large crystal chandelier hung from an eighteen-foot ceiling. A small table stood in the middle of the entryway, and a bouquet of dead flowers drooped from a vase in the center of it.

Beyond that, white couches and Tuscan-inspired lamps matched the doorway arches. Soccer balls sat on a high shelf along the far wall. Even with the sports memorabilia, it was still beautiful and regal.

But nothing compared to straight ahead. Colossal sliding glass doors led to a pool with a complete view of the Vegas strip.

Coleman stood off to one side, motioning to the couches. "Please sit."

On the way to sit, Kennedy almost tripped over a stack of designer suitcases piled along the door.

After saving her face from another set of bruises, Pagonis stared at the mountain of luggage. "Are you going somewhere?"

"Nah, mate. Just got back. What's this about?"

"We wanted to talk about the letters you wrote to Chuck Perrault and the Vegas Victory Soccer Club."

"Football Club."

"What?"

"It's a football club, not a soccer club." Coleman snorted. "Yanks."

"You wrote a few letters—"

"Yeah, that bastard wasn't playing Markham on the post."

"That's no way to talk about a dead man." Why she was defending Chuck, Kennedy had no idea. But it felt disloyal to let this guy talk shit.

"Yeah, I heard about that. Although maybe now we'll have a decent shot at the finals, eh." The asshole had the nerve to laugh until he saw no one else thought he was funny. "I mean, it's a sad thing and all."

"Where were you Saturday?" The detective was nonplussed. Kennedy was plussed.

"California."

He had an alibi. Dammit. She so wanted this asshole to be the guy. She wanted to be the one to slap the cuffs on his arrogant little wrists.

"Why were you in California?"

Kennedy stood and looked out the back window. She didn't care why he was in California. She only cared that he wasn't here. The backyard was amazing. A large veranda overlooked an infinity pool that overlooked the entire Vegas skyline, including the valley surrounding it.

"Did you drive or fly?" Pagonis asked.

"Nah, too far to drive. I can't get away from the website that long."

Kennedy smiled at the implication that the website would somehow fall apart if he took an extra couple of hours to drive the desert. On the right side of the room, a door stood ajar.

"What airline did you use?" Pagonis asked.

"Oi, where're you heading, miss?"

Kennedy ignored him as she peeked inside. The room was covered in sports memorabilia. Not just soccer balls and signs. There were framed and hung jerseys. Lines of cleats in clear boxes sat on a ledge along the wall. But the soccer shrine wasn't what caught her eye.

"Don't go in there."

Kennedy heard Coleman say the words, but they didn't

stop her from pushing open the door the rest of the way and stepping inside the room.

Hanging on the walls were pictures. What looked like every player from the Vegas Victory, with strings connecting those pictures. Alex Volkov was circled with a starter flag. Tad Markham's picture was crossed out with "Torn Meniscus" written across the front. It was like the lair of a serial killer.

Be cool. She took in a deep breath. "Detective?" From the desk, Kennedy picked up a yellow notepad with Markham's name crossed out.

"I told you not to come in here." Coleman stormed into the room, Pagonis on his heels. Pagonis glanced at the pictures, then pulled Kennedy behind him as he rested his hand on the butt of his gun.

It was sweet. And condescending. And if she lived through this, she swore she'd hit a meeting—just to make sure she didn't actually hit him. She didn't like being treated as if she couldn't handle herself just because she didn't generally pee standing up.

"What is this?" Pagonis nodded toward the wall of crazy. Kennedy heard the distinct sound of his holster snap opening.

"It's not what it looks like." Coleman snatched the notepad from Kennedy's hand.

"It looks like you have an obsession with the Vegas Victory." Pagonis drew his gun at the same time he pulled out his cuffs. A slick move, and under different circumstances Kennedy would have given him a thumbs up. Pagonis planted his feet. "Is this why you killed him?"

"What, no. I had nothing to do with that." Coleman dropped the notepad as his hands raised over his head.

"You can imagine my confusion when I look at this wall."

Coleman's hands didn't move. The guy looked terrified.

But, then, most people weren't used to having a gun pointed at them. "Not an obsession. I'm just really into football. I'm the president of the Las Vegas National Football Pool."

"The what?" Pagonis lowered his gun, but he was still on guard. His stance was coiled cobra, ready to strike.

"It's on my computer." Coleman motioned to the desk. "I can show you."

Pagonis nodded, and Coleman sat down and pulled up a website. "The Real Football Pool. I got sick of American football mucking it all up."

"You run this entire website?"

"The site and the company. I made two million dollars last year."

"From betting?" Pagonis holstered his gun and secured it.

"Nah, I get a cut of the sign-up fees. The fees cover the site maintenance, and I manage the money and member bets. It's a full-time job."

Kennedy motioned to the serial-killer wall. "Why do you need all this information for a pool?"

"I'm a statistician. I set the odds." Coleman clicked a tab and a new screen came up. "The site is like the Expedia of gambling. There's links to the Xiongmao Casino Group. People can see all the different bets and places to bet."

Kennedy couldn't look away from the wall. "Why did you send Chuck a threatening email?"

Coleman laughed. "Tired of him making poor choices."

"Because he was costing you money?" Pagonis asked.

"I was making plenty of money. I just hate watching them lose. Vegas is my home now, it's bloody embarrassing watching them lose. Why would I kill him? I had a good thing going. Anyway, I was in California when he died, picking up a new server after my old one crashed."

Coleman opened a folder and spread out the papers inside. "Check my flight and my hotel."

Kennedy barely glanced at them. Something on the serial-killer wall wasn't adding up. According to the notes stuck to the pictures, Burkhead was on injured reserve, and Tad had a torn meniscus. In small letters, the note said "out for six months".

Where did Coleman get this information? "How did you know about Tad's injury? It hasn't been announced yet."

Coleman laughed, but his eyes never left the computer screen. "Well, I saw the way he was hit at the game." Either he was really enthralled with whatever was on the screen or he was lying.

Kennedy voted for option number two. "And you can tell he'll be out six months from how he was hit?"

"What can I say? It's a gift." Coleman's hospitality dried up faster than his logic. "I have work to do. We all done here?"

Pagonis nodded. "We'll be in touch."

"Feel free to call my lawyer anytime."

Kennedy smothered a snort. Pulling the lawyer card already? Something struck a nerve.

Pagonis followed Kennedy out of the office and out the front door. When they were safely outside, he leaned against the car. "I don't think he did it."

"I don't either, but he was acting squirrelly."

"He's getting inside information. That's probably his gift." Pagonis opened the Explorer's door and leaned against it instead of getting behind the wheel.

"Agreed. But isn't that illegal?" Kennedy was pretty sure she'd seen an episode of *Law and Order* on the topic. Being a Chicago cop, she didn't see many insider information crimes or gambling rings. Maybe Vice or some other divisions did, but not her.

"It's hard to prove." Pagonis shrugged. "That's probably why he's nervous. He wouldn't want to burn his informant."

Kennedy opened the passenger door. "Coleman said he wouldn't kill Chuck because he had a good thing going. Could Chuck have been the informant?"

"That would be stupid. Chuck could've lost his team."

"If it wasn't him, who could it be?" Kennedy angled into the passenger seat. "Markham?"

"He wouldn't have anything to gain," Pagonis said, getting in the car. "In fact, if it got out, he'd lose the upper hand in negotiations."

Which was the same thing Darcy said. "Alex Volkov?"

Pagonis drummed his fingers on the steering wheel. "He's Markham's best friend."

"Yeah, but Markham is the star." Kennedy didn't like Volkov. The arrogant jerk could be a backstabber. That wasn't outside of the realm of possibility. "Jealousy can be a strong motivator."

"He protected him in our interview. Turns out they're high school friends. What about the doctor?"

"Doctor said he didn't know until a couple days ago."

"Could he be lying?"

"I don't get that impression." And not just because he was dating her best friend. "He was pushing for Tad to get the surgery."

Pagonis started the engine, and Kennedy put on her seat belt before saying, "Too bad Markham doesn't have a girlfriend." It was always the significant other. She didn't have to be a cop to know that. Which was why she needed to get the spotlight off Darcy.

"There's no one current, but he does have an ex-boyfriend."

"Boyfriend?" She didn't see that one coming. "Could it be him?"

"He's a physical therapist. He's been out of town at some conference, but he'll be back tomorrow."

Kennedy smiled. She had another lead, and she was going to follow it until Darcy was no longer in the crosshairs. But first she needed to hit that meeting she kept promising herself.

CHAPTER 26

Another meeting in the bowels of the church basement, the smell of sugar and coffee permeating the air. Given the early evening time slot, the circle of chairs was full. The accountant, Joanna, and the Diandra were all accounted for.

Betty started the meeting. Tonight, they'd be covering step six—admitting they were ready to have God remove defects of character. God had his hands full if he thought he'd remove all the defects of character in this group. Two of today's attendees had bloodshot eyes and a handful of cookies each. Another one was clearly drunk, because she couldn't sit in the chair without swaying.

That didn't even cover all the problems going on behind the scenes in this group. And yes, Kennedy was including the mountain of issues she had in her life.

Diandra bounced in her seat. If Kennedy hadn't already met her, she'd think Diandra was on something. But that was Diandra. Bouncy. Talkative. The way she leaned forward and back, she either had to go to the bathroom or she was dying to tell everyone the next chapter of the Zeke saga.

Betty ignored the bouncing and the swerving and the bloodshot eyes. This was a no judgement zone. She turned to the accountant. "Brad will be reading for us today."

Huh, accountant had a name. He looked like a Brad. Dirty blond hair slicked back in American Psycho fashion. Impeccable suit. He wasn't bad looking, in a useless desk-jockey kind of way. Stereotyping was bad, but Brad read from the Big Book with all the enthusiasm of a professional basketball player watching paint dry.

When the monotone monologue was over, Kennedy and most everyone clapped. There were a few who either thought they were critics, or just didn't want to be here and were taking it out on Brad.

"So, everyone, who would like to go first?" Before Diandra could jump out of her chair, Betty said, "I know you had something to share, Brad?"

He nodded. "My name is Brad and I'm an alcoholic."

"Hi, Brad." That sounded so much better when there were more than three people responding.

"I've...." Brad slid two fingers into his shirt collar and tugged. The tie loosened. His tongue did not.

"It's okay. We're here for you." Betty showered him with her sunshine of a smile.

"I don't know." Brad let go of his collar and strangled his tie instead. "My wife just announced she's engaged to my best friend. I thought we were trying to work it out. I've done everything I'm supposed to do. I've stayed sober and come to these meetings." His lip curled when he said, "these meetings."

Kennedy could relate. There was something about being told you had to go that made them all the more excruciating.

Brad hunched in his chair. "What's the point? I'm not going to get my wife or my kids back."

"You're not doing it for them, Brad," Betty said in her calming voice. "You're doing it for you. I'm so sorry you're going through this."

Brad snorted. "I just don't see the point."

Betty's smile never wavered. "The point is you deserve better. Your family still needs you to be there for them. Your kids only get one father. Did you call your sponsor?"

He nodded. "I'm not backsliding, but I want to."

"Don't give up." Betty smiled harder. "I'm so proud of you for making the right choice."

Brad shook his head, like it didn't matter. Which in his mind, it probably didn't. Kennedy had those days too. It was one of the reasons she made sure she hit meetings on the regular.

Betty raised one finger. "Don't shake your head. Remember how you were two months ago? You would have taken a drink. You would have come back here feeling powerless and back at square one. But instead, today you beat the urge."

"Millions of people get through the day without taking a drink," Brad said. "It doesn't seem like that big of an accomplishment."

"Millions of people smoke, drink, do drugs, eat unhealthy foods, gamble, lie, steal... take your pick." Did Kennedy say that out loud? Everyone was looking at her. So, yes, she'd used her outside voice. "Just because millions of people aren't picking up a bottle doesn't mean they don't have their own demons."

"She's right, Brad." Betty smiled. "And what's your name?"

"I'm Kennedy."

"Hi, Kennedy."

"Did you want to share?"

She didn't want to share. She never did, but it only

seemed fair since everyone else was offering their stories. "I'm a cop. I see people at their worst." Sometimes it made life hard. Sometimes she knew why she had a drinking problem. "And this week my best friend's husband was murdered." What could she say after that? She wanted to complain, but why? She wanted to cry, but that wasn't her thing.

Betty didn't even blink. "Murdered. Oh my goodness. Are you okay?"

"Okay?" If using a very loose definition of the word she was probably okay.

"I'm sorry, of course you're not okay. Your best friend's husband died."

Kennedy didn't have the heart to correct her. He didn't just die, he was murdered. Violently. And in Kennedy's mind, it did count as okay. "I wanted a drink. Many times. The last time I took a drink, I crashed my car into a building. Apparently, drive and reverse look similar with beer goggles." She laughed. There was no humor in it. It wasn't funny. "That night. I walked into a domestic. A husband and wife were fighting and the neighbors called it in. Nothing unusual. We get those a few times a night. Nothing new."

How many times had she walked into the homes of people arguing about the silliest of things. Money. Sex. Shopping disasters. "This one time, a man bought the wrong cheese and his wife started throwing slices at his head. He had her arrested for assault."

The group laughed, but there was a hesitancy, almost like they knew something bad was coming.

"Yeah, it was funny. Things like that happen. Sometimes as cops, we leave these couples embracing and making up. Sometimes we separate them. One or two of them get escorted to jail, and they find their way to go on with life.

However that new life looks, they move on. But not this time. We were too late."

Kennedy took a breath. "This couple was fighting because the husband was cheating. From what we could get from the neighbors, they started throwing things. Then the wife grabbed a butcher knife. Their four-year-old son tried to separate them." Kennedy's vision blurred.

She could see the picture of him from the mantel in the haze. He was just a kid.

"When the wife tried to stab the husband, he pushed her arm away. The knife..." She couldn't say the words. They were too gory and too awful. "Let's just say the knife didn't go into the intended target."

Visions of that huge handle sticking out at his temple...

The blood...

"Four years old. The most beautiful green eyes. Mop top of brown hair. Sweetest little face. Their son was gone and for what? I couldn't stop seeing his face. I couldn't be alone. I couldn't close my eyes. He was everywhere. I can't even say his name. I've tried." Kennedy had dragged the mother away to jail kicking and screaming. The mother lost any semblance of sanity. And who could blame her? Her son had disappeared in the blink of an eye. Kennedy could barely function, and it hadn't been her son.

She was still in therapy for that. But she couldn't bear to hear his name out loud. When a mother started calling for "Tyler" in a store, her heart would race. She'd look over her shoulder, praying she'd see a boy with a brown mop top and perfect green eyes. She never did.

Another deep breath. "Hearing about Chuck's death wasn't the same, but it was hard. I knew him. I've known him for years. But I didn't take a drink. So hopefully that counts as okay." She choked on the last word and cleared her throat. Cleared her mind.

Betty nodded. "It does. Your job isn't easy, but you kept going. You should be proud."

Pride wasn't something that Kennedy associated with herself. She wiped away the tears. Not for a long time.

Betty smiled. And she must have realized that Kennedy's share-time was over because she turned to the group. "Anyone else?"

The circle sat quiet. No one wanted to follow that share. It was hard to top dead things and loss. Not that it was a competition. If it was, Kennedy didn't want to win.

"That's hard to follow, but this is all good news." Diandra cleared her throat. It seemed to be the thing to do. "Hi. I'm Diandra and I'm an alcoholic."

"Hi, Diandra."

"So, I did it. I got back together with Zeke. And it's been amazing."

Kennedy glanced around the group. A few people winced. The others appeared bored. Only Diandra seemed to think this was amazing. Even Betty's smile disappeared. Yep. Only Diandra.

"He still works at Caesar's," Diandra continued breathlessly, "and we snuck through the back door of Absinthe and watched the show. Oh my goodness, it was amazing. So hilarious, I almost peed my pants. Then we went and had the best crab legs on the strip."

Best crab legs? Kennedy ears perked up. Diandra continued to talk about the show. Which, to be honest sounded amazing. If this was a normal Vegas trip, Kennedy would consider taking in the show as well. But nothing about this trip was normal.

"Those shows are notorious for alcohol." Diandra sat up straighter in her chair. "But I didn't drink a drop."

Betty seemed to like that answer. The smile that was starting to wither came back full strength. "Good job.

You've come so far." She motioned for another person to share, and the stories flew.

Kennedy listened to all the outpouring of emotion, and then they finished up for the evening. As everyone dispersed, she all but pounced on Diandra by the snack table. "Do you have a minute?"

"Sure." Diandra poured more coffee and turned to Kennedy. "That was a rough story."

"Yeah, thanks." Kennedy did not want to get back into that. "This may sound weird, but where did you get those crab legs?"

Diandra giggled and leaned closer. "I don't even remember."

"But you said you weren't drunk." Kennedy would bet that Zeke the dirt bag boyfriend talked her into drinking again. That was why you stayed away from boyfriends when alcohol was the glue to the relationship.

"I didn't drink." Another giggle. "We went into the phone booth and did a little…" Diandra lifted her fingers to her nose and sniffed. In Chicago that meant cocaine.

"Coke?" Kennedy used her cop voice. She didn't want Diandra to think there was any judgement. That judgement was probably why she hadn't mentioned this part of the night during the meeting.

"Just a little. The back door is a freaking phone booth. We went in there to make out and have a personal party." She shrugged. "But I didn't drink a drop. Back in the day, I would have drank my weight in vodka after the drugs. I'm getting better."

"Sounds like it." Kennedy thought about ending things there, but really? It was not sounding better. "If you need to be drunk or high to have fun with your boyfriend, maybe he's not the guy for you."

"I don't need to be drunk."

Kennedy held up her hands. "It's not my business."

Diandra hid her pout behind the lip of her coffee cup, and water pooled in her eyes. Crap.

Kennedy might have been a bit harsh. She waved and headed out the door because there was way too much emotion in this room—starting with her own. She was making people cry now. But to be fair, she made herself cry first.

She was going to have to find a new meeting.

CHAPTER 27

"Are you sure you want to come with?" Darcy asked Kennedy later on that night. It really sounded like she didn't want Kennedy to tag along. Since they were halfway to Craig's, it seemed a bit late to ask that question for the tenth time.

And anyway, Kennedy wanted to go. "You shouldn't be heading to Craig's alone."

Darcy sighed as she seemed to come to terms with whatever was swirling around in her head. "I really need to get him out of that neighborhood."

Kennedy didn't bother agreeing. Darcy wasn't talking to anyone but herself.

Twenty excruciatingly silent minutes later, Darcy drove down the darkened street leading to Craig's building. "I hope these pills work. I've been worried about him."

Kennedy nodded. Not that Darcy could see, but again, it didn't feel like Darcy needed her input. Between losing Chuck and all the surrounding drama, Craig's health issues and running an entire soccer team, the woman needed a little bit of grace right about now.

"So, how did your day with the detective go?" Darcy

hadn't mentioned the detective or Kennedy spending time with the man at all. To say this was new was an understatement. Especially since Darcy had practically ignored her for two days because of it.

"It went fine. We interviewed Barrett Fischer Coleman."

"Who? Wasn't he on the grassy knoll?"

Kennedy smiled. Darcy cracked a joke. Maybe all wasn't lost. "Threatening letter guy."

"Oh. Did he do it?"

"Probably not. He was in California." Kennedy was still holding out hope that his ticket was fake.

Darcy flinched. "Am I still at the top of the detective's list?"

"Probably."

"Oh." Darcy sounded so dejected. Another thing on her ever-growing list of concerns.

And this would not make things any easier. "Barrett Fischer Coleman was an interesting guy. He knew about Markham's injury."

Darcy pulled into a parking spot along the street in front of Craig's place. "How could he have known?"

"That's the question." Kennedy opened the car door. The street was quiet today. No drug dealers on the corner. No cars driving by, looking for their next fix. No old woman in the window. The absence of the leering was almost as disconcerting as when they were staring. It was like the calm before the storm or when a baby cried on an airplane. Something felt up.

And not just because she had to ask the next question that was probably going to piss off Darcy again. "Could Chuck have been selling secrets?"

"I wouldn't think so." Darcy didn't seem to get angry, she just paused for a moment. "That would jeopardize the whole club."

"Okay, so who else knew about Markham?"

"Apparently, Markham."

"Would he have told Coleman about this?"

"No." Darcy turned the car off, and sighed. "That wouldn't make any sense. If he ended up a free agent, he wouldn't have any negotiating power if word got out he needed surgery."

"Didn't Volkov know?"

"He did, but he wouldn't say anything." Darcy stared silently out the windshield for a minute. "I don't know. I don't think anyone would say anything. No one would gain from the franchise failing. The team is like a family."

They both angled out of the car and walked up to the townhouse. The curtains were drawn. The yard was a mess.

In other words, same old, same old.

Kennedy knocked on the door. Nothing. "Did Craig know you were coming?"

"I left him a message this morning."

Another knock. Another bout of silence.

Darcy glanced around. "Where could he be?" Another question that didn't seem to need an answer.

Kennedy leaned against the front window and used her hands to block the sun. Through a gap in the blinds she saw.... No lights. Nothing.

A loud snap came from her right. "Shit."

Kennedy turned, and Darcy held up half a Visa card. "Are you buying something?" Kennedy asked her.

"I'm trying to break into the house." Darcy leaned over, peering at the door. "And I lost my damn card."

"Maybe it only takes American Express."

"Funny." Darcy straightened up and sighed. She turned the half-card over in her hand as she stared at it. "This works in the movies. You slide the credit card in the door-jamb and the thing pops open."

"Let me try." Kennedy jiggled the handle and, surprisingly, it opened.

Darcy smiled. "I probably should have tried that first."

"It's been a stressful few days." Kennedy held the door open while Darcy walked through.

The house was messier than before—which was a feat since it was a hoarder's dream before. Now all the piles were tipped over. There was barely a path for them to walk through.

"Something is not right." Darcy kicked at the magazines and papers, making her way into the kitchen. Cabinets hung open—the contents splashed over every available surface. The counters. The floor. Everything, except the virtually empty kitchen table. One lone sheet of paper sat in the center.

Darcy picked it up. "I don't understand." She handed it to Kennedy.

I didn't mean to do it. The aliens won't be stopped. Sorry.

"What did he do?" Kennedy had a feeling she knew Darcy's answer, but she had to ask.

"I have no idea."

Yep. That was it.

Darcy put the paper back on the table. "What do we do now?"

"I have no idea." So far the morning was a bust. They hadn't gotten any answers. Did Volkov tell Coleman about Markham's injury? If he didn't, who did?

And where the hell was Craig, and was he okay?

CHAPTER 28

The next day, they still hadn't found Craig. They'd done everything but put out an APB. But Darcy didn't want to get blamed for another missing Perrault male, so they figured they'd handle it on their own. After a night of driving around alone in a strange city, they were playing a waiting game. And since she had to wait, Kennedy might as well get some things done.

She entered the stadium through the back tunnels. It was like she owned the place these days. Well, it was like she'd wandered the halls enough to find where she needed to go after only getting lost for ten or twenty minutes.

The good news was she found a cute little nook where mothers could feed their babies. The bad news was she found a dark corner where her boot stuck to the floor. She didn't want to think about why. Finally, a long dark hall with a light bursting from the end came into view. That had to be the field.

She walked out, and her shoes sank into the wannabe grass. The light blinded her before she remembered her sunglasses and slid them down over her eyes.

Players sat on the portable massage tables set up along

one side of the field, with nine or ten staff either massaging them or checking them over. One of them might be Markham's ex. She could rule out the women, but she wasn't close enough to read the men's name badges. The doctor stood on the side talking to Markham.

"Mark up," Coach Brighton yelled, and players scattered onto the field in a 3-5-2 formation. The only reason Kennedy knew anything about this was she had dated a midfielder who always gloated how the 3-5-2 formation had him playing as a center-back. Not that any of that mattered.

Most of the players were camped at the post, waiting for the ball. Volkov spun as he dribbled the ball between his feet. He shrugged off a defender and drove toward the space at the far post. The camped defenders scattered, trying to stop him.

"Get square!" the sideline coach yelled.

Volkov edged around a group of defenders. He found a gap and sent the ball flying toward the goal. The ball missed the net, soaring high over the pole. Two players high-fived.

Apparently, that was the wrong thing to do.

"Are you proud of that play?" Brighton stomped toward the high-fivers. "Are you proud that you left him wide open and he didn't hit the goal? You got lucky. Get back on the line." The coach swore a blue streak as he walked back to the sideline. There were word combinations she'd only heard at the precinct when a cop was injured on the job.

Kennedy crossed the front of the field and opened a small door leading to the stands. She walked up a few stairs and pushed down the seat on one of the metal chairs along the wall before sitting down. She glanced up at the empty stands. Unlike at a game, today they were eerily quiet. No energy. No rumble of an excited crowd.

"Lift your leg up! This isn't high school soccer," a coach yelled.

The team ran up and then down the field, the coaches yelling, players pointing. Volkov kicked the ball to another player, who Kennedy thought was named Dembele. That player switched feet and kicked the ball toward the goal.

Toward being the operative word.

The ball soared far right. The goalie didn't even move to stop it.

"All right. This isn't working." Brighton tossed his clipboard on the ground. "Run the field. If you're not going to try, why bother playing the damn game."

The coaches huddled as the players groaned.

"Looks like the coach is pissed." Pagonis stood over her chair, the sun glinting off his sunglasses.

"How did you get here?" If he came through the door she'd entered, she should have seen him.

"Came in the front." Pagonis pointed behind them, up the stands. "Looks like the players are having a bad day."

"Yeah. They're not leaning into their shots."

"You know a lot about the game." He sat in the chair next to hers.

"I watched Chuck play all through college. Darcy would drag me to game after game." Although it wasn't a total hardship. The guys looked nice in their shorts. Not that she was going to say that out loud. "Are you a soccer fan?"

He shrugged. "Not really. I like a good basketball game."

"Why basketball?"

"The pace. The skill."

"Soccer has skill and it's always moving," Kennedy pointed out.

Pagonis stared at the players. "Yeah, soccer is always moving, but sometimes the ball just goes back and forth in center field and gets stuck there."

"So what are you doing here?" Kennedy looked back at the men running the field. "Since it's obviously not to appreciate the skill."

"I wanted to talk to the physical therapist."

"All right," Brighton screamed from the field. "Grab a quick drink and we're going to run that play again." The team hobbled to the sidelines.

"Why are you here?" Pagonis smiled like he already knew. Which he probably did.

"Jon." She pointed at the tables still set up on the sidelines.

He smiled. "Interesting."

"Why is it interesting?"

"We're both here to talk to the same guy."

The water break over, the coaches screamed the team back onto the field. Volkov dribbled the ball down past the first set of defenders and twisted sideways, avoiding Dembele, who managed to strip the ball from Volkov and left him in the dust.

Volkov gave chase. His teammates followed, but Dembele was pulling the trigger on a goal before anyone could stop him.

Brighton slammed the clipboard onto the ground. "We're done. Get out."

The players ran off the field, but Alex Volkov looked into the stands and headed her way. She was a bit surprised he was running toward her without an angry frown. They didn't have an excited-to-see-you kind of relationship. They had more of a she-talked-and-he-was-bored-out-of-his-mind relationship. On top of that, he'd just had a crappy practice.

Alex ran up to the wall. "Hey, Darcy's friend."

"Hey, Darcy's Right Winger." Kennedy smiled. He seemed so friendly today.

"You should take a woman to something better than

practice for date." Alex leaned into Pagonis conspiratorially. "Especially if you want to get lucky."

"We're not on a date." Kennedy tried to smile, which was hard when she really wanted to throat-punch him. "So don't concern yourself with anyone getting lucky."

Alex raised his eyebrows at Pagonis. "Dodged that bullet."

Kennedy wanted to be angry, but Alex's accent had him saying dodge-ed. "No one dodge-ed any bullets."

Pagonis bit back a laugh—not very well, since Kennedy could see his chest move as he covered his mouth. "Mr. Volkov, we have a few questions."

"About?"

"Do you know Barrett Fisher Coleman?"

"No. Should I?" Alex's attention span had hit his limit—obviously. His eyes were scanning the field, probably looking for someone else.

"How about Jon Diaz?"

"Tad's ex?" Volkov nodded at the field. "He is working on Dembele. Does that mean I can leave?" He pushed away from the wall and ran toward the locker room. He didn't need permission, apparently.

"Let's do this." Pagonis stood up and offered his hand to Kennedy.

Kennedy ignored his hand and stood. "Let's do this." She headed onto the field with Pagonis on her heels.

Except his long strides meant he was in front of her, holding out his badge, by the time they reached the sidelines. "Jon Diaz. Do you have time for some questions?"

"Can you give me a minute?" Jon had Dembele's forearm in his hands.

"I'm good." Dembele shook him off.

"Take a pain reliever if your arm starts hurting again," Jon ordered.

"Thank you." Dembele nodded to Kennedy and Pagonis before running into the hallway leading to the locker room.

Jon gathered tubes and towels, shoving everything into a backpack. He looked up with long eyelashes and wide smile. "What can I help you with?"

"How long did you date Tad Markham?" Pagonis jumped into the questioning.

Jon lifted the backpack with a bounce. The guy was like a ray of positivity. "We were together for over a year."

"When did you break up?"

"Two months ago." Jon set the backpack off to the side before sliding the half-moon headrest off the end of the massage table. He dropped it next to the backpack before tilting the table onto its side.

"Were there hard feelings?" Pagonis reached out to hold the table.

Jon smiled. "Thanks. Not on my side. I'd already spent two years in the closet, and Tad needed to stay hidden."

"Why?" Pagonis pushed on the top as Jon angled a leg into the bottom of the table.

"Contract negotiations. His agent is convinced he'll lose leverage if he comes out. They pay a lot to keep his indiscretions out of the news. I don't have the energy to be an indiscretion." Jon folded the last leg.

"Did that make him angry?" Kennedy asked. It would be surprising if Tad wasn't angry. Big star with a big ego, being rejected by the physical therapist. "Or you?"

"We really didn't talk about it, since we were broken up. But I don't think he was mad." Jon shifted on his feet. "I wasn't mad. I was hurt, maybe disappointed. Playing straight is an antiquated concept. But people can't handle their stars being anything but what they expect."

"And what do they expect?"

"Besides straight? Infallible. Indestructible."

"Tad's injury certainly proved he wasn't that."

"No. Heaven forbid they find out he's human." Jon finished folding the table and snapped the bindings closed. He leaned it against his leg as he slipped the head rest in his bag.

"When did you find out about Tad Markham's injury?"

"I was at the game." Jon shook his head. "He'll be out the rest of the season."

"So you know about the torn meniscus?"

"Yeah." Jon's frown said he wasn't happy about his ex's bad luck.

"When did you find out about that?"

"Yesterday."

Pagonis watched Jon intently. "So you hadn't heard anything before then?"

Jon tilted his head. Thinking or stalling, she wasn't sure. "No. I knew he was injured because I was at the game. I had a feeling it was more serious than everyone was letting on, but I didn't know for sure."

"So, how did you find out?"

"How we find out everything here." Jon shrugged. "Rumor mill. It's alive and well at the stadium."

"Do you know Barrett Fisher Coleman?"

Again, Jon thought about his answer. "I don't think so. That's not a name of a player or staff member."

Kennedy was a pretty good judge of character, and Jon didn't appear to be lying. He was energetic and open—when he paused, he wasn't trying to figure out his next lie. He was being thoughtful in his answers.

"It's not a player or staff," Pagonis said.

"Oh." Jon adjusted the backpack on his shoulder as he lifted the massage table. "Can we start walking? I have an appointment in a few minutes."

"Lead the way." Pagonis stepped back as Jon headed toward the hallway. "So, do you know who Tad is currently dating?"

"I don't know her name."

"Her?" Kennedy blurted.

"His current beard, the redhead in Accounting."

"Miranda Scott?" *Also known as cult of personality, if cult was spelled with an n.*

"Yeah, that's her."

"If we have any more questions, we'll be in touch," Pagonis told him.

"Sure." Jon disappeared into the darkness of the tunnel.

Pagonis turned to Kennedy. "Miranda Scott. Did she mention she was dating Markham?"

"Not before my interview was interrupted." *By you.* He knew he was the one who'd preempted her interview. "I'm assuming she didn't say anything to you, either?"

"Not a word. Hmm." Pagonis motioned for Kennedy to lead the way inside the building. That *hmm* said exactly what Kennedy was thinking. Interesting. People didn't lie about who they're dating unless there's something to hide.

So what was Ms. Cult of Personality hiding?

CHAPTER 29

Kennedy led Pagonis past offices till they found Miranda's. Thankfully, she was sitting at her desk. She picked up a pen and crossed something out on the pages in front of her, looking deep in thought.

Pagonis knocked on the open door.

Miranda flipped her red hair over her shoulder as she looked up and smiled. "Detective. What brings you here?" She must have noticed Kennedy because her smile fell.

Pagonis stepped inside the office. "I was hoping I could ask a few more questions."

"Sure." She nodded to the chairs sitting in front of her desk. "I don't really have much to add."

"We want to talk about Tad Markham." Pagonis pulled out a chair and waited for Kennedy to take a seat.

"Oh." Somehow Miranda's smile fell even farther.

Pagonis sat in the remaining chair. "How long have you been seeing him?"

Miranda sighed. "A month."

"Why didn't you mention this when we spoke earlier?"

"We weren't talking about my love life. We were talking

about Chuck." Miranda set down her pen. "I'm married. It's not something I want announced."

"You're sleeping with the biggest soccer player in the U.S. How did you think it would stay a secret?" Pagonis asked, fortunately before Kennedy could say something less polite.

"Well, no one knew about it until now." Miranda scowled. "We're very discreet."

The detective cleared his throat. He didn't glare at Kennedy, but he didn't need to. His tone said it all. "Have you heard about the nature of his injury?"

"His torn meniscus?" Miranda responded, and Pagonis nodded. "Of course I knew about it."

"When did he tell you?"

Miranda rolled her eyes. "I noticed when he couldn't be on top any longer."

"Mrs. Scott, would it be better if we did this at the precinct? I can send a formal letter to your home…"

"That's not necessary." She sighed. "He told me a week ago. He wanted my advice."

"Your advice on what?"

"What to do." Miranda shook her head. "The club wanted him back on the field as soon as possible. They didn't want to have to pay for an expensive surgery with a lengthy recovery if they could just have him use personal trainers and physical therapy."

"What advice did you offer?"

"That he should follow his doctor's orders and get the surgery."

"Which doctor?" As far as Pagonis and Kennedy knew, the team doctor was in the dark.

"They had him see some outside expert."

"Why?" Pagonis asked.

"I don't know. I'm thinking because Doctor Guzman would've recommended the surgery. His brother was some football star who got railroaded a few years ago after a rotator cuff injury. He wouldn't ask Tad to make that type of sacrifice for his future." Miranda's voice rose as her cheeks flushed. "That other doctor didn't care about Tad or his career. That's probably why Chuck sent him to another doctor. They wanted to make sure he could play out the season. So what if one wrong move could put him completely out of commission."

"Why would Chuck risk permanently sidelining him?"

"I don't know. All I know is that there's a better chance he'll get closer to his old knee strength and mobility if he goes with the surgery. If they just use physical therapy, there's a chance it won't heal properly. He has an entire career to think about, not just this season."

"That must have been unpopular with Chuck."

"Not everything is about Chuck. Not that he knew that." Miranda laughed, but she didn't seem to find it funny. "Tad deserves to have a full career."

"Is that why you and Chuck fought?"

"Yes."

Kennedy thought about her conversation with Miranda—the one about Miranda and Chuck arguing about how to spend capital. Capital L for lies. "So you and Chuck didn't argue about real estate and VIP areas."

"No, we fought about that too. But we also fought about how Chuck didn't want to lose his star player."

"Wasn't there another way besides surgery?" Yeah, Kennedy was hijacking the conversation, but she actually felt sorry for Tad.

"Not a way that benefits Tad. They have him on ibuprofen with codeine, and steroids. They barely take the edge off." Miranda sighed. "He's too young to be in this much pain all the time."

It was nice to see Miranda's human side. She actually seemed to like Tad. Which didn't mesh with Kennedy's first impression that Miranda was sleeping her way down memory lane.

"Can I ask you a question?" Kennedy had no idea why she said that out loud.

"I think that's what you've been doing. So, yes."

"You weren't really dating Chuck."

Miranda laughed—a full belly laugh. "That's not a question, but no. We were old friends at best."

"Which doctor suggested the medication?"

"Darcy's latest boytoy." She sighed. "Dr. Guzman."

"Her latest boytoy? How many has she had?"

"I don't keep track." Miranda sighed again. "Honestly, Guzman was the first one I really knew about. But she's a master manipulator. She's probably had a train of boytoys—"

"Boytoy?" The detective's lips quirked up as he interrupted Miranda's hate-fest. "So what about this latest boyfriend?"

"He normally has his hands in everything when it comes to the players."

"So he knew about Tad's injury before this week?"

"No. He didn't know the full details. But I think he gave him meds." Which contradicted what Guzman had said.

"But you're not sure." Pagonis stood, and Kennedy could feel his disappointment. Pinning things on the doctor would put the spotlight closer to Darcy. "I thought he suggested the medication."

Miranda rolled her eyes. "I'm assuming he did."

"Thank you for your time." Pagonis nodded.

"It's not like I had a choice." Miranda looked down at the paperwork in front of her. She was done. Thankfully, so were Kennedy and Pagonis.

He walked out and Kennedy followed as they made their way down the hall. "That was interesting," Pagonis said after a bit.

"She's an interesting person." That was the nicest thing Kennedy could think of to say. Since the woman had no problem disparaging Kennedy's best friend, *interesting* was nicer than the multiple words that started with a B or a W and ended with *itch*.

"Why did you think Chuck was dating her?" Pagonis was fishing.

"Miranda and Chuck dated in high school. They were all hot and heavy until he met Darcy."

"That would explain her animosity." Animosity about covered it. "We should head back to talk to the boy toy." Pagonis laughed. "That cracked me up."

"Yeah, she's a regular laugh riot." Kennedy could admit it was pretty funny, even if it was at Guzman's expense.

"Do you think Guzman prescribed the medication?" Pagonis pressed the down button for the elevator.

"Maybe." Kennedy walked into the elevator after it opened. She clicked the button for the lower level.

Pagonis followed. "That does leave us with a problem, then."

"Problem?"

"We still don't know who this other doctor was."

That was one of the many questions that needed to be answered before she could leave. She needed to clear Darcy's name, and somehow this outside doctor had the key.

CHAPTER 30

Ten minutes later they were back at Louis's office on the lower level of the building. "Notice how all roads lead to this office?" Kennedy muttered.

Pagonis nodded as he opened the door. "I'm noticing that as well."

Destiny stood behind the counter, her twists now gathered into a ponytail. She smiled, and she was still gorgeous. "Good afternoon, Kennedy."

"Good afternoon."

Beth the office manager walked in the room. In contrast, her blond hair was tied back into a messy knot.

"I'm Detective Pagonis." He pulled his badge from his waistband. "I need to talk to Doctor Guzman." He slid his badge back into place.

Kennedy smiled at Beth. Beth didn't smile back.

"I'll go get him." Destiny disappeared down the back hall. She must be the personality of the office. Beth was there for dramatic effect.

Doctor Guzman strolled into the room. His face brightened when he saw Kennedy. "Hi, Kennedy, what are you doing here?" He glanced at the detective and his face changed when he noticed the shiny bling on his hip.

"I'm Detective Pagonis. I have a few questions."

"Sure." Guzman nodded to Beth. "I'll be in my office if anyone needs me." She nodded back.

Kennedy and Pagonis followed Guzman down the hall, past closed doors. Once inside his office, Guzman sat in the chair behind the desk.

"I want to talk to you about Tad Markham's test results," Pagonis said.

"I would need a warrant." The doctor leaned back. "HIPAA."

Pagonis pulled out his cellphone and swiped at the screen. He turned away from the two of them and walked into the hall, phone to his ear. "Latasha, I need to get a warrant…"

Guzman smiled at Kennedy. "So you two—"

"There's no 'you two'. We're two separate cops working a case. I'm trying to make sure this doesn't get pinned on Darcy."

Louis smiled as he stared at her, like he was reading her face—or her soul, as it were. "I can see that. You love her."

"She's my family. I can see you love her too."

"I do. Very much." He took a drink from a water bottle on his desk. "Then there's nothing between you and him?"

Kennedy laughed. "Detective Dour?"

Louis joined in. "Yeah, he doesn't seem to like anyone—but you."

"I think he's counting the moments till I go away." Kennedy needed to ask the next question, but she didn't want to piss the guy off. He seemed to be on her side, and she wanted to keep it that way. But she needed to know. "Did you know about Markham's test results before last week?"

He just looked at her, accusation in his eyes.

Kennedy shrugged one shoulder. "I needed to ask."

He shook his head, no animosity in his face. "I know. But I didn't know about it. I don't know why Chuck hid it from me."

"What about the medication that Tad received? There's conflicting information." Miranda thought Doctor Guzman prescribed it. Doctor Guzman thought he didn't. All Kennedy knew was that someone did.

"I talked to the pharmacist," Guzman said. "He never gave him the meds. So we have a call out to the doctor's office that gave him the MRI. Doctor Payton." Guzman seemed just as confused by all of this as Kennedy.

"Why was Tad sent to a different doctor? Don't you handle all the players here?" And from what Miranda was saying, he handled them like a helicopter parent.

Pagonis walked in the door, sliding his phone into his pocket. "I have a warrant en route."

"Perfect. Thank you. I'm sure you understand." Doctor Guzman smiled. "And as for Doctor Payton, I'm not sure why Chuck sent Tad to see him. I've been trying to figure it out. I don't know why there's all of this hiding."

"What was Chuck hiding?"

"The knee diagnosis. If Tad knew about this last week, he had to get it from someone. It wasn't me."

Pagonis leaned against the far wall. "Who would have given him the report?"

"All of our MRIs are handled through Henderson Imaging." Louis shook his head. "But the report was signed by a Doctor Payton. Normally the results are sent to my office first, not directly to the player."

"What about Markham's medications?"

"I will need that warrant to discuss that type of information." Guzman did look contrite, but he was right.

Pagonis pulled out his phone. "I have it here. Can I email it to you?" How he got that warrant so fast, Kennedy had no idea. In Chicago that would have taken a hell of a lot longer.

Guzman gave him his email address and they both tapped and swiped on their phones. Finally, Guzman opened a bottom drawer and pulled out a folder. "Here's the file."

Pagonis grabbed the folder and began sifting through it. He flipped over a page. Kennedy looked over his shoulder —nonchalantly.

LEFT KNEE AP, LATERAL, OBLIQUE VIEWS
　　CLINICAL INDICATION: Acute left knee pain
　　COMPARISON: None
　　FINDINGS: Small osteophytes about the knee and patellofemoral joints. Definite acute fracture. Trace suprapatellar joint effusion. Definite acute bony abnormality identified.

Most of the words went over Kennedy's head. First off, osteophytes sounded like something you'd find in a limestone cave. Suprapatellar sounded like something you found on the spaceship.

The detective turned the page. More gibberish. "So you prescribed a pain medication?"

"I offered, because he was in so much pain, after we were told there was a wait for the results. He declined."

"Is that normal? Don't you normally get test results right away?" Kennedy wasn't sure that was true, but this was a big-money franchise that relied on the bodies of their players. Test results seemed to be really important.

"Yes and no. They always tell us there's a backlog and then we get it in a day or two. When you're dealing with million-dollar bodies, backlog has a different definition."

"But his results took longer than a week." Kennedy

probably wasn't supposed to add her two cents, but she couldn't help it.

Louis didn't seem to care that she was asking the questions. "That's unusual, but it's happened. Last year we waited two weeks for a pathology lab."

"Didn't you follow up?"

"Destiny called a few days after the test, and they said it was lost."

"You didn't question that?" Pagonis seemed to be less accepting of what Guzman was saying.

"I did. We scheduled a retest, but then the results appeared."

Pagonis closed the file and dropped it to the desk. "Can I get a copy of this?"

Guzman pressed a button on the desk phone. "Beth, can you come back here?"

"What's going on?" Instead of Beth, Darcy strolled into the office.

"I'm talking to the police about Tad Markham." Louis stood and gave Darcy a kiss on the cheek.

"Why are we talking to them at all?" Darcy's smile seemed painted on.

Louis rubbed her arm and said in a soothing voice, "We have nothing to hide."

"Someone was sitting on the results after Chuck and Markham found out." Pagonis said.

Darcy started to say something, but Guzman interrupted. "We've sat on results, as you say, in the past. Markham would have wanted them kept quiet so he could negotiate."

"Since he was negotiating with Chuck, there wasn't much point." Pagonis wasn't wrong.

Kennedy could see how Tad wouldn't want the results out there, but Chuck... "If another team *was* trying to court him, Tad would want the results kept quiet but Chuck would want them made public. He'd get to renew Tad's contract for a song."

Guzman shook his head. "Putting that out there might help with contract negotiations, but the team would lose ticket sales. People like loyalty. And they want to see their own superstars play. When a team announces their star player won't be on the field for six months, ticket sales plummet."

Kennedy frowned. "Would he really have been out for six months?"

"He needs to have surgery. At least that's my recommendation." Guzman leaned back. "Chuck was trying to convince Tad to pursue rehab instead of the surgery."

"Can you blame him?" Darcy must have picked up on the accusation in Guzman's tone, because she jumped on the end of that sentence. "We can't survive six months without Markham."

Kennedy kind of hated herself for siding with Miranda on this. But the surgery was the right thing to do. "Six months is a small price to pay to ensure Tad has a future. Chuck was pushing him into sacrificing everything for one season."

"He wasn't pushing—but so what if he was?" Darcy crossed her arms. "We're talking hundreds of employees who rely on our revenue."

Pagonis stepped into the brewing argument. "Okay, so neither one would benefit from this information getting out, but who would?"

Darcy sighed. "Whoever sold the information."

"Sold?" Guzman seemed genuinely confused.

"Do you know Barrett Fischer Coleman?" Pagonis asked.

"No." Darcy shook her head.

The doctor shook his head, as well. "I haven't heard that name."

"Doctor Guzman?" Destiny said from the doorway. "Beth left for her other job."

"I forgot." Louis held out the folder. "Can you make a copy?"

"Are we done?" Darcy waited till Destiny left to ask the question. Her patience seemed to be wearing thin.

"A few more questions while I have you here. Do you know who your husband was dating?" Pagonis asked, like he was asking her favorite color.

"I have no idea. We didn't double date or gossip at the water cooler." Darcy slid her cell phone from her pocket, looking unfazed.

But Kennedy knew Darcy, and her eyebrow twitch said she was all kinds of fazed.

Pagonis continued. "Didn't you both sleep in separate parts of the house with your partners? You didn't bump into her in the kitchen before work? Or see her swimming in the pool one day?"

Only four people knew that information. Three of them were in this room. And since Kennedy was standing next to the detective… shit.

"I don't know where you got your information." Given the glare aimed at Kennedy, that was a lie. "My husband and I dated outside the marriage, but we didn't flaunt it. We were a team." Darcy's eyebrow twitched even more.

Shit. The twitching eyebrow.

Pagonis cocked his head. "But wasn't he leaving you?"

Darcy's face burned bright red as fury flared her nostrils. She was inches from catching a case for beating up a cop. Guzman reached for her hand, but she pulled away.

"Mrs. Perrault, can I help you?" Saved by the security guard.

"Yes, Bobby. Can you please escort these two out of the building." Darcy looked at Pagonis. "We are done here, right?"

"Yes." Pagonis nodded.

Bobby held up his arm and waited for Pagonis to exit the room before turning around.

"Wait. Her too." Darcy pointed at Kennedy.

Fear rooted her in place. Anything. But there weren't words. Darcy was kicking her out of the building.

"Ms. Romero?" Bobby's face didn't give away any emotion as he motioned her toward the door.

Darcy emotions were a little easier to read. She still had that fire in her eyes and anger in her clenched fists. Guzman had the good sense to look down as his girlfriend's best friend was given the perp walk.

Kennedy was thanking God she wasn't a crier. Although now would be a great time to start. She looked over at Pagonis. Not helping. The pity on his face was almost too much. She stopped looking at people and focused on the floor.

Step. Step. Toward the door.

Kennedy followed Pagonis toward the front office. Destiny met them, offering Pagonis the copied file. "Is that everything you need?"

Pagonis nodded.

"Great." Destiny turned to the waiting room. "Dembele, you can come back to the room."

Kennedy led the way out of the office. "There is so much mystery around this one little report."

"We need to talk to the doctor behind it." Pagonis pointed to the doctor's name on the report, complete with address.

"Doctor Payton." They reached the elevators and headed up to the main floor. Once her armed escort made sure she was outside Bobby disappeared inside, leaving Kennedy and Pagonis in the bright Las Vegas sun.

"That could've gone better." He was stating the obvious now. Fun.

"You could've let up on her."

"You know I couldn't have. I needed to push."

Pushing was sometimes needed, but this was Darcy. Kennedy's family. Kennedy's current landlord. And… shit. "I have Darcy's car."

"Is that bad?"

Kennedy waved at the stadium. "She just kicked me out of her building. I'm pretty sure I'm kicked out of her house. Can I use the car?"

Pagonis shrugged and made a face. "Probably to get to her house."

"Where I need to vacate the property immediately. I'm sure."

"Do you have somewhere to go?"

"Not really."

"I'd offer my place, but I have a studio with one bed in Henderson. Interested in sharing?"

"I'm good." She'd figure it out, but sleeping with the detective assigned to this case was not the way to go. The good news was she was in Vegas—home of hundreds of hotels. The question was, how long could she afford to stay at one that didn't scare her?

"Do you want to head back, or put off your housing situation for a bit? I'm going to talk to the doctor." He pulled out his keys.

"That sounds good." She had no desire to deal with the fallout from that spectacle. She'd been told over and over she couldn't leave town, but now she might not have a place to stay.

Which sounded like a problem for later.

CHAPTER 31

Almost an hour later, Pagonis pulled into the parking lot of a small two-story medical building on the south side of Las Vegas. It had started to rain while they were driving. A small microburst of downpour, followed by sunshine. Kennedy and Pagonis walked through puddles up to the white-trimmed light blue building and entered a small vestibule. On the wall by the elevator, a sign indicated that South Vegas Radiology—and Doctor Payton—were in room 201.

They took the elevator to the second floor. The door to room 201 was open, so they walked right in. A few patients, or maybe the drivers of patients, sat in the room reading magazines or looking at their phones.

A man sat behind the front desk and poked at the keyboard in front of him. He didn't look up. He didn't seem to notice that Kennedy and Pagonis were standing there at all.

"Excuse me?" Kennedy said. Keyboard guy held up an index finger in a wait-a-minute gesture without looking up at all. He took his pointer finger back and poked at the keyboard again. A pause. Another finger poke. Another pause. Another finger poke.

Finally, he looked up and smiled at them both. "Good afternoon, do you have an appointment?"

"I do not." Detective Pagonis flashed his shield. "I need to speak with Doctor Payton."

Pointer finger didn't seem impressed. "The doctor has a full schedule today."

"I'm sure he can make time to see me."

"*She* could, but she's fully booked for the rest of the day."

"Please ask her if she'd like to talk to me now, or if I should schedule something at the precinct."

Pointer's lip curled in a half smile, half sneer. He got up from behind the desk and disappeared through a door. A moment later he came out and smiled. "Please follow me."

They did. Through the door and past a few darkened rooms with large equipment. Kennedy trailed behind the men. One door stood ajar, and a pregnant woman with her blond hair in a ponytail sat inside. She appeared to be crying. Something about her seemed familiar, but her face was obscured by the tissue blotting at her face. The room must be used for consults or something because other than two chairs, a small sink in the corner surrounded by a tissue box and soap dispenser, the room was empty.

It was Beth the office manager.

Kennedy leaned in the doorway. "Are you okay?"

She struggled out of the chair. "Kennedy. What are you doing here?"

"We're here to see Doctor Payton."

"What are you doing here?"

"This is my other job." Beth wiped her eyes with the back of her hand.

"Excuse me." Pointer finger stood next to Kennedy in

the open door. He wasn't pointing, but his tone said he wanted to be. "The detective is in the doctor's office. I'll show you where to go."

Kennedy was pretty sure she knew where he wanted her to go. And she was also sure she didn't give a damn. "I'm talking to my friend Beth."

He glanced at Beth. "She's had a hard enough week, losing her fiancé. Can't you give her a break? She's pregnant."

The pregnant Kennedy knew about. But what were the odds it was a coincidence her boss and fiancé died in the same week? Kennedy saw Beth's face when realization hit. Kennedy knew. Beth knew Kennedy knew.

Kennedy took a breath. "I'd like to talk to her for a minute."

Pointer looked at Beth, who said, "I'm fine."

Pointer nodded and disappeared down the hall just as Pagonis walked up behind Kennedy. "Did you get lost?" He looked past her and his eyes narrowed. "Ms. Haas, right?"

Beth nodded, and sat back down in the chair.

"We came here to talk to Doctor Payton, to uncover how Chuck could've found out about Tad's knee before everyone else. Could you know something about that?" He stepped inside the small office.

Beth wiped her eyes. "I gave the reports to Chuck."

"And Doctor Payton allowed that?"

"She didn't know. I told her they were lost."

"Why did you give him the results?"

"He told me how having Tad out for six months would destroy the club." Beth mangled the tissue with both hands. "He needed to know if Tad's knee needed surgery so he could talk him out of it. They need every seat filled or they won't meet the balloon payment."

"The balloon payment?"

"He said he borrowed against the house, and he owed the bank a lot of money. If people don't buy tickets, he'd lose everything." She hiccupped. "We'd lose everything."

Kennedy grabbed another tissue and handed it to Beth. "How far along are you?"

"Eight months," Beth whispered between gasps.

"That's rough." Pagonis knelt down in front of Beth. He must have caught on to the *we'd lose everything* and the pieces fell into place for him. "When my first ex-wife was pregnant, that last two months were the hardest. I was out every night picking up peanut butter cups. She craved them constantly. Do you have cravings?"

She smiled as she dabbed her eyes with her left hand. "Pickles. I can't get enough of pickles."

"Sodium deficiency. Totally normal to crave pickles to get that extra sodium." He seemed to know a lot about cravings and deficiencies. Made Kennedy wonder how many ex-wife baby mommas were out there.

"Does your boyfriend run out and grab pickles?" Clearly, he needed her to say that Chuck was the father.

"No." Beth didn't look at him.

"Is the father in the picture?"

"Not really." Beth picked apart the tissue in her hand.

Pagonis looked at Kennedy, like she might know what the answer to the next question might be. She knew. It had to be.

"Who's the father?" Kennedy asked.

All the color drained from Beth's already pale face. "I have to get back to work." And she stumbled out of the room, nearly knocking Pagonis down as she disappeared into the hallway.

Kennedy sighed. "We sure know how to empty a room."

"Without getting an answer to our questions." He stood to his full height and nodded toward the door. "We're going to have to go back in."

She was afraid he was going to say that.

CHAPTER 32

Kennedy led Pagonis into the back offices. She didn't want go, but she was an adult. And a cop. And she didn't back away from a challenge.

They needed to know who the father of Beth's baby was. All signs pointed to Chuck. She was his type. Cute and blond.

They walked past empty room after empty room. They walked up to Doctor Payton's office. Beth stood in the doorway talking to the doctor.

"Excuse me." The detective whipped out his badge, probably for the doctor's benefit. "I'm Detective Pagonis. Beth Haas, I'm sorry to interrupt, but I need to speak with you again."

The doctor came around her desk and held out her hand. "May I help you, Detective?"

He shook her hand. "Yes. I'm here to discuss Tad Markham's MRI."

"I'm sorry. I can't discuss a patient's information without a warrant."

"I don't need to discuss Tad. I have the report." The

detective produced the paperwork from his pocket and handed it to her. "Was this provided by your office?"

The doctor nodded.

"When was this sent to Chuck Perrault at the Vegas Victory Football Club?"

"We don't normally send anything to the owners. The test results go to the physician's office. That day, there was a glitch in the computer system and we almost lost a day's worth of files. Thankfully, Beth was able to work with IT to fix it."

"Doctor, your patient is in room three." A woman wearing nurse scrubs came up to the door.

"Thank you. I'll be right there." The doctor turned from the nurse to Pagonis. "Do you need anything else?"

"Before we go, we just need to talk to Ms. Haas for a minute."

"Beth, are you okay to talk?" The doctor didn't make a move to leave. Everyone was so protective of her.

Beth nodded. "I'm fine." She slowly sat down on one of the chairs in front of the desk. "I owe you an apology. I shouldn't have run away, at least without answering your question."

"What is the answer?" Pagonis pulled out a notepad and pen.

"This is really hard. I don't want to lose my job. Either one of my jobs. I need them both." Beth nodded to the bun in her oven.

"Your job is safe." As Kennedy said the words, she hoped Darcy would stand behind them.

"Chuck Perrault is the father of my baby." Tears streamed down Beth's face. "I'm sorry. I'm so sorry. I didn't mean to hurt Darcy."

"Darcy will be fine. They were both seeing other people. It's okay"

"It's not okay. My parents raised me better. He was married, and I knew it was wrong."

Kennedy handed her a tissue. "I know this is hard, but can we ask a few more questions?"

Beth nodded.

Pagonis sat down across from her. "After you gave Chuck Tad Markham's test results, why did you hide them from the physicians?" His voice was calm, soothing. Kennedy was impressed.

"Chuck said he needed time to talk Tad into signing his contract. He needed the test results to encourage Tad to stay with the team and to keep him from having surgery."

"You mean the surgery that could save his career?"

Beth looked around the room, guilt in every movement. The woman should never play poker. "Yeah."

"Once you gave the report to Chuck, what did you do with it?"

"I sent a copy to Chuck and then I moved the all the files from the day to another place on the drive. That way, it looked like the folder got corrupted."

It was a pretty ingenious plan. Give her fiancé the information and make it unavailable until they were ready.

Pagonis looked up from his pad. "Was that before or after you gave a copy to Barrett Fischer Coleman?"

"Who?"

"How much did he give you for the report?" His tone didn't change, but there was an accusation to the words.

"How much what?" Either Beth was a great actress, or she had no clue what they were talking about.

"Someone sold Tad Markham's test results to a gambling magnate."

Beth frowned. "Why would I do that?"

"For money. To hurt Chuck." Pagonis didn't shrug, but it looked like he wanted to.

"Why would I want to hurt Chuck? He was going to marry me."

"Was he?" Pagonis studied his pen. The skepticism was clear. But whether it was for show, to get her off her game, or truly not believing her, Kennedy couldn't tell. Given how transparent Beth was, the need for games wasn't there.

"Of course, he was going to marry me." Beth's tears dried as anger took hold.

"Were you living together?"

"We were waiting for his wife to move out of the house and then I was going to move in." The realization of what she just said—or more importantly who she just said it in front of—must have taken hold because she stopped and stared at Kennedy. "I'm sorry. I didn't—"

"It's okay," Kennedy said, "but Darcy was never going to move out of that house."

"It's Chuck's house—"

"It was in both of their names."

"Oh." Beth's expression morphed from being contrite to baffled.

"I think we have everything we need." Pagonis stood.

Kennedy offered a soothing smile. Something to help Beth calm down and not think about the lies Chuck told her. After all, if he lied about that, what else was he lying about?

Beth nodded. "Do you need me to show you out?"

"No, we're good." Pagonis followed Beth out of the office, and she disappeared down the hall. "Why didn't Darcy move out of the house?" he asked Kennedy when they reached the elevators.

"It's her house too. Her name is on the deed. Everything they owned, they owned together."

Pagonis hit the button for the elevator. "Then why would Chuck have told Beth that Darcy was going to move out?"

The elevator door opened, and Kennedy practically jumped inside. Anything to finish this interrogation. "I don't know, but I would love to ask him." Although that wasn't going to happen without a séance.

"It must have been frustrating to have her husband giving her house away to his pregnant girlfriend." Although if Pagonis kept asking these types of questions, Kennedy was going to make sure he could ask Darcy's husband himself. He was trying to push it back on Darcy. Again.

"I wouldn't know. I have no idea what was going on in her head."

"But it is his child."

"And Darcy gave birth to two of his children. Those children don't just disappear because he knocks up someone else." Kennedy sighed. They weren't getting anywhere. Except out of the elevator. Finally.

Pagonis paused in the lobby. "The one thing I can't figure out— did Darcy leak Tad Markham's medical data? She wouldn't have anything to gain."

How optimistic of him. He only had one thing he couldn't figure out. Kennedy could make a list. "Exactly. She would lose everything. Beth mentioned a balloon payment that was coming due. They needed butts in seats. They didn't need rumors messing with attendance. So the question is who would benefit?"

"I don't know, but I think we need to figure it out." Pagonis held open the door as they walked out of the building, thus ending the inquisition for the day.

CHAPTER 33

Two hours later, Kennedy drove around the city of Las Vegas. Yeah, she was procrastinating. But the reality of the whole situation hit her after the detective dropped her back at the parking lot of the arena. Once she got to Darcy's and packed up her stuff, she'd probably never see her best friend again. Over twenty years of friendship just gone.

It felt so final. And her chest literally ached to think about it.

Over the years, Darcy had always been there for her. And Kennedy had been there for Darcy. To think that they'd never be there again… She just couldn't think about it anymore.

Kennedy drove the darkening streets and turned, pulling into the driveway. She parked the car and walked into the house. She waited. No one ran at the door, yelling. No one told her to get out. Nothing.

Selma walked into the living room carrying a broom. "Hello, Kennedy. Are you waiting for something? Do you need my help?"

"No. Thank you."

Selma swept the floor, swiping under the furniture. "Dinner's at six thirty."

Kennedy nodded. Not that Selma could see her. She wouldn't be around for dinner, anyway. Slipping off to her room, she stared at the clothes scattered everywhere.

She wasn't normally this messy, but her bathing suit was nowhere to be found the other morning. It was a nice a room. She'd enjoyed spending time here.

A tap came from the door as Kennedy pulled her suitcase from the closet. It could be Darcy, but that knock was way too timid. Given how Darcy was at the arena, the door would probably bust off its hinges with her knock. "Come in."

The door crept open, and Fanny peeked through the opening. "Are you decent?"

"Yep."

"Are you packing?"

"I'm just getting my stuff together." Kennedy hadn't thought about what she'd tell the kids. It was going to be hard enough losing Darcy. But losing these kids was going to be another level of hell. She'd been there raising them for so many years.

"I heard you talked to Beth today," Fanny said.

"I did." Kennedy stopped packing. This felt like a conversation that needed her full attention. It wasn't every day you found out you had a half sibling on the way. "What else did you hear?"

"I'm going to have a baby sister."

It's a girl. *Mazel tov.* "Is that a good thing or a bad thing?"

"I always wanted a sister." Fanny laughed. "Maybe not this way. Although it's typical. My parents are screwed." Fanny dropped onto Kennedy's bed. "Were screwed. Are. I don't even know what verb tense to use."

"Your parents are human. They were trying to make a

good situation out of a bad one." Kennedy believed that wholeheartedly. They'd spent so much time trying to make good out of bad. Just like Kennedy had tried to do with all the AA meetings. It was the reason the prisons were packed. It was the human condition. People paid for months or years because of one moment, one mistake.

"Infidelity always fixes a bad situation."

Touché. "They're human. We all do dumb things in the name of love." And heartbreak. *And other emotions we're too overwhelmed by to name.* "So you talked to your mom today?"

"Yep." Fanny sighed. "But we knew about Beth for a couple weeks."

"Really? Your mom knew about her?"

"Yeah."

"Was she mad?" Why the hell had she lied to Kennedy?

"Not mad. She was worried."

"Worried?"

"Worried we'd get forgotten. He kept talking about redoing his will to include the new baby, and he kept threatening to exclude us."

"But she's not even born yet." Kennedy couldn't understand why he'd redo a will for a child when they hadn't even validated paternity. Although maybe he wasn't as paranoid about that these days.

"He was just trying to piss Mom off."

"Was it working?"

"Always." Fanny laughed. "You know Mom."

"Did your brother know?"

"No. He's too busy with school."

"You know this gives you motive." That's probably why Darcy didn't tell Kennedy about it. She knew this wouldn't make any of them look good. And she'd do anything to protect her family.

"If I wanted my dad dead, I had so many other reasons. The list was long."

"You probably shouldn't say that out loud."

Fanny laughed, a hollow chortle. "Probably not. Considering. But I didn't want my dad's money. I have my own job."

"You're working for your dad over the summers."

"For now. But it's just to help my mom out and get some experience. I'll take that and my degree and I'll go run another team."

"Another team?" Kennedy believed what she was saying. Fanny had always been independent. She wasn't going to sit around and wait for her father's handouts. But run a team that wasn't her family's?

Fanny leaned in. "Don't tell my mom, but I want to be the GM of the LA Galaxy."

"LA? Why would you want to move to LA? Aim higher, Fantasia. The Chicago Fire would love to have a female GM, and then you could come stay with me. And we'd eat deep dish pizza and Portillo's every day."

"Every day?

"Okay, every day is a bit much. We wouldn't be able to walk around the block if we ate like that every day. How about once a week?" Kennedy had a feeling that deep dish and Portillo's wasn't luring Fanny to face Chicago winters, but she did want Fanny to come and visit her. But with everything that happened with Darcy—would Fanny ever want to see her again?

"I could do once a week." Fanny laughed. "As long as I can afford a personal trainer."

The two smiled at each other. This was the type of comfortable silence that Kennedy craved when she was back home in Chicago. Looking into Fanny's eyes, she could feel all the love and warmth emanating all the way to her toes. Kennedy wasn't sure if she should tell Fanny about the rest of today. It wasn't really her place. Fanny wasn't her daughter. It was Darcy's job to control the narrative for her own children.

And Kennedy felt so, so powerless.

"I know you two fought." Fanny's words didn't make Kennedy feel any more powerful.

"Ah." Darcy did tell her, then.

"She'll get over it."

"I'm not so sure this time."

"You're family. She has to." Fanny smiled. Her confidence was so sweet. Misguided, but sweet. "That's why you're packing."

"It's time for me to go." Home was the word that should've come next, but she couldn't leave. Not just because Pagonis told her not to, since he'd probably let her go now that she wasn't the main suspect. But Kennedy couldn't leave Darcy like this—not with a murder charge hanging over her head. Darcy might not want her help, but she was getting it.

"No matter what happened, you're still my Aunt Kennedy."

"You're still my Fantasia." Kennedy wrapped her arms around Fanny. She didn't want to let go. "I'm going to miss you."

"I'll miss you too." Fanny stuttered the words into Kennedy's shoulder.

"Dinner!" Selma's voice carried to Kennedy's room.

"We should go downstairs."

"Face the music." Deep inside her chest, a dirge played.

Face something, anyway. Kennedy didn't think it would be music. Either way, she'd worn out her welcome.

CHAPTER 34

ennedy's guess was right. Her welcome was a dilapidated jalopy rusting in the front yard. Darcy wasn't talking, just poking at her food like it stole her hubcaps. Charlie silently read a book as he ate his dinner. Guzman and Fanny kept sharing glances. Almost like they were trying to figure out how to escape.

As it was, Kennedy sat at the kitchen table and kept glancing at the front door. It was hard to breathe when Darcy couldn't even look at her.

The only source of normal was Selma. Thank goodness she still sat every night at family dinners or Kennedy would absolutely lose her mind. The woman seemed oblivious to the smog of anxiety filling the air. "So, what do you two lovebirds have planned for this weekend?" Or maybe she just didn't care.

Darcy didn't even answer. Selma sat with her spoon poised over the best damn gumbo in the city of Vegas and stared at Darcy, waiting for some sort of reply.

Louis set his spoon down and rested his hand on Darcy's. "We have a bye week, so we were going to take in a show."

"What about you, Kennedy?"

Kennedy shrugged.

Fanny leaned over toward Kennedy. "You should come with us. The new Cirque du Soleil is supposed to be amazing." God bless Fanny for trying to keep her included.

"I'm not sure." *that I'll even be in the state.*

Darcy snorted. "She's probably too busy with her boyfriend."

"I don't have a boyfriend." Kennedy had a chance to sleep in his bed and she turned him down. How much more not-boyfriend could there be?

"Are you sure?" Darcy's eyebrow arched. "You were basically eye-humping him at the field today."

"Mom!" Fanny said, outraged as only a teenage girl could be, at the same time Kennedy said, "Darcy!"

"What?" Darcy slammed her spoon onto the table. "She practically stuck her tongue down his throat."

"When? At what point was I even standing close enough to stick my anything near his anything? My tongue —" Kennedy briefly stuck out the appendage in question "—never left my mouth."

Darcy rolled her eyes. "I said practically."

"Well, good thing you cleared that up. Otherwise that would be ridiculous." Kennedy rolled her eyes. Yes. She had eyes that rolled too.

"Are you calling me ridiculous?"

Kennedy stood up. If they were going to fight, she wanted to be ready. It was a cop thing. "If the clown shoes fit."

"If I need my clown shoes." Darcy stood and leaned over the table. "Don't forget your hooker heels."

"I have somewhere you can stick my hooker heels." Kennedy started around the table. "I'd be happy to help, so you get the heel just right."

"Ladies." Louis stood between the two women like a dazed referee.

Kennedy slammed her fists onto her hips. "Do you want me to leave?"

"Yes."

"Mom!" Fanny's yell of protest cleared the haze of anger. No one spoke.

With each second of silence, Kennedy's lungs remembered how to work.

Darcy sighed. "Of course I don't want you to leave." She sat back down in her chair and picked up her spoon. Took a deep breath. "So, Fanny, how was your meeting with accounting today?"

"It was long and boring."

The small talk took over and Kennedy let the words flow, even though the air in the room still hung heavy. There was so much more brewing just beneath the surface.

Ding. Ding. Dong.

"I'll get the door." Selma bounced out of her chair. She practically ran toward the door. Even Selma was ready to run away from this crazy train. "Thank you so much."

Selma came back to the table carrying a box. It was smaller than a microwave, but larger than a cigar box. "It's for you, Darcy."

"Who's it from?"

Selma checked the label. "Major League Soccer."

She handed the box to Darcy, who shook it. There was no sound. "What is it?"

Something felt off. Weird package. Delivered at night. Kennedy lunged forward. "Maybe we should wait."

Darcy ripped the tape and opened the flaps. There was a loud pop, accompanied by Darcy screaming.

Kennedy ducked as white powder coated them all. "What the hell?"

"It's in my mouth." Fanny cried.

Louis checked the inside of the box and pulled out an envelope. The front had Darcy's name in cut-out letters. He opened the envelope and took out a card with additional pasted-on letters. "This is how easy it is to get to you and your family," he read.

"What the…." Darcy snatched the card away from him. "This message was for me. Someone wants to kill me."

"Maybe it was an accident." Selma seemed to be the only one not coated in white.

Kennedy snatched the card away from Darcy. "Shit." The card actually said *ThIS is HOw EAsY iT IS 2 GET tO You & yoUr FamILy*. Same difference.

There was a lot of screaming back and forth, until Louis yelled, "Please, everyone calm down. It should be okay. It's white. It smells like powdered sugar, but we can't take chances. I need you all to go take a shower, now." He grabbed a stack of kitchen towels and slowly draped them over the powder on the floor.

Darcy, who had gotten the worst of it, nodded. "Selma, even though it doesn't look like you were hit, please use the second-floor guest room. Everyone else use your own showers."

"Go now. I need to call the police." Louis held his cell phone to his ear. "Hello. An unknown substance was just delivered to our address. We need help."

The 911 operator on the line must have said something because he just nodded. "There are five of us."

Kennedy didn't hear any more of the phone call as she ran for her bedroom, stripped, and jumped under the ice-cold shower spray. Her skin pebbled as she ran a loofah up and down every part of her body. Twice. And then one more time.

She rubbed her face over and over—using soap. Then shampoo. Then conditioner, just to be safe. The water morphed from frigid to warm and back to frigid during her twenty-minute scrub.

When she was done, her skin was prunier than a California Raisin. And her clothes still weren't packed. Part of her wanted to pack and run far away. The other part knew she couldn't leave Darcy and the kids alone with everything going on. She never would. But this had changed things. Someone was aiming at her family, and they didn't know who. And they didn't know why.

But one thing was clear. Kennedy couldn't leave until Darcy's family— her family— was safe.

CHAPTER 35

few hours later, the police had bagged up and taken all of the contaminated clothing. They'd taken samples from the scene, and another crew was cleaning up the area. The police had come by, including Detective Pagonis.

Somehow, Kennedy managed to keep her lips off him. She almost mentioned that to Darcy, but she didn't think her friend would appreciate her sarcasm after someone tried to scare her.

And yes, thankfully it was just a scare. Preliminary tests said the powder was confectioner's sugar, but with all the drama as of late Darcy was getting security for the house. She was also paying security to follow her children around for the foreseeable future.

Kennedy folded a stack of clothes and put it into her suitcase. Darcy hadn't said a word to her. Well, she'd asked if Kennedy was okay, but once it was determined she was fine, the ice wall went back up.

Hotels were ridiculously expensive—which didn't make sense. She thought Vegas was the land of cheap hotels surrounded by opulence. Apparently, cheap hotels weren't as prevalent. Or if they were cheap, they looked like the roaches were regulars.

Did they have roaches in the desert?

A knock came from her bedroom door. Probably Fanny wanting to try to talk her out of leaving. Again. It broke her heart to have to go, but Kennedy didn't see much of a choice. "Come in."

Blond hair peeked around the corner, but not Fanny's. Darcy. "Can I come in?"

"It's your house." Kennedy felt the ice in her tone, and she tried to dial it back. But this whole thing hurt so much. Darcy didn't trust her. After everything they'd been through.

Darcy surveyed the room as she sat on an open spot at the edge of the bed. "You're packed."

"I figured you wanted me gone."

"I don't want you gone. I just want all of this over." Darcy leaned forward and stared at the floor.

Kennedy dropped onto the bed next to her, exhausted. "That's what I want, you know."

"I know." Darcy kicked at the bed skirt, her thoughts apparently a million miles away. Kennedy knew enough to let her get her head together. "I'm scared. Someone tried to hurt you at the tram, and now they're threatening my home. The cops think I did something."

"I'm here to help with the cops and I can help protect you."

"I didn't hurt Chuck. I loved him."

"Even with a new baby and him trying to get you to leave?"

"Try? Please. I wasn't going anywhere, despite his delusions. He couldn't kick me out, just make my life miserable." She laughed, with all the humor sucked out. "But he'd been making me miserable for years. I was good at ignoring it."

"For years?"

"Do you know how many times I pissed him off and he'd retaliate. He sold my favorite car a few years ago. He auctioned off that painting my dad bought us for our wedding. He'd throw his mistresses in my face or how many children popped up claiming that he was their father. He would deny it, but admit he'd slept with their mother. Like that was supposed to make me feel better." Darcy tried to say the words like they didn't matter, but they mattered. Given the hitch in her throat, it mattered a lot.

Kennedy sat on the bed near Darcy. "How many of the children were his?"

"Who knows. He'd take a test, and then all the gold-diggers would disappear. He used to show me the negative paternity test, but I stopped caring." If Darcy was Pinocchio, her nose would have just poked Kennedy in the eye.

"That must have hurt."

Darcy leaned over and put her head on Kennedy's lap. She curled her knees into her chest. They sat like that for a moment—like they use to sit and watch *Friends* late at night after the babies were in bed. "I missed this."

"Yeah." Kennedy pushed a strand of hair behind Darcy's ear as Darcy's eyes closed.

"In some ways, playing 'my two moms' with you was the happiest time of my life," Darcy murmured.

"We remember things very different." Kennedy twirled golden hair around her finger. "Remember all those lonely nights? You missed Chuck so much back then."

"I did because I didn't know what he was doing. I thought he was telling the truth when he said he was faithful. I thought we were a team. But he didn't care about anyone but himself."

"You couldn't have known."

"No. But I could've been smarter. Stronger. I could've run away with you and the kids. We could've found some nice guys, who didn't play sports or cheat or drink. You never would've had your second DUI and I would've had a normal life, raising my kids with a backyard and a dog or something."

Kennedy would love to blame her choice of men on all her problems, but that wasn't entirely true. "Maybe. But I still would've made the bad choices that led me to drink and drive. That was my fault. And removing Chuck from your life might've made some things easier, but Fanny and Charles deserved to know their father."

"He hurt them."

"Hopefully they'll learn from that and not make the same choices he made." Kennedy wanted to believe that. She'd lived so many mistakes and hadn't learned from them. But one could only hope Fanny and Charles were smarter and stronger.

Darcy snorted. "Can you imagine Charles sleeping with a different woman in every city?"

Kennedy laughed. "He's way too sweet to be that callous. And that's because of you."

Darcy smiled and snuggled into Kennedy. "I think it's because he watched how his father treated me. It wasn't easy for him."

"It made him into who is today." Kennedy smiled. "And think of it this way, if you didn't stick it out with Chuck, you wouldn't have that awesome pool."

Darcy laughed. A real laugh that reverberated into Kennedy's lap. Kennedy couldn't help the smile that spread across her face.

"That pool is pretty amazing." Darcy twisted a thread on the leg of Kennedy's jeans. "Please don't leave. I need you here."

"I'm not with the detective."

"I know. He's just a dick."

"He is, but he's keeping me in the loop."

"He still thinks I'm a suspect." Darcy spun the string around her finger, and tugged.

"Probably, but I think you're slowly moving lower and lower on the list."

"Great. Now all I need is for someone in my family to get injured and I'll be taken off completely."

"I think it's fine." Kennedy gathered Darcy's hair into a ponytail and smoothed it down. "I'll keep working with him and we'll find out who did this."

"I'm going to have a security guard here twenty-four/seven. Bobby just got here, so don't be afraid if you see people walking the house perimeter."

"That's not a bad idea."

Darcy sat up and swiped at her eyes. "Are you going to stay?"

"Of course." Kennedy leaned in and hugged her close. "You're my family."

"You're my family too." Darcy held on tight for a good minute until she pulled back, wiping her eyes some more. "Speaking of family, I've tried to call Craig's therapist, Doctor Martin again, but he's not answering his phone or returning my calls."

"Do you want me to go talk to him?"

"Would you? I have to deal with lagging ticket sales and repurposing my security team to a home security system."

"Sure."

"And I promise not to get bitchy about you and the detective." Darcy didn't make the Girl Scout salute, but Kennedy knew she was telling the truth. "I think he likes you."

Kennedy leaned in and whispered. "Between you and me?"

"Yeah?" Darcy actually looked excited to be getting some deep dark secret.

Kennedy looked left, then right, to make sure no one was listening. "I don't think he likes anyone."

"I think you're right." Darcy shook her head, laughing, just as a knock came from the bedroom door. "Come on in," Darcy said.

Bobby poked his head into the room. "Can I check this room?"

"For what?"

"I'm verifying all doors are locked."

Darcy smiled. "We'll take care of this room. I'm sure Kennedy has that under control. Can you check the kids' rooms? I worry about all the sliding glass doors."

Bobby nodded and slipped back out, gently closing the door.

Kennedy tilted her head toward the door. "It's good having your security team here."

"Yeah, I need people here I can trust." Darcy nodded and stopped to yawn. "I should go to bed."

The smile in Kennedy's heart didn't show on her face, but there was a glimmer of happiness. Darcy still trusted her. Kennedy hadn't messed that up. "I should too."

After Darcy left, Kennedy pulled out her pajamas and put them on. As far as she could see, everything was back at square one. Craig had disappeared. They had no idea who was threatening Kennedy and Darcy's family. She was missing something. Like it was right in front of her, but she just couldn't put all the pieces together. She needed to change things up. No matter what.

This had gone on long enough.

CHAPTER 36

The next morning, the sun was obscured by clouds, and rain threatened. Despite the gloom, the bright yellow awning outside the psychiatrist's office still managed to be cheery against the tan stucco. Kennedy walked into a busy waiting room, with a counter facing the door.

The man standing behind the counter looked up. "Good morning. May I help you?"

"I need to talk to Doctor Martin." Hopefully there was only one doctor with that name because she didn't know their first name. Hell, she didn't know if they were a he or a she.

"Do you have an appointment?"

"No. I just have a few questions." She pulled out her badge. Quickly. Just enough time for the man to see it was a badge and not enough time for him to see which city the badge was from.

He narrowed his eyes. "What was that?"

In theory anyway. "My badge."

"That's not a Metro badge."

They weren't the same shape and of course he'd notice.

"I'm working with Vegas Metro. I'm a police officer from Chicago." This time, she pulled her badge out and let the guy stare at it.

"I can't let you see anyone without an appointment."

"Look, Craig Perrault is missing. I need to know when the doctor saw him last."

The man looked torn. He obviously wasn't allowed to let rando's inside the inner sanctum without an appointment, but a missing patient was an emergency in Kennedy's book. Hopefully, this guy was reading from the same page.

"One minute." He entered a code into a door at the back of the room. It opened with a click, and he walked through. A few minutes later he came back. "This way, please."

Kennedy followed him through the door and down a hallway. Another door. Another code. They walked past open and closed doors. The murmur of people talking wafted from behind the closed doors.

They stopped at an open door, where another man sat at a desk typing on a computer. "Thank you, David."

The man from the front desk smiled and left.

The doctor stood up. "I'm Doctor Martin. You're here about Craig Perrault. I understand you're a police officer. I'm sure you understand I can't discuss my patients."

"I do understand, and I don't want you to violate anybody's privacy, but he's missing. We went to his house and found a note he left. He wouldn't leave his sister-in-law and her kids without telling them. We need to ask him a few questions— and get him back on his meds."

The doctor sat, and indicated Kennedy should, too. "The medication he's on sometimes causes memory gaps."

That did not sound good. Kennedy decided she needed the chair. "Gaps?"

"Like a double life. One when he's on the meds, and

another when he's off. He doesn't always remember what happens in the different lives."

"Got it. Do you know where he is?"

"No." The doctor sighed. "Look, I can't say anything, but maybe you can tell me what you know, and I'll agree or disagree."

"Craig was hiding from a large alien. The alien is male. Maybe real." Kennedy was pretty sure that was true. "Well, the alien isn't real, but the person could be."

Doctor Martin coughed to cover a small laugh. "It's okay to be nervous. This is an interesting situation."

"Could someone have taken him?"

"Maybe, but it sounds like he left to keep someone safe."

"Who?"

"Who would he do anything for?"

"Chuck. Darcy and the kids." Kennedy knew the answer to that one. What she needed to know was where Craig was. Because while he was hiding, someone made a very real threat. "Do you have any ideas where he might go? We've been trying to figure out where he'd hide if he needed to get away."

"Think like him. Where would the aliens not have access to him?"

What stopped aliens? Tinfoil on the windows. Metal roofs. "He said that Chuck and Darcy's house was safe because Chuck put metal in the roof like at Binion's."

"You checked his sister-in-law's house."

Bobby had done a thorough sweep of the house and grounds. Well, except for Kennedy's room. She took great care to handle that herself. "Yeah, he's not there."

"What about Binion's?"

"I'll have to check there." Really, anywhere with an anti-alien metal roof would work.

"Sounds like a good place to start." And he was right. It was at least a *place* to start.

"Thank you."

The doctor nodded and escorted her back to the entrance. "Reach out if you need me when you find him."

"I will." Kennedy left the doctor's office, and twenty minutes later found herself parking in the red garage at the Fremont Experience. She left the garage and walked down Fremont Street, past the casinos and napping neon signs.

She passed two scantily clad women in bright pink flamingo costumes, with pink feathers on their heads. They sashayed along the sidewalk, handing out cards for special drinks at the Golden Nugget. Just beyond them were the open doors of Binion's Gambling Hall and Hotel, the newest version of what used to be the famous Binion's Horseshoe Club.

Machines dinged and binged as she wandered the casino floor. Nothing. She didn't even know what she was looking for. Craig wouldn't play a game. He'd be hiding in a hotel room with windows covered in tinfoil.

She walked into the attached hotel and smiled at the front desk clerk. If Craig used an alias, she'd never figure it out. "Hi. I need to reach a hotel guest."

"Do you have his name and room number?" The woman at the front desk asked her.

"Craig Perrault. He said he was on the second floor." Yeah, she was embellishing. She found that the more confident you were about your statements, the more people bought it—even if it was a load of crap.

The woman clicked at a keyboard. Her face screwed into a frown. "I'm sorry, I don't have anyone by that name on the second floor."

"He gets confused. Maybe he's on the third floor."

"I'm sorry, but who are you?"

Kennedy pulled out her badge and did the flashy thing.

"I'm working with Metro." She shoved it back in her pocket.

"Of course, Officer. Craig Parrot."

"Craig Perrault." Kennedy spelled the last name.

"I'm sorry. There's no one here with that name. Could he have checked in under another name?"

Kennedy had no idea. "I'm not sure."

"I'm sorry. I would need a name to look him up." And the clerk did look sorry. It's not like she could give Kennedy a list of all the guests and Kennedy could telepathically pick out which one it might be. Although that would be convenient.

"Thank you." Kennedy walked away from the front desk. She was somehow back at square one. Again.

Darn it. She was seriously starting to hate that square.

Making her way back through the casino, she watched the machines blink and pop. Her eyes burned from the cigarette smoke. She had to get out. It wasn't like Craig was here, anyway.

She angled through the people pulling levers and clinking glasses. Women dressed in tight black skirts and black and blue bustiers and carrying trays walked around providing drinks to the glass clinkers.

She hurried through the crowd, but stopped when she noticed a black hoodie in a far corner. She turned. No hoodie. Her suspicions dragged her to the far corner. She'd swear she saw a black sweatshirt. But if there was one, it wasn't there now.

What she did find was an old woman wearing a floral muumuu and New York Yankee cap, a guy spilling bourbon on his dirty white tank top, and a blond woman in a UNLV sweatshirt. No one wearing a hoodie.

Not one.

Shaking her head, she headed for the exit. The fresh air of the Vegas valley was so welcome. The sun still was hiding and so far, so was the rain. Passing the flamingo twins, she watched the nooks and corners for a hoodie.

Nothing.

Apparently, she was seeing things now— random black hoodies at every turn. Maybe that tram attack freaked her out more than she thought. Well, it must have been if she was seeing hooded figures in corners. She should probably grab a meeting to talk about it.

At the car, she pressed the key fob just as a blur rushed past her. She turned. Not surprising, there was nothing there. Shit. She might need more than a meeting to help with this.

She locked the car doors and walked toward where the blur had been. Her gym shoes scuffed along the pavement but otherwise there was only silence. She angled around a car. No sound. Not one.

She headed back to the driver's side of the Jaguar.

Wah. Wah. Wah.

She spun to face the loud noise and the flashing lights— and a person wearing a black hoodie. She swore it was the same one on the footage from the train platform. Not that it mattered. She was being stalked by someone. It didn't matter if it was the same hoodie or a new one.

The hoodie twisted around and ran. Kennedy took off after them. Car alarms howled as hoodie bumped into car after car. They flung open the metal stairway door and disappeared. Kennedy followed, her shoes slamming against the cement stairs as she barreled down.

Hoodie opened the main-floor door to the outside, and light poured in until the door banged shut. Kennedy hit the release bar, shoving the door wide. She turned left, then right, as the rain drizzled down.

Of course it was raining.

She spotted the hoodie as whoever it was ran down the street, past the neon cowboy, bumping into people like a drunk pinball. Kennedy stepped up her game, running faster. She was gaining on them.

She pushed harder when Hoodie shifted direction and turned toward something called Evil Pie. Kennedy didn't want to know what that was, but it sounded kinky. The pizza in the window told her a different story.

Hoodie tripped, falling to their knees.

Kennedy jumped on top of Hoodie. Definitely a guy. He squirmed and twisted, and Kennedy refused to let go even as he managed to scramble partway to his feet.

"No." She braced her feet and yanked. He was too heavy to keep upright. She had two choices: let go, or fall. Hoodie decided for both of them when he tripped on his own feet and fell.

She clawed at the hood until the black material gave way. Blond scraggly hair popped out.

As well as eyes she recognized.

"Craig?"

"Don't hit me." He covered his face with his arms and laid on the ground. Unmoving.

"I'm not going to hit you, but you have to stop running."

He nodded, so Kennedy angled back. She still kept her hands clenched on the neck of his sweatshirt. "Why are you following me?"

"You were coming to see me." He didn't ask the question. He stated it like a fact.

"I was looking for you."

"Why?"

Oh no. Kennedy was getting some answers first. "Why are you wearing a black hoodie? Did you push me onto the tram tracks?"

"I did." Craig's frown matched his hunched shoulders. "I thought you were Darcy. It wasn't my fault you were wearing her jacket."

Kennedy blinked. "Why…why would you hurt Darcy?"

"I didn't want to hurt her. I was saving her. They were going get her."

"Who?"

"The alien was coming after her. They had a gun." The terror behind his words was unmistakable. And weirdly believable.

Someone or something was after Darcy. And given the message she'd gotten at home, this was no longer the rambling of someone off their meds. There might not be an alien, but someone was after her family. And they'd tried to get her before.

Kennedy needed to get Craig to the police so they could figure out who, before the baddies got to Darcy.

CHAPTER 37

ennedy managed to get Craig to come with her. She wasn't sure how. But he followed her to the Jaguar. He didn't run. Then he managed to stay inside the car. He didn't jump out of the moving car. Honestly, she thought at one point, he might do that. But somehow he was still in the passenger seat when she got to the stadium, where Darcy and Louis were waiting at a side door when they pulled up.

Darcy ran to the car and whipped open the passenger door. As Craig slid out of the car, she wrapped him in her arms. "Oh my goodness, you're okay." She looked him up and down before resting a hand on his cheek. "Don't you ever do that again. I was scared to death."

"I'm sorry. The aliens…"

"I don't care about aliens or anyone else. I care about you."

"I know. I'm sorry." Craig rocked back and forth, like he was looking for something. Or someone. Or maybe he was just looking for an escape.

Darcy must have noticed. "Let's go inside. Kennedy, leave the car here. I'll have security move it."

Kennedy followed them into the stadium and up to the owner's office. Darcy and Craig sat on the couch while Louis and Kennedy stood off to the side. Darcy needed to get him on-board with talking with the cops.

"Are you okay?" Darcy laid a hand on Craig's knee.

He nodded, but the look in his eyes seemed like he didn't believe his own head.

"Why did you run away?"

"I had to keep the alien away, but it didn't work. Somehow he found you." Craig clutched his stomach as a large gurgle came from that general direction.

"Are you hungry?" Darcy had to know that answer. The man was hiding in the middle of Vegas for who knew how long. He probably needed a hamburger.

"A little, but I don't want to be a bother."

"It's no bother." Darcy smiled. "Louis, can you go see if you can rummage up a spare sandwich from the team locker room?"

Louis nodded and disappeared out the door.

"So when did the alien find me?" Darcy leaned back on the couch.

"On the train platform. I didn't mean to hurt Kennedy. She was wearing your jacket." He looked so contrite as he peered at Darcy through his lashes. "I'm so sorry. I would never hurt you." Craig's voice shook.

"I know, honey. I would never hurt you either. We're family. But why did you push Kennedy if you thought it was me?"

"The alien was following you. Or your jacket." Craig shook his head. "He had a laser gun and he was going to use it. I had to save you."

"He had a gun?"

"Yes. So I pushed you out of the way before he could use it."

"What does he look like?"

Craig's face turned the color of ash as his voice lowered. "Tall and angry." Craig shook when he said "angry". Kennedy wasn't sure how angry *looked*, but she also wasn't sure she wanted to push Craig right now.

Louis came back with a paper bag. He opened it and pulled out a wrapped sandwich, a bag of chips, an apple, and a can of soda. He put it on the coffee table in front of Craig, who attacked the food like it was the first thing he'd eaten in days. And it might have been.

"Do you think you could tell all of this again? I know this is hard, but we need to talk to the detectives." Darcy smiled. She was trying to put him at ease.

He was too busy eating to need any easement. "If you think it will be okay."

"I won't let anything happen to you." Darcy nodded to Louis. "I want you to meet the lawyer first. She's going to help us with the police."

"Okay." Craig hoovered down the bag of chips in between gulps of soda.

Darcy looked over at Kennedy. "I think that's the best way to go."

Kennedy and Craig had a stilted conversation about this on the drive over. Not that Kennedy went into specifics, not with Craig sitting next to her with his hand on the door handle. She was afraid any words would spook him at that point.

But they had to play this right. There was no way Craig hurt Chuck, and there was no way that he'd meant to hurt Kennedy. But once all of this was out in the open, the police could grab hold of it and run all the way to an easy arrest.

She wanted to think that Detective Pagonis wouldn't drive that bus over a man with obvious mental problems, but she couldn't be sure.

They were taking a chance introducing him to Craig before he took his meds. But once he was on his meds, from what the doctor said, he wouldn't remember anything. They needed the information, no matter how ridiculous it sounded. And they needed Pagonis to keep an open mind.

Otherwise they were risking the freedom and sanity of a man who needed psychiatric help. Not three to five years behind bars.

CHAPTER 38

Louis stepped out again and came back with the lawyer. Brown hair pulled back. Dark pant suit. She looked like she could kick some ass. And she looked about ready to do so.

She walked over to Craig and smiled. Some of the serious dripped away from her face. "Hi Craig, I'm Brenda Kramer." She held out her hand and waited for Craig to rub his hand on his pantleg before he shook. "I'm here to help you talk with the police. They have some questions. If the questions aren't a problem, I'll let you answer."

"Why would they be a problem?" Craig frowned, making him seem less fragile. That could be an issue if he snapped and took responsibility for things he didn't do or didn't understand.

"I just want to make sure all questions paint the family and you in the most positive light. You know how sometimes the police can misinterpret things that are said. It's my job to make sure that nothing gets confused." She was talking to Craig like he was a child, but Craig didn't seem to mind. "So you don't have to worry about anything. You just tell the truth. Tell them everything you know, and if I say that they need to stop asking a question, you can stop answering. You also don't have to answer any questions you don't want to, and I'll make sure they understand. We're a team. Okay?"

Craig nodded.

"Wonderful." Brenda looked over her shoulder. She nodded at Kennedy and Louis "Can you get the detective?"

Louis nodded and disappeared. The doctor was turning out to be quite the little retriever—food, lawyers, and cops. Kennedy should ask if he had any crab legs.

Darcy stood, picking up a cup of coffee from her desk. "I don't think I introduced you to my friend Kennedy. Kennedy, this is the team lawyer, Brenda."

One lawyer?

Kennedy walked over and shook her hand. "It's nice to meet you, but I figured there'd be a team of lawyers for the team."

"I'm general counsel. The captain of that team, as it were. We're keeping the numbers small today." Brenda nodded to Craig. "This isn't something that needs a lot of...drama."

In other words, they didn't want to overwhelm Craig. One lawyer instead of a gaggle of them. Given Craig's mental state, that wasn't a bad idea.

A minute later, the doctor led Detective Pagonis in the door. The detective nodded to everyone in the room and sat in the chair diagonal from the couch. "Craig Perrault. We've been looking for you."

Craig opened his mouth, but the lawyer rested her hand on his. "That's not a question."

Pagonis scowled at her. "And you are?"

"Brenda Kramer. I represent the Vegas Victory."

"I'm sorry, I didn't realize the team was under investigation."

Brenda smiled. It was a sweet smile, which included a

glint in her eyes that said she would be happy to throw down with the detective if he wanted a fight. "I represent the interests of the Vegas Victory Football Club, Detective Pagonis. Mr. Perrault is family of the owner of the team. Therefore, he is included in those interests."

"I didn't know this was going to be a formal inquisition." Pagonis somehow accused Darcy and Kennedy with a matched set of glares.

"It's nothing formal." The lawyer blew off his comment and his dirty looks. "It's common practice for a man of Craig's stature in the community to retain counsel."

Pagonis looked Craig up and down, lips quirked. True, Craig was a mess. Dirt from the tussle on the sidewalk. His hair looked like a light socket was involved in its styling. Craig did not look like a man of any stature—let alone one who retained counsel.

Not that Pagonis said any of that, but he was probably thinking it. They all were. Instead, he simply nodded, frowning. But this wasn't about his happiness. This was about protecting Craig. And no matter what happened, Kennedy wanted that to happen.

"Where have you been, Mr. Perrault?" Pagonis glanced at the lawyer. "Is that an appropriately worded question?"

She nodded.

Craig licked his lips. "I was hiding."

"From whom?" The detective pulled out a notepad, pen poised.

Craig looked at Darcy, like he was asking permission. She smiled and nodded. "Tell him the truth."

"The aliens."

"Aliens." The pen sagged. "Are we talking illegal or E.T.?" By the tone of his voice, it was obvious he wasn't taking this seriously. And he needed to.

"Can I talk to you?" Kennedy motioned for Pagonis to follow her into the hall. She closed the door behind them and pulled him down about twenty or so feet—just far enough for privacy.

"Aliens?" Pagonis was using that tone again. And the raised eyebrows told her he was inches away from sending them all to the funny farm. "If Chuck's brother is unstable, why am I just hearing about this now?"

"He's got some issues, but he's very protective of his family. He wouldn't hurt them."

"And you know this how?"

"I've spent time with him. I've talked with him. I know he doesn't make a lot of sense. But there's truth in there somewhere. I know it. He's the one who pushed me onto the tracks."

"What?" All the tension in his body appeared to move to his shoulders.

"Yes. Just listen to him."

"Why am I not arresting him?"

"He thought I was Darcy and he was trying to protect her. There's more going on here than is on the surface. And we need to talk to him while he remembers everything." Kennedy didn't want to go into all the details of the medication issue. Pagonis was having a hard enough time believing Craig could offer anything of value, and adding the whole medication layer probably wouldn't help.

He sighed and nodded. They both returned to Darcy's office, and Pagonis sat back in the chair. "Mr. Perrault, I have a few questions. Are you ready?"

"Yep."

"It's got to be hard being Chuck's brother. He has a beautiful wife and family. He has the soccer team. It would make anyone jealous. Were you jealous of your brother?" Accusing right out of the gate. Kennedy shook her head. It was like he hadn't even been in the hall a minute ago.

"No."

"Don't you want those things?"

"Yes." Craig hung his head. "But I wouldn't take Chuck's stuff. I want my own things. I wasn't good like Chuck."

"How was Chuck good?"

Craig twitched one shoulder. "At soccer. Being a husband." At soccer, yes. As a husband, Chuck left a lot to be desired, given he knocked up the blond down the hall. Not that Craig knew any of that. "But my brother wasn't happy."

"Were you happy?"

"No, but I had a reason. My brother was just miserable." That Craig could recognize that even without meds was amazing, since Chuck couldn't figure it out and he supposedly didn't need meds.

"Why was Chuck miserable?"

"He needed money. It was always about money with him." Craig frowned. "But he had everything. He just was too blind to see it."

"What was your reason for being miserable?"

"They tell me I hit my head in an accident a few years ago."

"Do you believe them?"

"Sometimes my head hurts. So maybe." Craig touched his temple. "I think the doctors are working for the aliens. I get so tired of hiding from them. They always find me. They always found Chuck."

"Would your medication help?"

Craig wrinkled his nose. "No, the doctors want to keep me slow so I can't protect my family."

"Like you protected Kennedy?"

"That was an accident." Craig's eyes widened, and he looked at Darcy.

She gave him a smile that said he was doing great. The tightness in her shoulders and her twitching eye said she was about to end the interrogation or the detective. One of the two.

"Why did you push Kennedy onto the tracks?" Pagonis re-poised his pen.

"I didn't want the alien to shoot Darcy with the lasers. But I didn't know it was Kennedy and not Darcy, but I would've saved Kennedy, too. She's like family. Darcy thinks so, anyway."

A burst of warmth crawled up Kennedy's spine. She'd gone from being *not* family to *like* family in a little under a week. She was moving up in rank.

Pagonis nodded. "So someone was pointing a gun at Kennedy, but you thought it was Darcy."

"Yes."

"Can you describe the alien? Is it a man or a woman? Tall or short?"

Craig stared at the wall. "Man. Tall."

Pagonis kept on. "Have you seen the alien anywhere else?"

"Just once. Yelling at Chuck."

"Just once? So the man didn't come to the games or hang around the stadium?"

"I don't know. I haven't been to any games yet." Craig shook his head. "I didn't want to lead the aliens here with all the people in the stands."

"Where were they when they were yelling?"

"In Chuck's office." He pointed at the desk. "Right there."

"And did you see this happen?"

"I was in the bathroom" —Craig pointed at a door that led to a private washroom— "when the alien came in. I should've known not to come. I led him here. I'm sure of it. And then I saw him."

"What did you see? Did you see his face?"

"No, I didn't want to leave the bathroom." He sagged

against the couch. "I opened the door just a little, but all I saw was his back."

"Why didn't you come out?"

"I was scared."

"But you know it was a man."

"He was big. Tall." Craig shook his head. "I should have come out."

"No, then you'd be hurt too. It doesn't seem like the alien knows you saw him. That's good." Pagonis nodded, almost friendly. "You're here today to help us because you stayed out of sight."

Chuck's slouch straightened. He puffed out his chest just a bit. The reassurance seemed to give his self-esteem a little boost.

"When you were watching them, did you hear what they were saying?" Pagonis asked.

"It was so loud. There were spurts and static. I couldn't understand."

"Did you make out any words?"

"The alien was telling Chuck that he wanted money. He said he'd be sorry and he'd get what was coming to him."

"Is there anything else about the alien that you remember? What was he wearing? Did he talk different?"

Craig tilted his head. "He talked like regular. He wore all black."

"You saw them argue here, right?" Darcy asked.

Chuck nodded.

"Could it have been a security guard? Black pants and a black polo shirt?"

"Don't the security guards wear blue?" Pagonis scowled.

"Blue are outside contractors. Guards employed by the club wear black."

Craig seemed to be thinking about it as he leaned

forward and finished his soda. "It could've been a security guard."

Darcy stared at Louis with wide eyes. "We need pictures. Now."

"What's going on?" The lawyer was smart enough to see that this was not good news.

"The guards employed by the club are the ones watching my house and the kids." Darcy stepped around the desk and picked up the handset for the desk phone. "I need the employee files for the current security guards right now. It's urgent."

There was someone talking on the other end, but it was impossible to understand what they were saying. "Bring it upstairs now," Darcy snapped. She slammed the phone down and turned to Louis. "Call Charles."

Louis swiped at his cell phone as Darcy dialed the desk phone.

Louis spoke first. "Where are you?...Are you okay?... Stay at your friends and don't leave. Don't talk to anyone, especially security guards from the club."

"I can get some officers over to him." Pagonis got on his phone. "Can you give me the address where Charles is located?"

The two men's discussion was interrupted by Darcy slamming the handset down. "She's not answering. Kennedy, try her cell phone."

Louis moved his phone away from his ear. "Have you tried her friend Magda?"

Darcy shook her head and pressed in another number while Kennedy called Fanny's cell phone. "It went straight to voice mail," she said a moment later.

Shit.

CHAPTER 39

Five minutes later, Kennedy stood in front of Craig holding up a file opened to a photo of one of the security guards. She'd joke about looking like Vanna, but they didn't have time. And nothing about Fanny being missing was funny. "How about this one?"

The guy in the picture didn't exactly have the tall-alien look, but she wasn't going to skip anyone. They needed to be thorough.

"No." Craig shook his head.

"Fanny isn't with her boyfriend." Darcy's voice held the panic of a parent looking for a missing toddler in a big-box store.

"We'll find her." Louis laid an arm around her shoulder. "Who should we call next?"

"I don't know."

"What about where she gets her hair cut? Or a spa? Or any hobbies…" Pagonis was on his phone coordinating the Metro response. They'd already moved Charlie to an undisclosed location. They were sending people to the stadium.

Kennedy put down the first file and picked up the next one. When she opened it, a big man with black hair and a crooked smile stared back from the photo attached to the front cover. She showed it to Craig. "Is this him?"

His head swayed side to side. "I don't know."

"Could it be him?" Pagonis asked Craig.

"It could be," Craig said slowly.

Pagonis took the file. "I need a background check on a David Friedman," he said into his phone.

It wasn't the smoking gun they needed, so Kennedy chose another file. "How about her?"

"No. It wasn't a female."

Kennedy knew that, but she had to ask. One more file left. Bobby, the guard she'd met the first day.

"David Friedman has four kids and serves as an assistant rabbi at his synagogue." Pagonis shrugged. "I have someone going to pick him up, but I doubt he's our guy."

She showed Craig the picture. "What about him?"

Craig's eyes lit up and he pointed. "That's him."

"Are you sure?" Kennedy didn't want this to be true. Bobby had been to the house. He was polite and said ma'am.

"Yes."

Kennedy handed Pagonis the folder. "This is him."

"I need you to run another name. Robert Burnett." He took the file and rattled off the information. Name. Date of birth. Social security number.

"Bobby?" Darcy shook her head. "He wouldn't do anything…"

Kennedy watched Pagonis, saw his face change with whatever he just heard. "Understood. Send a car to his house." Pagonis shoved his phone in his pocket. "Darcy. We need to get you somewhere safe."

"What? Why?"

"Robert Burnett died ten years ago in a fire."

"Maybe it's a different Robert Burnett. He said his name

is Bobby. That's a common name." Darcy clearly didn't want to believe it. Heck, neither did Kennedy. The guy seemed so nice. But that was how the good criminals got you.

Pagonis tipped his head, eyebrows raised. "Not with the same social security number."

"So that's not his name?" Darcy asked, voice rising.

"Probably not. He lied about who he was. Which means he had something to hide."

"We wouldn't have hired him if we knew," Darcy protested. "The background check would've caught this."

"Depends on the background check company you use," Pagonis told her. "Sometimes they just make sure the person doesn't have any convictions and don't check much else."

Darcy dropped into the chair behind the desk. "What about Fanny?"

"We're going to put out an APB on her and Bobby," Pagonis said. "We'll release the picture of them both. We'll put all our resources toward finding her. Was he anywhere near the house today?"

"Yes. He was posted out front this morning."

"When you called the house, did Selma say if he was still there?"

Darcy bit her lip. "He left at noon. Chloe is there now."

"Have you been able to get in touch with Fanny at all?" Pagonis asked what Kennedy was thinking. This felt more like a bad dream than anything that could happen in real life.

"No." Darcy shook her head. "I've tried everyone I can think of. I called the place where she gets her hair done and the spa we sometimes go to when she's in town..." Darcy's voice broke on the last word.

Louis wrapped his arm around Darcy. "Can Metro send someone to find her?"

Before Pagonis could say that there was nowhere to send an officer—they couldn't have cops knocking on random doors looking for her— Darcy's desk phone rang.

She dove for the phone like it might run away and picked up the handset. "Darcy Perrault." A pause. "Who is this?" Her voice had dropped an octave.

Every sound stopped.

Everyone stopped breathing.

Or that might have just be Kennedy.

The caller was saying something, but only Darcy could hear. Pagonis mimed putting it on speaker. Darcy head jerked in a nod and she pressed a button.

"… Two million dollars in small bills." It was definitely a man's voice.

"Bobby, why are you doing this?" Darcy asked, calmer than Kennedy would have been.

"You know why," Bobby snapped.

"No. I don't."

"Your husband really didn't tell you, did he?" He snickered. "What a piece of shit."

"Tell me what?"

"It was better when I didn't know who my father was. At least then I could pretend he wasn't a complete waste of space." Bobby sighed. "Give me the money you owe me and you can get on with your life. If you try anything, I'll kill her."

"Please don't."

"Then don't do anything to force my hand," Bobby shouted. "Two million dollars. Small bills. Meet me at Roman Plaza at Caesars Palace. Three PM. And make sure you come alone. I wouldn't want anything bad to happen." The line went dead.

The room was silent except for Pagonis tapping on his phone as Darcy sobbed and Louis held onto her.

"How are we going to play this?" Kennedy had her own theories, but this wasn't about her.

Darcy's tears stopped. It was like Kennedy's question just dried up the well. "We'll give them the money and get Fanny back."

And just like that, they had a plan.

CHAPTER 40

Twenty minutes later, Kennedy sat next to Darcy in the backseat of the unmarked while Pagonis drove them away from the stadium.

"If you can, go to the bank on Warm Springs," Darcy suggested.

Pagonis nodded as he merged into the lefthand lane. Louis and Craig had gone with a police escort to the undisclosed location to meet up with Charles. The lawyer had gone off to ensure that Darcy didn't get arrested for using the money in the safe-deposit box.

"Is there going to be enough to cover the whole amount?" Kennedy leaned back in the seat.

"I don't know." Darcy twisted toward Kennedy. Their heads were inches from each other. Their foreheads almost touching. "I'm hoping between the safety deposit box—if he hasn't already emptied it— and the safe at home, I'll be able to cover it. I was going to use that money for the bank payment. I figured giving them part of what we owe them might encourage them to refinance the balloon payment that's due."

"It's a lot, huh?"

"Twenty-five million."

Kennedy must have misheard that. "Dollars?"

"I didn't realize he'd taken on that much debt." Darcy's eyes filled with tears.

"When did you find out?" Kennedy couldn't even imagine owing that much money.

"This week. I went over the books. The worst part is going to be telling the board of directors. They'll think I had something to do with all this shit."

"I'm sure they'll be able to see you couldn't have known."

"They won't care. All they'll care about is keeping Chuck's name out of it. It's easier to blame me. I'm going to lose the club, but who gives a shit. I just cannot lose Fanny."

"We'll get her back." Kennedy couldn't even fathom the alternative. She just hoped that the money was still there. Otherwise she'd start asking everyone to empty their pockets if they came up short. Kennedy had a little over three hundred dollars. That wouldn't put much of a dent in the two million needed.

Darcy reached for her arm. "Will you come with me into the vault?"

Kennedy hadn't wanted to invade Darcy's privacy, but letting her best friend out of her sight was not on the agenda for the day. "Of course."

Pagonis pulled into the parking lot of the bank and killed the engine. Before Kennedy could open the door, he turned to look at her and Darcy. "I need you both to stay close." He nodded toward the bank. "I'll stay in the front while you two go in the back."

Kennedy nodded, and they all left the car. Darcy headed for the front door, duffel bag in hand. Pagonis reached for Kennedy's sleeve. "Keep an eye on her. Don't let her go off on her own."

"Agreed." Kennedy followed Darcy inside.

Darcy walked up to a bank employee. "Good morning. I need to open my safe deposit box."

The employee smiled. His black hair was tied back into a bun. His skin was deep like his dark suit. "Good morning. I'm Jackson. I can help with that. Can I see an ID?"

"Sure." Darcy held up her driver's license.

Jackson took it, seemed to look it over for a minute and then nodded. "Let me get the key, Mrs. Perrault. "

Jackson went into an office and came back holding a set of keys. "I have the key. Please follow me, Mrs. Perrault."

They walked down a back hall, past a reinforced door with a large spoked handle, into a room off the main vault. Safety deposit boxes of various sizes lined the four walls, and a metal table stood in the center of the room.

Jackson crossed the room to one of the lower boxes. It was bigger than a breadbox. He inserted a key, turned it, and indicated that Darcy should do the same with her key. "I'll give you a minute." He stepped out of the room and shut the door.

Darcy pulled out the large metal drawer and set it on the table. She opened the lid and pulled out a folder and couple of boxes with jewelry-sounding names. Cartier. Bulgari. She set them off to the side. Underneath, Kennedy saw banded stacks of money. Crap—but in a good way. That looked like a lot of money.

Darcy took out two stacks, and then pulled out ten more. "We're about eight hundred thousand short."

Crap—not in a good way. "Do you have enough back at the house?"

"I'm not sure." Darcy packed the bundles into the duffel bag. "We'll have to stop there before we head to Caesars. Can you hand me those boxes?"

Kennedy handed the jewelry boxes to Darcy. "Why is he having us meet him at Caesars? Aren't there cameras?"

"There are a ton of cameras in the casino, but we're meeting outside in the plaza."

"There aren't cameras?"

"Some, but not as many as there are inside." Darcy clicked the lid closed on the drawer. "Basically, it's a busy area, so they'll be a bunch of people and it's out in the open. Few cameras. It makes sense. Especially since we know who it is." Darcy picked up the bag and opened the door. "We're done."

Jackson came back in and lifted the drawer, sliding it into its slot. He turned his key as Darcy turned hers.

They walked out of the room and parted ways with Jackson when they hit the exit of the vault.

"Are you okay?"

Darcy sighed. "I'm trying to be. I'll feel better when Fanny is home safe."

"Do you think Bobby is Chuck's son, or is this a cash grab?"

"Who knows." Darcy shifted the bag as they walked past Pagonis, and nodded. "I hate to think that Chuck has another kid out there—more than the two and a half he already has—but it wouldn't surprise me."

Darcy slid into the back seat on one side and Kennedy on the other. Pagonis got in the front. "Do you have enough for the drop?"

"No." Darcy leaned back and shook her head.

"So where are we going now?" His eyes met Kennedy's in the rear-view mirror.

Darcy closed her eyes. "My house."

Pagonis mouthed into the mirror, "She okay?"

Kennedy shrugged. Dead husband. Cheating. New baby. New adult son. Darcy was getting to know her late husband in a whole new way. And it wasn't a good way. Darcy wasn't okay.

She had no idea if Darcy would be okay for a long time.

CHAPTER 41

Two hours later, Darcy had gathered the rest of the money from the safe at home. Which meant at least that concern was gone. They weren't sifting through the lint in their pockets trying to find change or panhandling on the strip.

Pagonis pulled up to the front door of Caesar's and parked at the end of the emergency lane. He turned to face Darcy and Kennedy in the backseat. "I'll have you two go around the valet stand to the plaza. I'm going to head to the stairs on the other side."

"Are you sure we should go alone?" Darcy looked outside the car like the sky might bite.

"You're not alone." Pagonis looked confused.

"I know you're coming with me," Darcy said to Kennedy. "But it's not like you're allowed to carry a gun or anything."

"Hopefully, it won't come to that. But I can handle things." Kennedy placed a hand on Darcy's. "I have your back."

"I know."

"Always."

Darcy squeezed Kennedy's hand. "I've got your back too."

"I know. So let's go out there and bring Fanny home."

"I love you." A tear slid down Darcy's cheek.

"I love you, too." Kennedy patted her hand. "Again, always. Let's go kick some ass."

Darcy nodded.

"Go left." Pagonis stepped out of the car. "I'll be around the other side."

Kennedy followed Darcy past the long line of people waiting for taxis. They walked up the stairs to the plaza—an open space with people laughing and walking around. To the right was an entrance to Caesar's. To the left was a red and white tent with the words *Absinthe* along the side. Although the tent wasn't actually a tent, but a building. Probably a good idea not to house an entire Vegas show under cheap plastic.

She'd heard of Absinthe, right before she'd heard about the best place to get crab legs. It was the laugh-out-loud show with a back door where people could snort blow and hook up with their boyfriends. Hopefully Diandra wasn't around giving blowjobs for free drinks.

Kennedy walked toward the entrance. It was a cool setup. Maybe she'd actually see it one day—when all this crap died down. "Do we know where we're supposed to meet him?"

"No."

Ringing came from a table next to the front doors of the tent. Darcy looked at Kennedy—like she might know why tables were magically ringing. Kennedy approached the table and picked up a vibrating cell phone.

"Did someone lose their phone?" Darcy asked.

"Maybe." Kennedy waited until the call went to voicemail. "We'll take it to lost and found when we're done here." She didn't have the mental bandwidth to worry about someone else's phone right now. She went to slide it into her pocket, but the phone vibrated in her hand.

She looked at the screen. *Pick up.*

Okay, then. She answered when the phone rang again.

"She was told to come alone." No pleasantries.

"I wouldn't let her come alone."

"Fine." The gruff voice sounded annoyed. Join the club. "Give the phone to Darcy."

Kennedy tilted her wrist. "It's for you."

Darcy took the phone. Put it up to her ear. After a moment, Darcy nodded. "Fine." She clicked the phone off. "He wants me to go inside."

"Inside what?"

"Inside the tent." She pointed to the front doors of Absinthe. "Alone."

Of course, alone.

"He said he has someone watching the door."

Kennedy couldn't follow her in. But she didn't need to. She knew of a secret entrance. "Don't worry."

"Don't worry?" Darcy had panic written all over. "I'm going in there all by myself. What if he didn't bring Fanny."

"I'll be in there."

"But he's watching."

"There's another door." Kennedy leaned in. "Take a minute to breathe before you go in. I'll pretend to leave, but I'll be right behind you if you need me."

Darcy nodded.

"Go in and get our girl." *And don't die.* Kennedy didn't have the heart to say that last bit out loud because she barely had the heart to think the words at all.

CHAPTER 42

Kennedy stepped back with her hands up, signaling a retreat to any onlookers. "I'll get you a drink for when you're done."

Darcy nodded and faced the door. She wrapped her hand around the handle and took a deep breath. Then she repositioned the huge duffle bag of money and pulled. The door swept open and she slid inside.

Kennedy walked toward Caesar's and looked back. When Darcy and the area in front of the door was out of sight she veered left around the tent-building, looking for a door. Diandra said something about a phone booth, but she also said she'd been high on cocaine so how much of it had been true? Kennedy dodged a garbage can and a set of tables and chairs. No hidden doors. Although, that was kind of the description of hidden.

Kennedy didn't have time for hidden. She needed to find a way into the building before she gave up and created one herself. Before she could plan further than using one of the garbage cans to bang against the side of the building, she noticed a lime green box sticking out the side of the tent. Building. Whatever.

It was about six feet tall, with bars over little windows. The phone booth. It was attached to the side of the tent. She jogged over and slid the folding door open. On one side was an old-timey phone. The fact that a hanging phone was somehow old-timey would depress her later. But right now, she needed to know how to get inside the building.

She lifted the phone and pushed on the wall facing the tent. Nothing. Locked.

She tapped on the switch hook. No dial tone. No door magically opening.

Dammit. She wanted to jiggle the handle—maybe kick open the damn door. But she needed to keep quiet. She couldn't let Bobby know she was here.

A few feet down, the side of the tent popped open and a waiter walked out pushing a cart filled with dirty glasses. He headed toward Caesar's.

An open door.

Kennedy ran over and opened the door. It was dark inside, but looked like a small kitchen area. She followed the wall to an opening. That led to the main stage area—where Darcy stood across from Bobby. He looked like hell. Scraggled hair. Shadow on his face that was way past five o'clock.

He sat in a chair and tapped his finger on the table in front of him. "Give me the bag."

"I just need to see Fanny."

"You can see Fanny after you give me the bag." Bobby slammed his fist on the table.

Darcy cringed. "How do I know if she's okay?"

"She's my half-sister. Why would I hurt her?"

"Why would you kidnap her at all, Bobby?" Good point, Darcy. "If that's even your name."

"I'm just trying to get what's mine. My inheritance from a man who couldn't even be bothered to come and see me."

"He might not have known you existed." Darcy had

mentioned that kids had come out of the woodwork for years, but not one of them passed a paternity test.

"He knew. My mom brought me to see him when I was five."

Five?

Bobby kept talking. "She brought the paternity test. He knew. He just—never cared."

"Why didn't you tell me?" Darcy shook her head. "All you had to do was ask me. Come to me. I would have understood."

"Right, like when I asked my father and he tried to fire me. He threw me out of the building. But I showed him. I made a deal with my bookie, sold him information about the team. Dear old Dad found out and threatened to have me arrested. It's not bad enough he took away my job, he wanted to take away my life. What kind of fucked-up father does that?"

Darcy shook her head as a sigh slipped past her lips. "He wasn't very good at handling surprises." Or treachery, apparently. Selling team secrets could've led to Chuck's own stint in jail.

"Yeah, he wasn't good at handling a lot of things." Bobby sprang to his feet and reached out his hand. "Give me the bag."

"You don't think I would've helped you? I trusted you with my family. I trusted you more than I ever would've trusted Chuck."

Although that might have just been a way to gain Bobby's confidence, Darcy probably meant every word. Honestly, Kennedy would've trusted a Kardashian with a credit card before trusting Chuck with… well… anything.

Kennedy slid inside the room, keeping out of sight of the Darcy and Bobby standoff. The room was round. One big open space. She dropped to her knees and scooched up to a metal pipe trellis decorated with fake flowers. She was hidden, barely. A large sheet of fabric poured down from the center of the room, surrounding the small stage. Other than the tables and chairs for patrons, there was nothing in the way of cover.

"I just don't think I should give up the money without my daughter." Darcy slid her arm over the bag and clutched it to her body. "It's my daughter."

Sliding on her knees, Kennedy moved from one table to another. Trying not to touch them. Trying not to make a sound.

Bobby pulled out a knife and Kennedy shoved to her feet. Her body was in clear view of the two people across the room. Shit. She dropped to the floor. *Be cool, Kennedy.*

It took everything in her not to jump over the ten or so tables and whoop his ass. But they still didn't know where Fanny was. They couldn't make any move until they knew where she was being kept.

"You have a choice. You give me the bag, or I take it. If I take it, there will be pain. Do you want to go pick up your daughter covered in blood? Hasn't this been traumatic enough for her?"

Darcy sighed and lowered the bag, setting it down in front of her. Bobby dragged it over by the strap and slid it onto his shoulder. "Your daughter is here." He stuffed something in Darcy's hand. Fanny's location. That was all they needed.

Kennedy jumped. Her shoes squeaked. Shit. There went the element of surprise. She ran flat out toward Bobby, but he turned and ran for the front door.

Oh hell no.

Kennedy pivoted. Lunged. So close. She shoved a table out of the way and dove for him.

Bobby turned, swinging the bag behind his back. His hand came forward.

The glint of the knife hit her first.

CHAPTER 43

Kennedy's knees hit the floor. She looked down. A knife stuck out from the front of her body. She pulled her fingers back. Soaked in red.

She reached for Bobby, wrapped her hands around his arm as pain needled down her side.

Bobby scooted backward, eyes bulging. "I didn't... you weren't supposed to be here."

"What did you do?" Darcy's face appeared in front of Kennedy.

Bobby staggered a step back. "I didn't mean to do it. This wasn't how it was supposed to go."

"It doesn't matter what you meant." Darcy stared at the handle of the knife and started to cry. "I don't know what to do."

Kennedy took a deep breath and nearly screamed. Darcy, Bobby, the entire room—everything slipped out of focus for a long, horrible moment. She wanted to tell Darcy to find Pagonis, but Bobby would run. So far, the shock seemed to have nailed his feet to the floor. Any words might frighten him off.

Out of the corner of her eye, movement. Pagonis was in

the room—albeit on the other side. He needed more time to get to Bobby. He needed to keep that element of surprise. The one Kennedy lost.

Kennedy didn't look at Pagonis straight on. Distract. She shivered. "Bobby, can I borrow your coat?"

He nodded. He really wasn't a bad guy. Although the knife sticking out of her gut would beg to differ.

"Thank you." Kennedy smiled—and somehow even that made her wince. "Bobby, you don't seem like a master criminal. Why all this?"

"I don't know. I just wanted to get to know my dad. I know he didn't want me, not as a son. But I thought I'd finally get a chance to know him as an employee. When I told him who I was, he called me a liar. He wouldn't even listen."

"Then why are you going after the money?"

"I have to get away. I can't stay here anymore, after what I did."

Kennedy guessed that what he did to Chuck was the unfinished part of that sentence. "What happened?"

"It was an accident."

Thirty-seven puncture wounds. That's how many times Chuck was stabbed. How does one accidentally jab a knife into someone thirty-seven times by accident?

"He fired me," Bobby said, "and I saw the test results for Markham on his desk. I took a picture and sold it to my bookie. Somehow Chuck found out. I don't know how. But he asked me to come in and talk to him. I thought he felt bad for how things ended with us. I thought he was going to ask me to come back to work." Bobby's eyes teared as he spoke. "He just yelled and called me a thief and a liar. He said he thought I just wanted to get to know him but then I stole from him. I tried to explain that I had been angry, but he wouldn't listen. He kept calling me names. He wouldn't stop."

"That must have been hard."

"I just wanted to fit in. For so many years I dreamed of meeting my dad and doing all the father/son things that dads do."

Kennedy started to shake her head and decided any movement was a bad idea. "You know he wasn't like that. Charles lived with him, and Chuck never even played a game of catch with him." To be fair, Chuck tried to teach Charles soccer, but Charles hated it. Since his son didn't want to play his game, Chuck chose to do nothing with him.

Sometimes Kennedy really hated Chuck for all the pain he caused to everyone around him. Let's be real—she'd always hated him. He was a narcissistic, selfish dick. She tilted to the side and pain radiated down her side, stealing her breath.

"I'm sorry." Bobby did indeed look sorry. He looked from Kennedy to Darcy—but Darcy's attention was focused across the room.

Pagonis.

A giant cop-sized blur silently careening toward them.

Pagonis was still too far away to reach Bobby. Darcy was a civilian, and there was nothing she could do to stop him.

That left Kennedy.

Kennedy angled forward till her fingers could wrap around the strap of the duffel bag. Pain speared through her middle. She didn't care. He wouldn't leave without the money. And she wasn't letting go.

Bobby yanked at the bag, sliding Kennedy along the floor on her knees. There was no word to describe the pain. Tears pierced her eyes. She couldn't hold on.

She had to let go.

Let go. Her hand didn't listen. It wouldn't listen when

she tensed her core and a scream echoed in the room. Her throat dried as she realized the scream came from her.

Darcy's hand wrapped around the bag next to Kennedy's. She yanked on the bag, taking the brunt of the pulling and tugging.

"Give me the bag!" Bobby twisted his hand in the strap and jerked back. The bag didn't move. Darcy gave them leverage. Apparently Bobby didn't like that. His eyes narrowed as he lifted his foot and aimed his heel at Kennedy's face. She had to keep Bobby busy. She had to keep him here.

Kennedy closed her eyes and turned away. At least he was aiming for the face and not the stomach. A whoosh of air blew past her.

"Get down." The detective's voice was welcome—which was different. "You are under arrest."

Darcy peeled Kennedy's fingers from the duffel bag as Kennedy slumped against her. She closed her eyes and stopped listening. The perp was in police custody. The money was in Darcy's custody.

And hopefully, one of them would be calling an ambulance because Kennedy didn't think she had much more blood to lose.

CHAPTER 44

Three weeks later, Kennedy sat in a chair next to Darcy's pool taking in her last day of Vegas weather. She was going to miss the sunshine. She'd miss the mountains. She wouldn't miss being the center of a murder investigation—so there was that—and it was time to get back to Chicago and real life.

Darcy strolled outside carrying three glasses. One was for Craig, on the chaise lounge with his eyes closed, and she tapped his shoulder with the glass.

He shook himself awake and snatched at the drink. "Thank you."

She set another glass on the table before sitting in the chair next to Kennedy. "Are you done cleaning your house, Craig?"

His smile was genuine, but it didn't glow like it had before. He also wasn't erratic and talking about aliens, so there were tradeoffs. He tended to be less social on the new meds. Quiet and reserved. "I've gotten everything out, now I just need to fix it up and put it on the market." He got to his feet, glass in hand.

Darcy had invited him to live in the guest house over

the garage, and since there wasn't anyone chasing him any longer, he'd agreed. She offered to let him stay in the house, but he probably wanted to be away from the noise. With Fanny moving back in, and the doctor moving his stuff into Darcy's room, the house had taken on new life.

"I will buy you all the furniture in all the world." Darcy yelled as he walked away, before leaning over and whispering, "I don't want anything that lived in that townhouse living in my home."

No argument there.

Selma opened the sliding glass door with a whoosh. "Miss Kennedy, you have a guest."

A guest? Kennedy looked past Selma. Pagonis nodded at her. "You look good."

"Thanks." Kennedy shifted in her chair. She definitely looked better than she felt.

"Would you like a drink, Detective?" Selma offering him basic hospitality without cringing was new. The two had come to some sort of truce while Kennedy had been in recovery. He'd come to check on the family—and Kennedy — a few times, not that the fact meant anything at all. He was just worried about his previous prime suspect.

She wasn't in denial. Previous prime suspect worry was a thing. She'd Googled it.

"No, thank you, Selma." Pagonis sat in the chair across from Kennedy. "I have to get back to the office." He faced Kennedy. "I know you're leaving tomorrow, so I wanted to see how you're feeling."

Kennedy didn't want to complain, but getting stabbed sucked. "I feel better, but…"

"…it was like you were stabbed or something." He actually made another joke.

"Yeah. Like that." Kennedy laughed. Carefully.

"It'll get better." He leaned back and took in the sun.

"Were you stabbed before?"

"Second ex-wife." He didn't look over at her. Which was good, or he'd notice her eyes were probably the size of soccer balls. Two ex-wives. So far.

"Why?"

"I accidentally broke her mom's vase."

"A vase?" Darcy said. Kennedy agreed. Who got stabby over a vase?

"It was a family heirloom." He turned to Kennedy. "I guess it meant more to her than I did."

"Hence the reason she's an ex." Kennedy knew she should let the conversation go, but she just couldn't. "So how many ex-wives do you have?"

"Why? Are you looking to apply for the position?"

"I have enough problems, so no thanks."

Pagonis smiled. He really was endearing when he behaved in human fashion. Gorgeous teeth. Eyes that sparkled. A face that said *sit on me*.

She was not applying. Or sitting. Or anything.

She just had to keep reminding herself of that.

"I've been married three times." He stared out over the pool.

"What happened to the third ex-wife?"

"She never made it to ex. She passed away a few years ago in a car accident."

"I'm sorry to hear that," Kennedy said.

"So am I." Darcy took a drink of her water.

"Thank you." He cleared his throat. Kennedy knew that sound. Share-time over.

Sharing about his life, anyway. She had other questions. "So what's going on with Bobby?"

"He's been arrested. No bond. He's claiming temporary insanity. Some lawyer might be able to get him off on a lighter sentence, but he'll be going away for a very long time."

Kennedy had figured Bobby would try an insanity plea.

"It's better than the accident he was claiming before."

"Yeah, once is an accident. I'm not sure thirty-seven times is accidental." Darcy shook her head. She'd come to terms with all Chuck's bullshit. He'd made his bed, and all the fornication led to him dying in it.

Fanny walked out onto the back patio. "Detective?"

He gave one quick nod. "How are you feeling after your ordeal?"

"Thankful to be getting back to normal." Fanny sat on the edge of the pool. "Well, as normal as things will get. My mom won't let me out of her sight."

Darcy snorted. "You make it sound like I have you handcuffed to my wrist."

Fanny's face screwed into a frown. "Please don't do that."

"That does sound like a great idea." Darcy tapped on her chin with her index finger. "We could do everything together. We'd be like conjoined besties."

Kennedy laughed. Pagonis snickered.

Fanny did not. "More like conjoined detesties."

Kennedy grasped Darcy's hand. "I don't want to come back here for any more mysteries. So, how about we don't do things that make Fanny want to kill you?"

"Fine."

"Well, if you're ever in town again, look me up." Pagonis looked Kennedy up and down as he stood up. Not in an *I want you* way, more like he was staring at a bird with a broken wing. "It was interesting working with you. Have a great trip."

"Thank you." Kennedy braced herself to stand up.

"Don't get up. I'll show myself out." He disappeared through the sliding glass door.

"I should go too." Fanny stood. "I'm reminding you I have two classes tonight. Don't send the detective after me."

So, yeah. That happened. Darcy somehow forgot Fanny had two classes on Thursday nights and called the police when she didn't come home promptly at eight. Fanny apparently almost died of embarrassment. Thankfully, dying of embarrassment was not a thing.

"Second class is over at ten, correct?"

"Yes. I'll come straight home." Fanny leaned over and gave Darcy, a hug and kiss. She angled and gave Kennedy the same hug and kiss. "Have a safe trip. And thank you."

"Anytime, kiddo." Kennedy thought that sounded good, but then again… "I take that back. Let's not do that again. Ever."

"Deal." Fanny stood up. "I love you, Kenn."

"Love you too, Fantasia."

And with that, Fanny left, leaving Darcy and Kennedy alone with the swoosh of the mini waterfalls at the edge of the pool.

"Thank you so much, Kennedy." Darcy smiled. She raised her glass. "To friendship."

Kennedy held up her drink. "To friendship."

CHAPTER 45

Later that night, Kennedy sat in the circle of the AA meeting. Diandra's bounce was gone. Brad was buried in his phone, his suit and coat impeccable. Kennedy recognized a few people from her last meeting. The one where she bared her soul.

She wasn't sure if she should even come back, but something drew her here. Something unresolved.

Betty was reading from the Big Book today. Kennedy had missed a few meetings, so they'd moved on without her. They were talking about leaving the past behind.

Kennedy had spent so much time blaming herself for everything that happened over the years. It was hard to get sober when you carried the baggage of the past around like a lead balloon.

When Betty finished reading, she looked at Diandra. "Would you like to share?"

"My name is Diandra, and I'm an alcoholic." Diandra's eyes filled with tears. "Zeke left."

"I'm sorry." Betty really did look sorry, even though she had to know it was coming.

"He said I'm no fun anymore now that I don't drink. He

said that he loves some girl named Seduction and he wants to marry her. What kind of name is Seduction? Unless you're a porn star." Diandra shook her head. "She is a porn star, but, whatever."

"Did you have a drink?"

"No." Diandra gave a small, watery smile. "I didn't. I decided if he doesn't like me sober, he doesn't like me for me."

"Good for you," Betty said.

"Yeah." Diandra nodded as fresh tears flowed. "It just hurts. He told me he loved me, then a couple days later, he was gone."

"That has nothing to do with you. That man doesn't like himself." Kennedy heard the words, and was shocked to hear them in her voice. But it was true. "Men like that hurt others because they're broken and they want you to be broken, too."

"I don't want to be broken anymore." Diandra swipe at her cheeks.

"And you're not." Betty smiled. "I call this a big win. You didn't let yourself backslide. You are stronger than you give yourself credit for."

Diandra nodded, wiping away more tears with the back of her hand.

"Anyone else want to share?"

Kennedy raised her hand. "My name is Kennedy and I'm an alcoholic."

"Hi, Kennedy."

"It's been three hours since I wanted a drink and almost ten months since I've had one. I used to try to numb the pain with a well-placed drink. But getting stabbed—" Pause for gasps. "—made me realize that pain is a part of life. Trying to numb it is only making it worse. I need to embrace it. So I'm going back to school. I've spent too much time trying to stop the chaos after it's in full swing. I want to help people and children before the chaos takes hold. I want to jump into the pain instead of trying to outrun it."

Betty tilted her head. "It sounds like you're moving on."

"Yeah." She was moving on, she was doing what she needed to do to make herself happy, and she was ready to cut out anything that didn't. Because even though she'd made mistakes over the years, she deserved more than she was letting herself have. She was done paying for the guilt of the past.

EPILOGUE

ne Year Later

Kennedy sat in a seat in the Vegas Victory training field bleachers, taking in the Vegas weather. One year ago to the day, she was a prime suspect in a murder. So much had changed. She leaned her head back. But not the sun. It hadn't changed one bit, and she was okay with that.

"Volkov, move down the field!" Coach Brighton yelled as he threw down his clipboard. On the sidelines, a physical therapist helped Tad Markham stretch. His surgery had gone well, but it had been a long road to recovery. From everything Kennedy had heard, he was playing better than ever.

Darcy dropped into the seat next to Kennedy, and a moment later Craig walked up the stairs from the field. "I'm heading out." He was a whole new man. He'd been on his meds for the past year and he was helping out full-time with the team.

"Can you wait till I'm done?" Darcy said. "I can drive you home. I just need to talk to the coach first."

"Nah, I'll call the service." Craig looked over the field, where the players were running back and forth after the ball. "Do you need me to stay?"

Darcy shrugged. "I just need to give him next year's player wish list."

Craig leaned against the seat in front of Darcy. "Is Billy Porter on the list?"

"Yes." Darcy pulled a sheet of paper from a file folder in the bag at her feet. It was a list of names, with handwritten numbers lining the margins.

Craig glanced over the list like it was about to self-destruct. "Good. Olufemi Musa made the list."

"I told you I'd keep Billy and Olufemi on the list."

"That's smart." Craig smiled.

Darcy took the paper back and returned it to the folder. Craig took out his cell phone. "Should I see if Fanny wants a ride back to the house?"

"She brought her car because she's going out with her boyfriend tonight." Darcy leaned back and shielded her eyes from the sun overhead.

"Okay." He tapped at his phone.

Kennedy liked this Craig. The one that wasn't yelling about aliens and making friends with critters— which turned out to be rats burrowing into piles of stuff in his house. To be fair, the other Craig was nicer to her—if you ignored the pushing her onto tram tracks—but this one was mentally healthier.

"I'm out." Craig nodded at Darcy and gave Kennedy the side eye as he headed up the stairs.

Kennedy frowned at his back. "What was that about?"

"Who knows." Darcy shook her head.

"Are you sure I can stay at the house? Maybe he doesn't want me there."

"It's my house. You're staying." Darcy's clipped tone said there was no arguing. "Anyway, he's still in the guest house. You won't even have to see him—unless you come here. He's always here."

Kennedy laughed. "Always here, huh?"

"He wants to be more hands-on at the club."

"Ah." Kennedy knew that was a sore subject. Craig might not be yelling about aliens and Darcy not knowing how to handle said aliens, but he was very opinionated about how the team should be run. And he liked to share those opinions.

"Yeah. But what can I do, it's a family business."

It was a family business now that Fanny was working in the marketing department. Beth was back after her six months of maternity leave, working full-time for the Vegas Victory.

Darcy figured it wasn't Beth's kid's fault his father had been an idiot. The kid deserved to be surrounded by family. And as long as Darcy didn't have to deal with Beth, she was good.

"The training field looks great," Kennedy said.

"Yeah, we were lucky we could find some silent investors to buy this property. The money covered the first payment of the balloon payment."

"What happens when the second payment is due?"

"Markham back on post has filled the seats. And Miranda has been diversifying our portfolio, so we should be able to cover it."

"It sounds like you have it all under control."

"I don't know about that." Darcy nodded toward the team. "Their winning streak is what's keeping us in the papers."

"Look who found her way back from Chicago." Feet scuffled behind Kennedy as someone walked down the metal steps.

And she knew that voice. A year later and she still could pinpoint that voice anywhere. "Surprisingly, there wasn't a group of Metro waiting at the gate trying to keep me out of the city."

"I tried to set that up, but we were afraid you'd find another way in." Pagonis stood over Kennedy. It was hard to see him with the sun shining in her eyes, but she had a feeling he looked edible.

"You look good." He nodded at Kennedy before turning to Darcy. "Darcy."

"Have a seat, Detective." Darcy smiled. "To what do we owe this visit?"

"I heard Metro was getting a new transfer and I thought I'd check on her."

"She'll be official, with a badge and everything." Darcy practically bounced with joy. She'd been begging Kennedy to come back to Vegas, and honestly, since she could attend college anywhere, there wasn't much for her back in Chicago.

Pagonis gave Kennedy a sideways look. "Yeah, you won't have to flash a Chicago badge and pretend it's Metro any longer."

"You knew about that?" Thankfully, Las Vegas Metro didn't hold it against her when she requested that transfer.

Pagonis quirked his lip. If he wasn't wearing sunglasses, she had a feeling she'd see his eyes rolling. Of course he knew she'd been flashing her badge. He saw everything.

"Get off my field!" Brighton yelled at the players, and they didn't waste any time scattering like roaches.

Darcy popped up from the seat and grabbed her bag. "I need to talk to him so we can leave." She had the folder out before she was across the field.

Brighton yelled at the players about dedication and sleeping and other topics that Kennedy didn't bother listening to. The men ran off the field like they were being chased by rabid fans. The coach's screams died down as the field emptied.

A familiar face ran up the stairs toward the seats where Kennedy and the detective sat. "Darcy's friend!" Alex Volkov ran a hand through sweat soaked hair.

Kennedy nodded at him. "Darcy's Right Winger."

"Back for vacation?"

"No. I'm here for good." She'd sold her possessions and hopped on a plane as soon as she got the acceptance letter from University of Nevada in Las Vegas.

"Really." Alex leaned down and smiled. He was good looking, in a barely out of college kind of way. "You go with me."

"Go where?" She couldn't remember making any plans to go anywhere with the team.

"I think he's asking you out." Pagonis looked like he was trying not to smile.

"I'm sorry. I don't date players." And she meant that in more ways than one.

"Your loss." Alex winked and ran down to the field, disappearing into the tunnel to the locker room.

"I think you broke his heart," Pagonis said.

"I highly doubt that." Kennedy didn't bother shaking her head because he knew that was crap.

At least, he should have. "I think he was a bit disappointed."

Apparently, he didn't know. In fact, if she wasn't so sure, she'd swear the detective was jealous. "Detective Pagonis, I think you're mistaken."

"You can call me Miles."

"You have a name." She always assumed he had a name, but she never thought she'd learn what it was.

Miles—that was going to take a while to get used to—laughed. "Yes, my parents didn't name me 'Detective', Romero."

"You can call me Kennedy."

He leaned in. "I think I like Romero better."

Kennedy's eyes hazed over as she breathed in the mint from his breath. He was so close she could taste him. And she kind of wanted to taste him. But not. The whole not-dating-where-you-worked thing.

"Are you both ready to head out for dinner?" Darcy returned, her bag slung over her shoulder. "Let's head out."

"I'll bring the car around." Miles dangled his keys on his finger as he walked up the stairs.

"What was that?" Darcy looked at his retreating back.

Kennedy might have been watching him too. Not because she was into him, but because she didn't want him to trip up the stairs. It was thing. Google it. "What was what?"

"You were practically eye-humping him."

"This again." Kennedy couldn't have her loyalty tested again.

Darcy smiled. "No. It's a good thing. A little officer fun-time."

"Gross." Kennedy curled her lip. "He's a coworker now."

"A little complication." Darcy smiled as she faced the field. The remnants of the team were moseying into the tunnel. The fake grass glistened in the sunlight. A silence hung over the field. "We are really building something great here." She inched close to Kennedy and intertwined fingers with her. "I don't think I could've gotten through any of this without you."

Kennedy squeezed her best friend's hand. "That's the beauty of our friendship—you never have to."

EXTRAS

Thank you for supporting an independent author. It would be great if you could leave a review or a rating wherever you purchased this book, or on Goodreads.

Would you like to know when my next book is available? You can sign up for my new release email list at http://www.vanessamknight.com or like my Facebook page at http://facebook.com/vanessamknightauthor.

ABOUT THE AUTHOR

Vanessa M. Knight has always enjoyed writing, and once she found mystery and romance, she was addicted. She props her laptop in the suburbs of Chicago with her family and menagerie of four-pawed claw-babies (AKA cats and dogs.) That laptop has partnered-in-crime to write contemporary romances with a dash of humor and splash of snark.

When she has a few moments to spare, you can find her singing off-key (but she assures everyone it's still considered singing), reading, kickboxing, or killing a few brain cells as she stares at the many sitcoms and dramas available through the Internet and TV.

For more information on Vanessa, including her Internet haunts, contest updates, and details on her upcoming novels, please visit her website at www.vanessamknight.com.

OTHER BOOKS BY THIS AUTHOR

MYSTERY

Christmas Cookies Mysteries

Swing Into Murder

Roxy Horne Novels

Come Die with Me

Vegas Victory FC Novels

Deadly. Set. Vegas.

ROMANTIC SUSPENSE

Chicago's Finest Series

Second Time's the Charm

Stark Raving Mad

Stealing Vegas

Final Strike

Busted Series

Busting In

Busting Out

Busting Through

CONTEMPORARY NEW ADULT

Ritter University Series